Foxgloves, Fancy Fungus, and Fatal Family Feuds

by

J L Wilson

Foxgloves, Fancy Fungus, and Fatal Family Feuds

Cover Art by *Kim Mendoza*

The Wild Rose Press
PO Box 708
Adams Basin, NY 14410-0706
Visit us at www.thewildrosepress.com

Publishing History
First Crimson Rose Edition, 2011
Print ISBN 1-60154-912-1

Published in the United States of America

The man wore a prosthesis, an artificial right arm ending in a hook sticking out from his blue plaid flannel shirt under his denim jacket. When he saw Livvie, he took a step back. "What are you doing here, Liv?"

My first thought was, how can this guy be a cook? He's got a hook. He's a cook with a hook. I plastered a smile on my face and prayed I wouldn't giggle.

"Cassie, this is T.J. Watson," Livvie said. "Tom, this is Cassie Whittington."

I automatically held out my right hand then stopped, embarrassed. He smiled and held out his left hand, taking mine in an awkward but firm grip. "Good to meet you." He had a low, rough voice with a trace of Texas or some other American West state. "Olivia's talked a lot about you. She was right. You do look like Gidget."

I shot Livvie a disgruntled look. My resemblance to Sally Fields has haunted me all my life. I hoped when my hair turned gray it might change, but apparently it didn't.

"What are you folks doing here?" he asked.

Livvie said hesitantly, "I was worried when you said you couldn't come. Is something wrong?"

T.J. looked back at the building behind him. "Yeah, I think you could say that." His voice sounded almost bemused.

I peered around him. "Is there a problem—" I took an involuntary step forward when I saw what I thought I saw. "Is that—" I leaned to one side.

A body lay on the floor just inside the door, a pool of blood making a dark stain in the chest of the white chef's uniform.

Dedication

To Houdini, my portly feline muse,
and his companions (Opie, Pandora, and Mia).
Whenever I need a plot point to be clarified,
I can count on them to provide me
with the diversion I need.

Chapter 1

"As your lawyer, I advise you not to advertise the fact that you want to kill Sheila Peavey." My ex-husband Charlie looked amused, but there was a hint of exasperation in his voice. "If she turns up dead, you're liable to be a suspect."

"That bitch deserves to die," I muttered.

"Cassie, that's irrelevant," Olivia Whittington Carlyle, Charlie's sister, said. "There are a lot of people in the world who are a waste of skin. All Charlie is saying is don't tell all and sundry you'd like to be the one who wields the machete and weed Sheila out of the gene pool." She sipped her tonic water and regarded me with amused affection. "I'm sure you want to kill John, too."

"A lot of people want to kill John," Charlie snapped. "Our dear brother is a pain in the butt and a jerk to boot."

We were sitting in Charlie's second-floor condo on the shores of Lake Minnetonka, Minnesota, in a pricy building in the pricy suburb of Orono, west of Minneapolis. Charlie's sailboat was docked at the Yacht Club down the street and we were enjoying the sight of a late October sunset from his spacious living room, whose floor-to-ceiling windows framed a spectacular view. My day-off Friday afternoon was wrapping up and I was relaxing, happy to put my feet up and chat with my exes.

"Sheila got away with murder," I pointed out as I sipped the martini Charlie made for me. I felt mildly guilty about the drink. Livvie was on the wagon and I hated putting temptation in her path, but she appeared content with the 'tonic and a twist' Charlie handed her. "All John has done is contest your grandmother's will and prevent me from inheriting the estate."

"It's just your opinion about Sheila and her involvement in murder. The police don't have proof so they had to release her," Charlie said as he mixed another cocktail. Charlie is two years older than my fifty years. His thick dark hair was just starting to show touches of gray and there were lines around his eyes and mouth, but that only added to his George Clooney-esque appeal. He also goes for a long run several times a week, an action that keeps his tall, leggy physique lean and muscular. To top off his good looks, Charlie is also rich, unspoiled, and one of the nicest people I've ever met. When a Higher Being was handing out Packages, Charlie was at the front of the line and he got the deluxe edition.

"I still can't believe John is trying to prove that Grandy Theo was not of sound mind." Livvie smiled wryly. "She had one of the soundest minds I know. Grandy knew what she was doing when she left her estate to you."

"Now if you said you want to kill John, you'd have a lot of company. Just about everybody I know wants to kill John, myself included." Charlie came back to the couch, balancing a perfect appletini decorated with a thin slice of apple from the Whittington orchards. "But when it comes to Sheila, because your...um...paramour is related to the Peavey case, you'd better keep your mouth shut."

Livvie almost choked on a sip of tonic water. "Paramour? That's an interesting word."

"Give me a better word, then. Cassie and Sam

2

are sleeping together. What should I say? Somehow boyfriend-girlfriend sounds too odd at our ages. Bedmate?" He waggled his eyebrows at me, but his green eyes weren't laughing. I saw a hint of his displeasure in their depths.

"Sam's not related to the case," I protested half-heartedly. "He's been cleared."

"Sam Barlow was married to Shelia, who divorced him to marry Mike Peavey, the victim. Peavey stole Sam's ideas for a new hybrid shrub and there was a patent dispute. Sam was going to sue him for a share in Peavey's company. There was a lot of bad blood between them and that always looks suspicious, no matter how airtight Sam's alibi is." Charlie recited the details of the homicide that occurred the previous spring with a lawyer's crisp precision, not surprising given the fact that he's a contract lawyer.

"How long will it take before John's lawsuit is thrown out? Cassie deserves the money Grandy wanted to leave her." Livvie stood up and went to the window. I envied her tousled ash blonde hair and svelte, rich-girl good looks. Livvie was what Paris Hilton would look like in twenty years if she went natural. Livvie was at least six inches taller than my five-foot-three and she probably weighed just a little more than my one-hundred-twenty. Where I was short and stacked, Livvie was long, lean and tennis-y beautiful.

"The court has to gather depositions from people who knew Grandy. That will take time because I'm sure they want to be thorough since the estate is valued at almost twenty million."

I had seen only a trickle of the money due to me from Charlie's grandmother, so I wasn't overly worried. I wasn't depending on the cash. It was a windfall and it hadn't really fallen yet, so to speak. "I'm sorry it's created such bad blood in the family."

"Cassie, there's always been bad blood between John and the rest of us." Livvie turned from the window to smile at me. The dark blue slacks and striped blue-and-white 'sailor' top picked up the navy blue of her eyes, artfully made up with cosmetics. Livvie always looked well-put-together, but since she quit her social drinking she looked fresher, somehow, as though a layer of fuzziness was peeled away and the true woman was emerging.

"This is over the top, even for John." Charlie scowled then settled back, propping his left ankle on his right knee, his dark khaki pants and white shirt making him look like an ad for Ralph Lauren's Polo.

I, of course, was the frump of the bunch in my 'good' jeans, red T-shirt, and white sweater. I chose my wardrobe to honor the memory of the woman whose ashes we earlier tossed over the side of Charlie's boat—Theodora Penningford, Charlie's grandmother. Red, white, and blue was her favorite color combination because she was an unabashed patriot until she died the previous spring. Today was the ash-flinging party on the lake with her descendents. I was a de facto member of the family, having been raised with the Whittingtons from childhood. Plus I was supposed to inherit most of Grandy Penningford's estate, an inheritance that had caused months of anger from Charlie's brother, John.

"I still say Sheila should be in jail," I maintained, jerking the subject back to the murder that had ensnared me the previous spring.

When Love Came to Town blared out from Livvie's Coach handbag on the couch. She whirled and pounced on it. "That must be T.J. I wonder why he's late." She took the bag and wandered toward the foyer behind us.

Ah. That explained Livvie's anxious behavior. We were going to meet the new Man in her life. I'd heard rumors about the mysterious T.J. Watson, the man Livvie met at Hazelden, an exclusive alcohol and drug treatment center north of the Twin Cities of Minneapolis and St. Paul. I looked back at her over one shoulder. She had a cell phone pressed to her ear, smiling. "Livvie looks happy," I commented in a low voice.

"I think she is. When she read me the riot act last spring about you, I told her to take a look at her own life." Charlie smiled wryly. "Little did I realize she'd actually do it and check into a treatment center."

"Ouch. I didn't realize she chewed you out."

"She told me to back off when you started...seeing Sam." Charlie took a long swallow of appletini. "She reminded me, rightfully so, that you and I were divorced and if I wanted to be a part of your life, I had to speak up."

I longed to get up and walk away from Charlie's perceptive eyes, but I restrained myself and stayed put. "You never spoke up."

He was silent for a long moment, staring at the contents of his glass. Then he looked at me and I saw my own confusion reflected back at me. "I'm not sure, Cassie. I love you, but is it the right kind of love? We were married so young and we've been divorced so long. I still love you, but..." His face darkened under his tan with a charming blush. "Believe me, I've lusted after you enough since our divorce."

"You've had girlfriends galore, too. You weren't exactly starving for female company." I set down my glass with a trembling hand. Charlie and I had danced around questions about our relationship for years. Those questions began to take center stage in recent months, mainly because of my involvement with Sam Barlow, whom I met the previous spring. "I know some of those girlfriends wouldn't mind another chance."

"You mean Kathleen?" He drained his glass in one swallow. "Sorry. After the way she confronted you last spring—that's over."

"I meant Janelle Rimes."

Charlie's head whipped around so fast I thought I heard his muscles scream. "You and Janelle have been talking about me?" His usually light voice was deadly calm.

"I've seen a lot of Janelle lately since she's the lawyer assigned to work with me on settling Grandy's estate." I ignored the warning tenseness I saw in his hand holding the glass and barreled ahead. "She hasn't settled down with anyone since you and she broke up."

"Really?" His eager question told me a lot before his mask settled back in place. "It doesn't matter. Janelle and I broke up years ago." He shrugged. "Besides, like I said before, she's too young for me."

I snorted. "Most men would jump at the chance to go out with a gorgeous thirty-something lawyer."

"We broke up years ago. She's moved on."

"Three years. Don't you think you could—?"

"No." Charlie stood up and went to the drinks table again, dumping some ginger ale and ice into a tumbler. "Janelle broke up with me because I wouldn't commit to a relationship."

"You wouldn't commit because of me," I said gently.

"What about you?" he countered. "Why didn't you change your name when we got divorced? You kept the Whittington name." His green eyes regarded me accusingly. "And what about Sam? You and he have been together for seven months now. Are you afraid to commit to him? Or is it just a passing thing?"

I decided to focus on the part of his speech I wanted to address. I wasn't ready to discuss my relationship with Sam with anyone, even myself. "Change my name to what?" I considered picking up my glass but was pretty sure my trembling hand would make a spill likely. "My father was a murderer. I'm not going to change my name back to Wheelock."

"You could change it to anything. But you kept the Whittington name. Cassie, you married me because you wanted to be an official part of our family. You could change your name and still be a part of the family. You—" Charlie broke off when Livvie walked back into the room and resumed her seat. "Problems?" he asked when he saw her worried face.

"T.J. can't come. He got tied up at the restaurant." Livvie gnawed on her lower lip. "He asked if you could give me a ride home, Charlie, since Cassie is borrowing my car."

"Restaurant?" I asked, happy for the diversion.

"He's a saucier." Livvie sipped her tonic water, her eyes narrowed deep in thought.

"I beg your pardon?"

"A sauté chef."

I blinked rapidly, trying to absorb this information. "Like, in a kitchen?"

"Yes. He's saucier at *La Suzette du Paris*."

This required a big sip of gin on my part. *La Suzette* was one of the most expensive restaurants in the Twin Cities metro area, specializing in authentic French cuisine. The restaurant was located in a small house on Lake Minnetonka, a ritzy location near on one of the secluded bays on the west side of the lake. Guests could arrive by boat or road, and reservations were impossible to obtain. "Really?" I glanced at Charlie. *You rat,* I thought. *You knew and didn't warn me.* Charlie smiled innocently at me and raised his glass of ginger ale in salutation.

"But you guys met at Hazelden?" I asked then

7

wanted to slap myself for such a stupid thing. What did I expect her to say, *Yeah, we met during rehab?*

"He volunteers at Hazelden during orientation for new people. He's one of the alumni."

"How did he become a cook—er, I mean, a chef?"

"He was a cook in the Navy during Viet Nam. When he got out, he ran into some problems. After he got straight, he went to culinary school." Livvie recited these facts almost absent-mindedly, her eyes on the window where twilight was falling.

I did some rapid mental math. If T.J. served in 'Nam, he had to be in his late fifties at the least. He was probably fifteen years older than Livvie.

"T.J.'s son is the pastry chef at the restaurant," Charlie murmured.

A son? Livvie's mystery man had a son? I drank off my martini, trying to assimilate the information being tossed my way.

"Another drink?" Charlie asked with an innocent smile.

I shot him a murderous look. "Ginger ale, please." I held out my glass and glared at him as he sprang to his feet and went to the drinks cart nearby.

"When I got out of rehab, I, well, I—" Livvie sounded bewildered, as though she could barely remember the experience. "I felt I had to meet him. His story—the one he told at orientation—was so intense. I called the restaurant and was told I couldn't get a reservation." She looked at Charlie, who had his back to her as he poured my drink. I, however, had a good view of the smug look on his face. "So I called my big brother and he came through for me."

"Amazing what a bit of name dropping will do," Charlie said. "My legal firm has a standing reservation at La Suzette. We take clients there occasionally." He dropped a slice of lemon into my drink and rejoined us, handing me my glass with a wink. "Has T.J. had any more trouble with that other chef? You mentioned it the last time we all had dinner together."

I shot him a disgusted look. *Dinner together? How chummy were they?* The least he could have done was prep me for a few of the surprises I was getting.

Livvie stood and paced to the window. "It's an ongoing battle with them." She sounded distracted but her back was to us so I couldn't see her face. "This bothers me. I know he wanted to meet you, Cassie. That's why we arranged for him to pick me up at your house later, so I could loan you my car. Do you think maybe we could stop at the restaurant? That way I can get a ride with him and you can just take the car."

"That's fine." I eyed the tense line of her shoulders. "Do you want to go now?"

"Could we?" She whirled and smiled with relief. "It just bothers me."

"Not a problem." I set my refilled glass on the end table. "I appreciate the loan. My Jeep needs to go to the shop again."

"Your Jeep needs to be retired," Charlie muttered.

I frowned at him. "Not all of us can run out and buy a new car when we need one." I got to my feet and settled my JC Penney leather bag on my shoulder.

Livvie picked up her far-more-pricey leather bag and held out her car keys. "Why don't you drive? It'll be good practice. You're going to be borrowing it for a while."

I took the keys warily. While it was nice of Livvie to let me use one of her cars, I wasn't sure I liked the idea of being responsible for a fifty-thousand dollar vehicle. Had I known I was going to be driving today, I would have limited my alcohol consumption. She saw my hesitation. "Oh, go ahead. It won't bite. I told you, if you like it, you can just buy it from me. I was going to sell it anyway." She led the way to the doorway, grabbing her matching blue jacket from the chair as she passed.

"See you tomorrow?" I asked as Charlie escorted me to the door. "At your father's party?"

He bent over and gave me a cheek kiss. "Maybe. Drive carefully."

"No shit. It's a Lexus."

He laughed. "You'll be fine."

"Talk to you later, Charlie." Livvie gave him a brief hug then hurried out into the hall. I followed, dragging on my denim jacket as we went.

When we emerged into the side parking lot, the sun was just starting to set, angling through vivid leaves. I've always said autumn and spring were Minnesota's rewards for enduring the icy winters and humid summers. This autumn was even prettier than many I remembered. I looked down at the keys in my hand as assorted exterior and interior lights came on in a red Lexus GS in front of us. Soft illumination highlighted the side mirrors, the foot wells, and a spotlight even shone onto the steering wheel and center console. "Whoa. What happened? I didn't press any buttons."

"The car reads the keys and it automatically opens," Livvie said. "And lights your way."

I slipped into the driver's seat and stared down at the unfamiliar controls. "Is this a space ship or a car?"

Livvie laughed. "Just follow the lights." She pointed to a series of illuminated spots that led to a button on the dash.

"What's that?"

"The start button. Just press it."

I did and the car purred to life. "Wow. Where're

the mirror thingy and the seat thingy and all that?"

She showed me a control panel that slipped out of the console. Soon we had the car adjusted to my shorter self and I put it into gear, driving slowly out of the parking lot. "Go right at the traffic light," she said. "We can stay on this road almost all the way to the restaurant."

I did as she directed, thankful there was still enough daylight for me to easily see the road. I was busy trying to familiarize myself with a car so much bigger and more powerful than my ancient Jeep Wrangler. Livvie stared out the front window, her face anxious. I tried to find a topic of conversation to divert her attention. "I thought it went well today at the flinging."

She grinned briefly. "Yes, it did. John wanted to throw you overboard, his wife got seasick, my sister avoided me, and most of the assorted grandkids acted like assholes."

"A typical Whittington outing." I steered cautiously through an intersection. "Has T.J. met the family?"

"Most of them at one time or another. You're the last one. Like I told T.J., you're more of a sister to me than Becky is."

I couldn't quibble with that description of our relationship. Livvie and Becky weren't on speaking terms since Livvie slept with Becky's second husband seven years earlier.

"I wanted T.J. to be there today. He knew how important it was to me."

"Why today? I mean, besides the ash-flinging, that is." I looked nervously from one side to the other. The road was now just a narrow ribbon of pavement, with huge expanses of water on either side. Minnetonka was one of the biggest lakes in the state and I felt like it was all waiting to suck me and the expensive car I was piloting into its grasp.

"We needed to talk to you and Charlie about something and we wanted to do it together." Livvie glanced at me then out the window. "It can keep."

She fell silent and I was grateful. The lake now loomed only on the left side of the car. I vaguely recognized this part of the metro. The home I was supposed to inherit—Grandy Theo's mansion—was southwest of here, on another part of the lake. I spent many a summer afternoon boating through these channels and bays with the Whittington family.

We drove about four miles when she said, "Go left at the intersection there. Then take the first right. The restaurant is a mile south, on the right side of the road facing the lake."

I made the turn into a tree-lined older part of the lakeshore world. Buildings faced the lake on our right with their signs on the road, pointing in to their parking lots. The sign for La Suzette was a white wooden shutter, almost hidden by trees. A short drive led to two buildings. "That's Hell House," Livvie said as she leaned forward to stare at a smaller white frame house on the right. "That's what they call the kitchen building. The dining room—the Feed Bag—is in the other building." She gestured toward the square blue building next to the white one. "When the owners expanded the business they decided to just buy the neighboring house rather than add on to their existing one. The buildings are connected by walkways. You can park there." She pointed to a few spots next to the smaller building where a motorcycle was already parked near a sign that said *Staff Only*.

"Where is everybody? It's Friday night. I thought the place would be jumping." I carefully maneuvered the car next to the Harley, breathing a sigh of relief when we rolled to a stop.

"It's only open on weekends in the fall and

winter and the buildings have been under construction. They're renovating the dining building, so T.J. has been on vacation for the last couple of weeks." Livvie opened her door before we stopped, springing out and going to the back door. Before she got there, it opened and a man stepped out on the wooden steps.

My first thought was *What's a biker doing here?* Scuffed boots, worn jeans and a denim jacket with appliquéd patches made him look like a refugee from Sturgis. Then my next thought was *This is a man who's seen some hard times.* He was tall but a bit hunched, as though protecting himself from a blow. His brown and gray hair was short and stubbly, topping a triangular face that narrowed to a smallish chin with a shadow of gray beard. The set line of his mouth was like a slash in his face, hard and inflexible. He reminded me somewhat of Eric Clapton: Eric post-drugs and getting older. A man at peace with himself and the world, but not forgetting the blows dealt him along the way.

Then I saw this man wore a prosthesis, an artificial right arm ending in a hook sticking out from his blue plaid flannel shirt that in turn stuck out under his denim jacket. When he saw Livvie, he took a step back. "What are you doing here, Liv?"

Holy shit. It was him. T.J. I made a mental note to give Charlie a lecture the next time I saw him. He needed to prepare me for shocks like this. My first thought was, *how can this guy be a cook? He's got a hook. He's a cook with a hook.* I plastered a smile on my face and prayed I wouldn't giggle.

"Cassie, this is T.J. Watson. Tom, this is Cassie Whittington."

I automatically held out my right hand then stopped, embarrassed. He smiled and held out his left hand, taking mine in an awkward but firm grip. "Good to meet you." He had a low, rough voice with a trace of Texas or some other American West state. "Olivia's talked a lot about you. She was right. You do look like Gidget."

I shot Livvie a disgruntled look. My resemblance to Sally Fields has haunted me all my life. I hoped when my hair turned gray it might change, but it didn't.

"What are you folks doing here?" he asked.

"I was worried when you said you couldn't come. Is something wrong?"

T.J. looked back at the building behind him. "Yeah, I think you could say that." His voice sounded almost bemused.

I peered around him and took an involuntary step forward when I saw what I thought I saw. "Is that—" I leaned to one side, trying to get a good look.

A body was lying on the floor just inside the door, a pool of blood making a dark stain in the middle of the chest in the white chef's uniform.

Chapter 2

"What is it?" Livvie started to move toward the door.

"Don't go in." T.J. barred her way by raising his arm.

I ducked under it and hopped up on the first step. "Who is it?" I stared with fascinated horror at the man on the floor. "Is he..." He had to be dead. There was too much blood. "Did you call the police?"

"Why would he call..." Livvie's voice faded away as she peeked past me. "Oh my God. It's Robert. What happened?"

"I haven't called the police. In fact, I was hoping to leave before anyone got here." T.J. sounded more exasperated than worried, as though finding dead bodies was an everyday occurrence.

"Haven't called the police?" I whirled, which made me almost level with his eyes since I was standing on the stoop. "You're crazy. It's a homicide. You have to call the cops."

"How do you know it's a homicide?" Livvie asked faintly.

T.J. put an arm around her and steered her back toward the cars, a few feet away. "You look pale, Livvie. Sit down."

She leaned against the motorcycle as I stepped down and joined them. "There's blood," I said. "It's got to be homicide." I reached into Livvie's car and grabbed my handbag. "We're calling the cops. If we don't, we're accessories or something."

"Don't."

The single word made me stop and turn to stare at him. "Is that a threat?"

"Of course it's not a threat. But Paul was here. I need to give him time to get away."

"What?" My voice came out in a small shriek. I looked around frantically. The street was just a car length or two away and traffic was meandering past, unmindful of a dead body lying so nearby. I saw the lake ahead of us, sparkling in the last of the setting sun. It was surreal. We were standing here talking while a corpse was lying on the floor.

"My son, Paul. He works at the restaurant, too. He's the pastry chef. He was here when I got here." For the first time since we arrived, T.J. looked worried. "Paul has had trouble with the police in the past. I don't want him involved in this."

I resumed my hunt for my cell phone. "That's bullshit. You can't just hide someone's involvement in murder."

"According to you, Sheila Peavey has," Livvie said faintly.

I glared at her. "That's different." I extracted my phone and dialed 9-1-1. "I'm sorry, T.J., but the cops have to be called."

"I know. I guess I was just hoping..." He looked at the restaurant. "I was hoping I wouldn't mess Paul up too much again."

I didn't have time to decipher his cryptic comment. "I need to report a dead body," I said to the operator.

****

"What's taking so long?" Livvie muttered fretfully two hours later as we sat in the lobby of the Mound Police Department. We had been hustled there by officers who descended on the restaurant.

16

We were interviewed separately, then 'released' to wait.

It was just like being in a bank lobby right down to the tile floor and a big counter topped by thick glass behind which two impassive police officers sat. Glaring overhead lights made it almost cheerful with pictures of the lake on the walls and even a carved pumpkin sitting on a table. Livvie and I huddled together in two of the five blue upholstered chairs. We each stared, fascinated, at the door with the electronic lock that led into the back rooms where we were interviewed.

"I'm so glad you're with me." Livvie held my arm tightly, her eyes bright with unshed tears and worry. "That lawyer Charlie brought looked competent, didn't he?"

We had called Charlie when we got to the station and he arrived immediately, followed almost as quickly by a criminal lawyer from his office. They both disappeared into the depths of the police station, leaving us to fret in the waiting room.

It was the third time Livvie asked me that question. "He looked good," I reassured her.

"I wish Billy Armstrong could be here," she murmured. "He's the lead defense attorney for Charlie's firm."

I patted her hand. "This guy looks competent. He said he would work with Mr. Armstrong on anything that needs to be done."

Livvie nodded distractedly but I doubt she even heard me. Billy Armstrong was a former Minnesota Viking football player with a reputation as a tough attorney. I had no idea the law firm where Charlie partnered fielded such a prestigious lineup. I started to ask if T.J. could afford it, then I remembered. Livvie would undoubtedly handle all the expenses.

"I'm surprised they let us drive here," she said, her eyes not straying from the door as though she could will it to open and expel T.J. "I thought we'd be taken in the squad car."

I didn't mention how closely we were tailed as we followed a squad to the station house. "I guess we look trustworthy," I said weakly.

"What do you think is taking so long?"

I put my hand over hers on my arm. "It's the police. They're probably just being thorough." I glanced nervously at people who walked past, all of them heavily armed, uniformed, and official-looking. I've had an abnormal fear of guns most of my life. Or maybe it was a normal fear based on my abnormal childhood. I had seen my father murder someone right in front of me then watched him being shot just inches from my face. That experience left me with a heightened awareness of guns and those who wielded them.

Regardless of the reason, the sight of firearms always makes me break out in sweat. I kept my eyes either on Livvie or on the door so I could block out the view around us but my focus was shattered when a woman strode into the waiting area from a door on the far side of the counter, escorted by two police officers. She made a beeline for us. "What did T.J. do?" she demanded in a voice that seemed to fill the small space.

I leaned back in my chair away from any potential threat as Livvie leapt to her feet. For a minute, I thought she'd take a swing at the woman, then she stopped, a sad expression replacing her anger. "Michelle, I'm so sorry for your loss."

Her quiet words acted like ice water on a cat. The woman stopped and stared at Livvie, her face contorting. She looked about my age with chin-length black hair, dark green eyes, and pale skin with just a hint of color on her cheekbones. I had a doll when I was a kid and this woman was a dead ringer for Sassy Susie, right down to the stylish clothes and short, somewhat stocky build. *Hunt club hussy,* I thought. *All that's missing is the riding crop and boots.*

"What did T.J. do?" the woman asked again, her voice choked with grief. She dug a hankie out of a coat pocket and sank into the chair next to Livvie, her shoulders shaking. The police officers who escorted her backed off, going to the counter to talk to the officer sitting there.

I eyed the woman critically. Having grown up on the fringes of High Society, I was a connoisseur of drama queens and I knew an act when I saw it. Or maybe I was just a bigger cynic than I liked to admit. Livvie, charitable soul that she is, leaned near the woman and whispered consoling words. She saw me watching them.

"This is Michelle de Garmeaux," she whispered. "Robert's wife." She used the French pronunciation of 'Robert' and whatever the last name was, so it took me a second to process the words.

"The dead guy?" I whispered in return.

"Michelle Bedford," the woman corrected. "I didn't change my name when I married. Robert and I felt it would be better that way, so we could keep the business side and the culinary side separated." She pronounced it 'kew-linary' and once again I frowned, trying to decipher her meaning.

Livvie nodded, taking Michelle's hand in hers and giving it a little squeeze while the other woman dabbed at her face with her hankie. "Michelle is co-owner of La Suzette with her husband, who is— was—the *chef de cuisine.*" Livvie correctly interpreted my blank look. "Robert was the head chef and T.J., Paul, and other chefs reported to him."

"The restaurant was our dream," Michelle said with a delicate little sniffle. "Robert so loved having his own restaurant. That's why I bought it for him. I hope T.J. didn't bring trouble with him. Paul swore his father wasn't—" She stammered to a halt.

Bought the restaurant for him? That piece of property was probably worth a couple of million which meant Michelle was probably worth multi-millions. "Trouble? T.J.?" I looked at the set line of Livvie's jaw and knew she was struggling not to snap some reply.

"T.J. and Paul's mother were married when they were teenagers. She died while T.J. was in Viet Nam. T.J. became addicted to drugs when he got out of the Army." Livvie explained the sad story in clipped, quick words. "The pain from his injury combined with some problems he had when he got out, and, well, he got addicted. Paul was raised by his grandmother. He and T.J. were estranged for years. Then T.J. got treatment and he and Paul reconciled. That was sixteen years ago."

"T.J. had a hard time kicking the drugs," Michelle said in a low, angry voice. "I wasn't sure if we should hire him, but Robert insisted. He said T.J. had real talent."

There are two sides to this story, I thought. *I wonder what T.J.'s side is?*

Livvie's nostrils flared as she drew in a long, steadying breath. "That was almost sixteen years ago. T.J.'s been straight ever since."

My glance slipped past Livvie and I saw rage flash in Michelle's heavily made-up eyes before it was suppressed. Was something happening that Livvie was unaware of? My stomach clenched. T.J. wasn't still an addict, was he? Surely Livvie would know.

My cell phone buried in the depths of my bag chimed *I Can't Tell You Why,* my ringtone of choice for Sam. I murmured an apology and got to my feet, pulling out the phone as I walked to a small alcove nearby where several vending machines displayed chips, pop, and candy.

"How're things going with Richie Rich?" Sam's cheerful voice asked. "What time do you think you'll get home? I'll be off work by nine. Is that too late for some company?"

I pressed the phone to my ear, so happy to hear his voice my knees wobbled. I've only known Sam since the spring, but I relied on his pragmatic, straightforward outlook on life. "Sam, you won't believe what happened." I stammered out a somewhat coherent explanation of what transpired since I talked to him earlier in the day.

"So let me get this straight. Livvie's guy, T.J., works at a restaurant and his son works there, too. And T.J. is an ex-addict and now the owner of the restaurant has been killed and the restaurant owner's wife is throwing suspicions on T.J.?"

"Yeah," I muttered. "It sounds complicated."

Sam snorted with laughter. "Complicated? You should talk. Your family is the king of complicated, isn't it?"

I straightened at this blunt assessment. "I'm not sure that's fair, Sam."

"Your father killed Livvie's mother. And your mother acted as a nanny and raised the kids." Sam spoke quietly but I heard an undertone of anger in his voice. "Then you married Charlie, the son of the woman your father killed. That's pretty complicated."

My continuing, albeit tenuous, relationship with Charlie was a sore point with Sam. I settled for saying, "I saved Charlie's life that day and he saved mine. We have ties beyond a failed marriage. I suppose to an outsider our relationship is a bit unusual."

There was a long pause. "Way to put me in my place, Cassie."

"Oh, Sam, please. You know what I meant."

"Yeah, I suppose I do."

I tried to decipher his emotion from his tone of voice but couldn't. With Sam, it was always hard to interpret his feelings. He was very adept at hiding them. "Charlie and I have come to an understanding," I said.

"Yeah. You'd rather not understand what's going on." He didn't give me a chance for rebuttal. "So what does the lawyer say about it all?"

I was vaguely aware of a large presence on my right. I darted a glance that way and realized I was blocking the entrance to the snacks. A big man in a blue uniform regarded me with impassive politeness.

"Sorry." I bobbed out of the way and meandered back to Livvie, who watched as Michelle spoke with a man who had just arrived from outside. He was short and muscular, his bald head gleaming in the bright lights. He looked like a boxer or a bouncer. Michelle looked angry and upset, shaking her head vehemently.

"I've got to go, Sam. Something's happening."

"Should I stop by tonight?"

I hesitated. "I'm not sure how long I'll be. Why don't you call me later?"

"Are we still on for tomorrow?"

Tomorrow? What were we doing…? "Oh, yeah. Sure." Sam and I were due to go to one of his cousin's wedding then to a Halloween costume party thrown by Charlie's father in the evening. It promised to be an interesting day of social contrasts.

"The wedding's at noon then we've got lunch afterward and the reception, which is another word for beer brawl. What time does the party at Little Lord Fauntleroy's start?"

I sighed. "It's at the Horse and Hunt Club. I think dinner is at seven with dancing afterward."

"Oh, boy. Can't wait."

Livvie now stood with Michelle and both of them were looking at the man with concerned looks. "I have to go, Sam. I'll call you if I can later."

"Doesn't matter how late. Call me."

"Will do."

"Cassie?"

"What?" I started to pull the phone away.

"Take care."

"Right." I hurried to Livvie as she sank back into her chair.

She rubbed a hand against her forehead. "I get these stupid headaches. It's part of detox, or at least that's what my counselor said. He said that when I get stressed and I don't drink, I'll get headaches. God, it hurts so much."

I plopped my purse on the seat next to me and dug a hand inside. "I've got some aspirin, hold on."

"It won't help. They're killer headaches." She closed her eyes briefly, lines of pain etching deep grooves around her mouth. At that moment she looked every minute of her forty-two years. Then she opened her eyes and I saw panic there. I put a hand on her arm, leaning forward to lend strength, if not hope.

"That's Michelle," she said in a low voice.

I looked at the man. "His name is Michelle, too?"

Livvie smiled briefly. "Sorry. It's Michael. Robert used to call him 'Michel.' That's the French pronunciation of his name."

"That must have been confusing," I said, looking from the male Michel to the female one.

Livvie frowned. "I don't know. There's a slight difference in the way it's pronounced. I suppose if you're trained to hear it...I think the other chefs call him Mike. He works at the restaurant, too. Someone saw Paul there," she said in a low voice. "The police are talking to him, too." Livvie looked past me as a door opened, then jumped to her feet.

Charlie emerged from the back rooms with the lawyer I glimpsed earlier. Livvie rushed to them and

Charlie enfolded her in a hug. He still wore his boating clothes and a leather jacket but the man with him was in a tailored suit, the dark gray fabric of his coat matching the touches of gray around his curly red-brown hair. I joined them, skirting past Michelle Bedford and the chef, who watched us suspiciously.

"Cassie, this is Rob Renard, one of the criminal defense attorneys in my office. Rob, this is Cassie Whittington, my ex-wife."

If Charlie's fellow attorney was surprised to be introduced to Charlie's ex-wife, he didn't show it. Of course, I was using Charlie's legal firm to help navigate the financial morass of Grandy's estate, so perhaps everyone in the office knew about our complicated past. I shook his hand. Rob Renard was a tall, big-boned man with pretty amber eyes, the color of dark honey.

"Thank you for coming," I said. "I know how worried Livvie is."

"I'm just filling in. Billy wasn't available but he asked me to sit in. Mr. Watson hasn't been charged, so he's free to go." Renard looked at the glassed-in area, where several people in uniform were conversing. "It'll be just a minute, but he'll be released."

"Does he have to come back?" Livvie asked anxiously.

Renard and Charlie exchanged a worried look. "Possibly," Renard said. "They just wanted to talk to him tonight, but don't be worried if he's asked back. I think they'll need more details from him later."

"Where's Paul?" Michelle Bedford demanded. "Mike said they wanted to talk to Paul, too. Is he there?"

The man with her pushed her out of his way and stared belligerently at Charlie. "Paul had nothing to do with this. T.J. is lying if he said he did."

"Hey, wait a minute," I said. "You've got it wrong. T.J. didn't say anything about him. In fact, T.J. was—"

Thankfully, whatever I might have said was lost when the door once again opened and T.J. Watson stepped out.

Livvie flew into his arms and he enfolded her in a hug, his craggy face briefly softening as she cried on his shoulder. He looked up from her to Charlie and nodded once in acknowledgement then he murmured something to Livvie, who raised her head and smiled tentatively at him. His glance flickered to Michelle and the man with her. He frowned then tucked Livvie protectively under his arm as they sidled by.

"Thanks for coming with her," he said to me as Livvie moved to one side. "I'm glad Olivia had someone with her." His arm tightened slightly and the hook, almost hidden by his denim jacket, shifted and glinted in the bright overhead lights.

I didn't mention that the police had not given me an option. "Not a problem." I looked at Renard. "So we can go now?"

"That's not fair," Michelle said shrilly. "Tom, you can't just desert Paul."

T.J.'s jaw clenched. "I'm not deserting Paul. We'll wait until we're sure he's okay." He glanced at Renard. "Right?"

"I wouldn't advise that," Renard said cautiously, but T.J. was already moving to one side, talking to Michelle and the man in a low voice, Livvie listening in.

"What's going on?" I asked.

Charlie grimaced. "The head chef was stabbed."

"So? When did it happen?"

Renard looked at the small notebook in his hand. "Sometime last night. Mr. Watson has an alibi but it's not one hundred percent tight. I suspect the police will want to talk with him again. You'll need more high-powered legal counsel than me when that happens."

"Can Billy help?" Charlie asked.

"Yes, I already talked to him. He'll be available tomorrow." Renard started walking toward the door where T.J. and Livvie stood. "Mr. Watson's motorcycle was impounded but he has a release form, so he's free to go."

T.J. had his arms around Livvie and she was huddled against him, her face pressed to his chest. My heart constricted at the woebegone look on her face. "I hope there's nothing wrong," I muttered.

"What do you mean, 'nothing wrong'? He's accused of murder." Charlie shot me a wry look. "The police have him at the top of the 'persons of interest' list."

"You know what I mean. I hope he didn't..." I didn't want to even voice the thought.

"I know." Charlie put an arm around my shoulders and gave me a squeeze. "I know."

"So why is T.J. at the top of the list of suspects?" I asked Renard. "Surely other people have means, motive, and opportunity." I smiled at Charlie's surprised look. "I read murder mysteries in addition to those steamy romances I love."

Renard stopped and stared at me. "You, too?"

"What?"

"Sorry. Nothing. My sister writes romance novels."

"Really? What's her name? Maybe I've read some."

Two small spots of color appeared on his cheekbones. "I doubt it. Anyway, Mr. Watson is under suspicion because of the means of death."

I looked at Charlie then back to Renard. "You lost me. You said he was stabbed?"

Renard looked at T.J., whose right arm encircled

26

Livvie's shoulder.

His hook gleamed in the overhead light.

"He was stabbed by something that looks remarkably like a hook."

Chapter 3

The door to the back offices opened again and a tall, thin man emerged, flanked by two policemen. When the man saw T.J., his face darkened to an almost purple shade of red. "You bastard," he snarled. His voice was low and rasping, almost painful sounding, like a voice ruined by cigarettes or illness.

"Paul, I didn't—" T.J. started across the lobby to the man but Michelle Bedford intervened, putting a hand on T.J's arm.

"Get out of here, Tom," she snapped. "I'll handle it."

The man named Mike interposed his bulk between T.J. and the man who glared at us all. So that was Paul, T.J.'s son. I looked over my shoulder as Charlie herded us out of the police station. Paul was a rangy man dressed in jeans and a jacket, his thick curly dark hair mussed and wild-looking. His unshaven face and wide, suspicious eyes gave him a haunted look. "Let's go, Cassie," Charlie murmured.

"Get out of here before they change their minds," Renard said to T.J. "You can talk to your son later."

T.J. cast one look back at Paul then he followed Livvie out of the station. She said something to him that made him put his arm around her. It looked like he needed the support. I lagged behind them to give them privacy. "Livvie is letting me borrow her car," I explained to Rob Renard, who walked with us. "My car needs to go to the shop."

"Your car needs to go to the junk yard," Charlie muttered.

"As I said before, Charlie, not all of us can run out and buy a new car when we need one," I snapped, peeved at his peevish tone of voice.

"I'm rich, Cassie. I'm not stupid. I know what it's like to worry about cash." Charlie shot me a look then grimaced, glancing at Renard as though to indicate I was being unreasonable.

"Bullshit." I tripped over the uneven sidewalk and twisted my ankle. "Damn."

Charlie put his arm around me, helping me balance. "You always act like I'm so removed from the things that are affecting you and Sam."

"How did Sam get involved in this?" I asked, jerking away from him. I hurried to catch up to Livvie and T.J., not sure I wanted to hear Charlie's answer.

"I'm sure Sam is worried about his business. You told me the store isn't doing that well this year."

"That has nothing to do with me being able to buy a car."

"Of course it does. Once you get the inheritance, you won't be as dependent on him. And Sam won't have to worry about money. He won't have to worry about the business."

I stopped and stared at Charlie, open-mouthed. "What do you mean?"

Charlie stopped, too, and put on his best innocent expression. For all I know it was sincere, but I doubted it. "You and he have been together now for almost seven months. I'm sure he's assuming it's a serious relationship."

"So? I mean, why? What does that have to do with anything?"

Renard had stopped, too, and now watched this

exchange like a spectator at a tennis match, his head going back and forth between us.

"Isn't that what you said to me? You told me that Kathleen thought our relationship was serious because we were together so long. It seems to me you and Sam are in the same boat. I'm sure Sam has some thoughts about the future."

"What's that got to do with the inheritance?" I glanced to my left, where T.J. and Livvie were standing near the sleek red car parked under one of the streetlights. A fine mist started to fall, bathing everything in a soft glow. The crisp autumn air held the scent of damp leaves and wood smoke. Someone nearby had a fireplace going

Charlie's handsome face held an expression of thoughtful concern but I thought I saw a curious, hooded look in his green eyes. "When you first met Sam, you had just found out about Grandy's inheritance. Then things got tied up in court and now...well, I'm sure Sam could use some help. Some financial help, that is."

It slowly dawned on me what Charlie was implying. "You're saying that Sam is sticking with me because he wants money."

"No, not that." Charlie sounded totally unconvinced.

I took a step closer to him. I only came up to his chin but I stared him down. "You're full of shit, Charlie. Don't presume to comment on my love life when yours is such a mess." I spun and strode across the parking lot to Livvie.

"Cassie, I didn't mean to offend you."

I stopped, stared at him, then turned and kept walking. "Cut the crap, Charlie," I shouted over my shoulder. "You're an asshole."

"Now just a minute. You need to think about it, Cassie. It's quite possible—"

I tuned him out as I dug Livvie's keys out of my

pocket. "Ready to go? I'll drive, okay? Do you want to get the motorcycle? Or to your house? Or to Livvie's house? Or do you want to drive?" I was so angry I barely heard my own words.

Livvie looked from me to Charlie. "You go ahead and drive." She held out her hand to T.J. "Where's the directions? I'll sit in front and navigate for Cassie. You don't mind, do you, T.J.?" She looked anxiously at him as he handed her a slip of paper.

"I'm so glad to be out of there, I'd ride in the trunk if I had to. You girls get up front." He looked back at Charlie and Renard, who stood near Charlie's Jaguar. "I appreciate the help, Livvie. Your brother really came through for me."

"Her brother's a class-A, number one, flaming asshole," I muttered as I jerked open the car door and fell into the driver's seat.

"He's that, too, but he helped me and I won't forget it," T.J. said from the back seat, his voice amused.

I twisted on the seat to look at him. "You're a perceptive judge of character."

"Nah." He looked out the window. "I just know how it feels to love somebody and be afraid they don't love me back." He looked at Livvie as she slipped into the passenger seat then he looked back at the police station. "I need to talk to Paul."

"Paul is so pissed off at you he won't listen," Livvie said. "Call him tonight when we get home. Or better yet, call him tomorrow. Nothing you say tonight will make any difference."

I grabbed the steering wheel to still my trembling hands and managed to hit the ignition button. "Here we go," I muttered. Charlie stared at me as we drove by and I resisted the impulse to give him the single-finger salute.

"He's adjusting to the fact that you're in love with Sam," Livvie said quietly.

I concentrated on the road and the big car I was driving. "I don't know if I'm in love with Sam," I said just as quietly.

"Hmm." She turned in the seat to look at T.J. "What happened? Can you tell us what they asked and did?"

I looked in the review view mirror. T.J. was seated behind me, his face dipping in and out of shadow as we drove down the main street. "Take a right here?" I asked at the stop light.

Livvie consulted the map in her hand. "Take a left then go left at the next light. The impound lot is straight down the boulevard. We should see signs."

I glanced at the glowing dashboard clock, surprised to see it was past seven o'clock. "What happened, T.J.?" I peered at him in the rear view mirror.

"Paul called me and asked me to meet him at the restaurant. We've been closed—I mean, the restaurant's been closed—for the past few weeks for remodeling. We couldn't do the work during the summer because that's our busy time. If it was daylight, you could see the restaurant. It's on the other side of the bay, just there."

I hazarded a glance to my left where a dark expanse seemed to stretch into the night. If there was a bay out there, I couldn't see it in the darkness that surrounded us. I turned onto a divided road that wound through a commercial district, two-and-three story warehouses on either side of us. The mist changed to a fine drizzle and to my surprise, the wipers turned on automatically, which saved me the worry of finding the switch. "This car does everything but drive itself," I muttered.

"It's got automatic wipers, the headlights swivel when we make a turn, and it's got Bluetooth," Livvie said. "I thought the remodeling was done?" she said to T.J.

"I thought so, too. I didn't pay much attention to it because it didn't affect the kitchen. They were doing some painting and new windows and stuff like that."

I took the next left onto another boulevard. White posts marked the edges of the road, separating it from the lake stretching out on both sides. I prayed silently I wouldn't dunk us in the drink. "So what happened?"

"The restaurant is on the way to Charlie's condo, so I figured I'd talk to Paul then come meet Livvie so we could talk to you and Charlie about the wedding."

"Wedding?" I almost turned in my seat, remembering in time that I was driving and turning wouldn't be such a smart idea. "What wedding?"

"T.J. and I are getting married." Livvie took a deep breath. "And we wanted to ask a favor of you."

I recognized her tone of voice. This was Livvie's *I'm about to drop a bomb* mode. I've known her most of my life and I recognized it. "What kind of favor?"

"Would you sing at our wedding?" She looked eagerly at me. "You and Charlie? It's going to be next spring."

"Does your family know this?" I asked.

Livvie's jaw tilted. "Yes."

"Just her father, actually." T.J. corrected. "He was majorly pissed off."

"That's because it's like a repeat of his life," I blurted. "He married Livvie's mother and her mother—Grandy—almost disinherited her. Of course I'll sing. We'll both sing."

"We'd better check with Charlie on that," T.J. said. "He might not want to sing. For all I know, he might be as pissed off as Livvie's dad."

"I knew I could count on you." Livvie turned to peer at T.J. "Cassie and Charlie sing at all family events. They sang today when we tossed Grandy Theo. And they sang at her funeral, and Becky's son's wedding and ...I know just the song, too. I have it all picked out."

T.J. seemed amused by this fuss over a simple song. "It's going to be a small wedding," he warned. "Nothing fancy."

Since the Whittingtons were one of the wealthiest families in the Twin Cities, I rather doubted that, but I'd leave T.J. his fantasies. He would learn his mistake soon. The Whittingtons didn't do anything in a small way.

"First we've got to get past the small matter of a murder," I pointed out. "Go on with your story, T.J." I glanced at him in the mirror but he'd shifted position, moving out of my view.

"When I got to the restaurant, Paul was waiting for me in his car. We opened the back door together and we found Robert on the floor. That's when I called you, Livvie. I guess I wasn't thinking, I shouldn't have called you. I didn't mean for you to come over and get involved in this."

I tried to visualize it in my head but I was too busy trying to visualize a road. There's nothing like nighttime on a lake, and despite the occasional streetlights, I felt like I was floating, suspended between heaven and water.

"If it involves you, it involves me," Livvie said.

I didn't comment but my mind was whirling. Why would he call Livvie when he was sitting, metaphorically speaking, on a dead body? Why would his son wait for him in the parking lot? "Did you have the only key to the restaurant?"

T.J. hesitated before answering. "The door was unlocked."

"It must have been an intruder," Livvie said confidently. "Someone who broke in and surprised Robert."

As soon as she said it, I started to relax. She was probably right. The restaurant was in an expensive

34

neighborhood in a relatively isolated part of the peninsula and if it was late at night, it was just possible somebody did try to rob the place. "You said the police were interested in your whereabouts last night?" I asked.

"Yeah." T.J. sounded glum.

"You have an alibi, right?" I relaxed my death grip on the steering wheel. The land around us was widening, the lake now just on the passenger side. Straight ahead I saw welcoming land on both sides of the road. "Don't you?"

"Sort of."

I looked in the rear view mirror. T.J. was staring out his window, his face averted. I glanced at Livvie. She was staring straight ahead, her jaw tense.

"What is it? What's wrong?"

"T.J. and I had an argument last night," Livvie snapped. "He was at my house, but he left early when we disagreed."

I glanced at her again, then at T.J., who regarded her with a sad look. "Disagreed about what?"

"T.J. doesn't think we should serve alcohol at the wedding."

The statement was so ludicrous I snorted with laughter. "Well, duh."

"Cassie!"

"Hell, Livvie. You're both recovering alcoholics. Why would you serve booze at your wedding?"

"For my guests, of course." Livvie looked outraged.

"Oh, for cryin' out loud. Your guests will understand if they can't drink it up at your wedding." I peered ahead. "Is that it?" I saw a brightly lit expanse of concrete on the left side of the road.

"I think so." Livvie looked at the paper in her

hand then at me. "That's not what John said at Barb Monahan's wedding last year."

"John's as big an asshole as Charlie." I waited for traffic to pass then made a left into a wide driveway where two chain-link gates blocked the entrance. A small shed sat on the right side under a glaring light. As I pulled up a police officer in uniform stepped out.

"Give me the papers, Liv." T.J. reached his hand through the seats and Livvie handed him his 'release papers.' He got out and approached the officer.

"I've never been to a wedding where alcohol wasn't served," Livvie said absently, watching as T.J. stopped several paces away from the officer, who kept his hand on his service revolver as T.J. approached. She cleared her throat. "Actually, there was one other thing we wanted to talk to you about, Cassie."

I shot a wary glance at her. "Now what?"

"I'm going to put my house on the market. T.J. and I need to find a new home, one where we can start our new life together."

My jaw started to sag open. Livvie's 'house' was an old Victorian mansion on Lake Calhoun, in Minneapolis. It was probably worth about one or two million. "Where are you going to look?"

"Well, actually..." Livvie plucked at the crease in her pants then looked at me. "We were hoping we could buy Grandy Theo's house from you."

"What?" Grandy left the bulk of her estate, including a home on Lake Minnetonka, a home in Northern Minnesota, and a home in Florida, to me along with her cash assets, most of her investments, and any possessions not already designated to other people. The lawsuit John Whittington filed prevented me from accessing any of the funds except those needed to retain legal counsel to battle John— an ironclad provision Grandy put into her will. I silently blessed her foresight for that stipulation a hundred times over because my salary as an employee at Barlow's Landscape Center couldn't begin to cover legal fees.

"Would you mind?" Livvie asked anxiously. "Do you plan to move there?"

"Me, move there? No, I hadn't planned on it. I figured I'd sell it sometime. There's a lot of stuff there. Furniture and clothes and all of Grandy's things."

"I'd help you sort through it," Livvie said eagerly. "In fact, I talked to John about it. I didn't tell him about T.J. of course."

"God knows what John will do when he finds out you're getting married," I said.

"Oh, he'll pitch a fit. That's why I just asked him if he thought it would be okay if I put in an offer on the house. I didn't mention it would be my honeymoon home." Livvie smiled and blushed, just like a bride should. "He agreed to remove the Lake Minnetonka house from the list of disputed possessions." Livvie smiled at me. "So I'll pay you for the house, you'll have that money, and John can go piss up a rope about the rest of the money being tied up. I was thinking two million."

"For what?"

"For the house. Would that be okay? I called a friend of mine in real estate and she said that seemed fair. We should probably have an estate sale." Livvie regarded me thoughtfully. "Sue can do the appraisal and set up the sale. Once that's done, we can finalize on the house."

"Two million dollars?" I tried to force my beleaguered brain into coherent thought. Grandy's money was Someday Money that I might or might not get depending on what happened with John's objection to my inheritance.

This was Real Money. This was Right Now

Money.

"What does T.J. think of all this?" I peered ahead where the person in question was signing papers and taking keys from the police officer.

"It's convenient for him because it's across the bay from the restaurant, so he's fine with it." She smiled faintly when she saw the gates open and T.J. hurry through. "I'm so glad Charlie was there to help us."

My cell phone, buried in my purse on the console next to me, chimed *The Boys of Summer*, my ringtone of choice for Charlie. "Speak of the devil. The asshole is calling..."

"Cassie? This is Charlie. I wanted to—"

"What's going on?" I looked around frantically when Charlie's voice echoed in the car.

"—apologize for jumping on you about Sam earlier. I shouldn't have done that."

"It's Bluetooth," Livvie said, touching a button on the console. "It automatically answers your phone for you."

"I can't help but worry, though," Charlie continued, obviously unaware of my technological gaffe. "You're going to inherit a lot of money and..."

"What if I want to screen my calls?" I muttered. "Turn it off."

"You and Charlie should talk."

"Not while I'm piloting the Starship Enterprise. Turn it off."

Charlie's voice abruptly silenced as Livvie pressed the button. She rummaged in the glove compartment, pulling out a book, which she set atop my purse on the console. "Just read up on the car, you'll love it. You can keep it as long as you need it. The registration and a signed letter of consent for you to borrow it are in the console." She gave a little chuckle. "You know Charlie, he insisted on the legalities." We both heard the thrumming roar of a motorcycle. Livvie put her hand on the door pull but hesitated, looking intently at me. "Call Charlie. He's worried about you. He's right, Cassie. It's a lot of money."

"I don't care about the money. Neither does Sam."

She smiled. "Look, get a prenup. It'll go a long way to easing Charlie's worries."

"I'm not planning to get married."

"Well, if you do plan to get married, get a prenup. I'll call you tomorrow. And stop worrying. It was a break-in, pure and simple." She slipped out of the car and hurried to T.J., who was wheeling the motorcycle through the gates. His lack of arm didn't appear to impede his handling of the big bike. I watched as Livvie got on, taking the helmet T.J. handed her.

Olivia Whittington Carlyle, riding a Harley. Who would have thought? She waved to me as they drove past, T.J. lifting his fingers slightly before they made a left turn and disappeared into the night.

The police officer regarded me questioningly. I smiled and wanted to roll down the passenger side window, but I was afraid to touch any of the controls, fearing I might trigger an ejector seat. I settled for stepping out of the parked car and asking over the hood, "What's the simplest route to Pickaway from here?"

He recited a string of "left, then left in the park, right at the junction, straight on then left." I nodded, praying I was absorbing the information. I knew I was northwest of home and I had a general idea that if I managed to find Highway 44, I'd find my way back to my townhouse. I set off in the Starship Enterprise, driving slowly on the unfamiliar roads, thoughts of murder on my mind.

I had the feeling T.J. was lying about something,

but what? Was he lying about Paul's involvement in what happened, or his own? I came to an intersection and peered left then right. Left seemed the correct choice, but the road there wound away in a northerly direction. After a long hesitation, I went left and was immediately plunged into darkness as I rounded a turn.

I was on a causeway, a narrow strip of land between the bays of the lake. I struggled to remember a map of Minnetonka in my mind, but the lake was so big and had so many bays it was impossible. I drove for what seemed like miles, the road twisting and turning and the lake lapping nearby, small waves showing when the headlights bounced over the water. I came to another intersection and I took a right, praying that I was now going south.

Wrong choice, as the compass on the mirror attested. When I belatedly checked it, I discovered I was going west. The road turned again, meandering into a residential neighborhood. I made a left, hoping to double back the way I came, but there wasn't another left to be had. I made a series of turns and soon realized I was hopelessly lost. I turned around in a driveway and started back, but I must have made a mistake because the car didn't go back through a neighborhood full of houses. I was headed on another causeway, this one even narrower than the previous one.

I peered ahead, gripping the wheel nervously. A small blinking light inset into the dash drew my attention and I slowed almost to a crawl to stare at it. The amber glow was an icon of some kind, a lumpy-looking circle. A donut? I laughed shakily. "Yeah, right. Stop for donuts," I muttered.

A muted beep-beep-beep started chiming from somewhere overhead as though in response to my complaint.

I jerked the wheel in surprise, then slammed on the brakes.

Lake Minnetonka, dark and deep, was just inches from my front bumper.

Chapter 4

"Holy crap." I tried to swallow and almost choked because my throat was so dry. I put the car into park, ignoring the insistent beeping of the Donut Alarm. I slowly opened my driver's side door, the interior light adding a bit more illumination to the scene.

It looked like I was surrounded by water on all sides, except immediately behind me. "How the hell did that happen?" I turned cautiously to look back from where I came and realized I'd come down a small ramp. "Oh, shit."

I was on a boat ramp leading straight into the lake. Many coves and bays had these types of ramps. They were really just flattened spots of earth, graded to slope down gradually to the lake and make it easy for boaters to get their craft into the water.

I rested my head on the doorframe, drizzling rain striking my sweaty flesh and making me shiver. I raised my head to the sky. "Why me?" I called out. I peered through the blackness behind me and wondered if I could back up. The rear wheels were precariously near the edge of the ramp and one wrong move might send me into the water.

I slipped back into the car and rested my forehead briefly against the headrest, closing my eyes and steeling myself for a tricky bit of driving. The damn Donut Alarm was still beeping at me, the little glowing light annoyingly bright in the murky darkness. I started to turn to look behind me and as I did I saw a glowing white button above the rear view mirror.

"Thank you, God," I muttered as I pressed OnStar.

After a humiliating half-hour with a policeman, I discovered that (1) I'd managed to drive unerringly through a state park straight to a steep boat ramp and (2) the right rear tire was low on pressure, which explained the Donut Alarm. The lumpy circle was supposed to be a tire in need of air. Who knew?

The stoic police officer backed the car out for me and directed me to a gas station where, miraculously, the clerk on duty knew how to fill tires from the hose provided. I thanked her profusely, tipped her generously, and was home in another half-hour.

I parked Livvie's car in my drive and locked it. Or at least, I think I locked it. I pressed a few buttons on the key fob and it made some beeping noises, so I assumed it was protected for the night. I took the instruction manual with me into the house, snagging my escape cat, Houdini, as he made a break for the Great Outdoors. The portly yellow feline enjoyed dodging me and it was now a game with us: will Cassie manage to corral him? Or will Big Yellow make a run for it and escape the Big House?

My home phone was ringing as I set the struggling ten-pound beast on the entry rug. I made a dash for the phone but whoever was calling didn't bother with the answering machine. I poured myself a glass of wine from my handy Wine in a Box and sagged down on the couch in the living room to settle my nerves. Houdi plopped down and pressed his bulky self against me as I thumbed through the Enterprise's instruction manual. I'd taken only a couple of sips when the phone rang. I checked caller ID and with a sigh, I picked up.

"Are you okay, Cassie? I tried calling earlier at home and on your mobile but I was cut off. I left a message on your cell phone."

Charlie sounded anxious. I tried to sit up around fourteen pounds of yellow cat snuggled against my hip. "Livvie's car answered my cell phone. It's got a Bluetooth thing. What's up?"

"I wanted to apologize. It was out of line for me to suggest Sam was with you just for the money." He sounded honestly contrite. "It's just that you're not accustomed to what can happen when people find out you're loaded." He gave a short, bitter chuckle. "It awakens the oddest emotions in people."

"I'm not loaded, at least not yet. Did you know they're getting married?"

As always, Charlie understood my cryptic change of subject. He paused then said, "Livvie mentioned they were considering it."

"It's next winter. She wants us to sing."

"Sing what?"

"I don't know but I said we'd do it. So tell me, did you do a background check on him?"

"What? Of course I didn't."

"You don't lie well, Charlie. Come on. Spill." A fleeting thought made me wonder: could I even tell if Sam lied to me? I wasn't sure I really knew him that well. I sipped my wine and relegated the thought to the recesses of my brain to consider later.

"T.J. has a record," Charlie admitted. "It was when he first got out of the service. He was addicted to painkillers, probably because of his injury. He was arrested for burglary. He spent a few months in jail then he was released into a treatment center where he served out his sentence."

"But he's okay now, right?"

"He had some rough times, bouncing in and out

44

of treatment. He went into residential rehab in the Nineties and he's been straight ever since. He had cook's training when he was in the Navy and he's been working his way up for the past ten years. This position at La Suzette is the most prestigious job he's ever had."

A hissing sound whispered faintly behind me. I twitched open the curtain that covered the window over the couch. A steady drizzle was hitting the leaves in the gutter, making them rustle. The smell of wet leaves was strong, seeping in through the small opening at the bottom. It reminded me of the smell of the lake, so close to my car wheels. I gulped some more wine.

"From what I can gather, T.J. has a good reputation. Apparently de Garmeaux was going to retire and T.J. and the sous-chef were up for the job."

"Sous-chef?"

"He's the second-in-command. You saw him at the station. Mike Johnson."

"The ex-boxer?"

"How did you know he was a boxer?"

"He looked like one."

"The head chef was supposed to be making a decision soon on who got the job." There was a brief pause. "Do you and Sam have your costumes for the party?"

"Yep. Are you going?"

"I don't know."

"Janelle is going. We're meeting her there."

"Why?"

"We figured we'd get John drunk and gather information about his nefarious schemes." I tried to keep my voice light and not give away my ulterior motive for accepting the invitation to his father's party. "You should come."

"I don't have a costume."

I finagled my way around Houdi, leaving him nestled in the warm spot on the couch. "Guys have it easy. Just wear a pair of jeans, a T-shirt, and grease your hair and you're ready for a Fifties party." I shuffled out to the kitchen and refilled my glass. A sudden thought made me pause. "Did you run a background check on Sam?"

"What?"

"A background check on Sam. Did you?"

"Why would I do that?"

I recognized a stalling tactic when I heard it. Charlie was notorious for avoiding tricky subjects, which was odd given his tenacity as a lawyer. "Damn it, Charlie, you did." Then my innate curiosity kicked in. "What did you find?"

"I think you know."

"Humor me, okay?" I stared at myself in the cat-shaped mirror over the kitchen sink. My sweatshirt-gray hair was its usual tangle because I couldn't decide on a hairstyle. Keep it short? Let it grow? I was at the 'if I let it grow just another couple of inches it might be manageable' phase, but I wasn't sure I had the patience to wait out the stage.

Charlie recited his findings with dry humor and a touch of exasperation. "Sam Barlow, age fifty-six. He was in the Marine Corps for fifteen years, went to college after the service and got a Masters degree in Landscape Science. Married Sheila MacAndrews while in college, married for seven years, divorced for ten years. His ex-wife left him for Michael Peavey, who was murdered last spring. But hey— you know about that, right?"

"You're not good at sarcasm, Charlie." I wedged the phone next to my shoulder as I peeked into the fridge. I eyed the ten-year-old block of good cheddar but resisted temptation and settled for some crackers instead. "Continue."

"Sam's property sits on land inherited by Sheila

Peavey from her father, but she can't sell as long as the company stays in business. It's a stipulation in her inheritance. By the way, I got a property evaluation on the land. It's worth about a million."

I dropped the cracker box. "What? Sam's landscape business is worth a million bucks?"

"Not the business, the property. A developer wants to tear down his buildings and put up condominiums."

"Holy crap," I muttered. "The deed is ironclad, though, right?" I once again thanked a Beneficent Deity for Charlie and his knowledge of contract law. He was helping Sam and his sister, Mary, stave off Sheila Peavey's attempts to grab the land for herself.

"As far as I know it is. We still have a hearing on the matter, though. Now that Sheila's out of jail, it can proceed."

"Sam's business is mortgaged to the hilt, but you knew that, of course," Charlie continued.

I didn't know that, but I didn't let on. "A lot of landscape and nursery companies are that way," I said with what I hoped was cavalier dismissal. "One bad year can set them back a bunch."

"Sure." He sounded totally unconvinced. "So that's the scoop." He hesitated then said, "I hope you don't mind, Cassie. You stand to inherit a lot of money—"

"If your brother lets me," I interrupted.

"John's objection won't succeed and he knows it. He's just making trouble because he's pissed off that he wasn't given more in Grandy's will. You know how John is."

I did and that's what had me worried. John was like a bulldog when it came to getting his own way. If he wasn't happy, he made sure everyone around him was equally unhappy. "We'll see," I temporized. "I'm more worried about this murder thing with Livvie's guy."

"I've got the best people in my office working on it. If they can't help him, nobody can. Speaking of which, am I forgiven?"

"For what?"

"For implying—you know—about Sam."

"Given what happened with Livvie and her first husband, I suppose you were justified."

I could almost see Charlie's grimace as he remembered Livvie's abusive, unfaithful and manipulative late spouse. When Kenneth Carlyle died of a heart attack eight years earlier, everyone breathed a sigh of relief. "Thanks, Cassie."

Houdi came wandering in with his *where's the food?* meow. "I've got to go now, Charlie. I'll see you tomorrow, okay?"

"I'm not sure. A Fifties party?"

"It's for a good cause. Your father is donating the cost of the party to the local food shelf and all the bigwigs paid big bucks to attend. He expects the entire family to be there. Besides, you're getting to be an old stick in the mud. Get out. It'll do you some good. Talk to you later." I hung up before he could continue his *woe is me* arguments. There were times when I wanted to shake Charlie until sense percolated in his brain. He was handsome, rich and single. Some people would kill to be in his shoes. No, a *lot of people* would kill to be in his shoes.

That thought occupied me as I dumped some kibble in Houdi's dish and ice into my glass. Why would someone kill a chef at a restaurant? My brief brush with murder the previous spring inspired me to revisit my mystery paperbacks so I knew the usual motive put forth was either love or money.

Love? I knew nothing about Robert de Garmeaux, head chef. I took my wine glass and went to the den where I sat down at my computer and fired up a Yahoo search.

To my surprise, I found pictures and facts.

Robert de Garmeaux leaves position of Dean at Milwaukee's Le Cordon Bleu School to accept chef de cuisine position at prestigious Minnesota restaurant.
I sipped and read, digesting the information with my crackers. The pictures of de Garmeaux were a few years old, showing a tall gentleman with silver hair, a long, somewhat droopy face and dark eyes. The attached biography said he was in his late sixties and had a distinguished culinary career starting in France with stints in Switzerland before coming to the United States for teaching assignments at various schools. There was a brief mention of his marriage—his fifth—and then assorted reviews of the restaurants followed.

I next did a search on Michelle Watson, but found little. Then I remembered. Livvie introduced her as Michelle Bedford. She must have gone back to her maiden name. A quick search of Michelle Bedford turned up a wealth of Internet gems, most of it recent.

Michelle was from California. I found a picture of her with Saul Bedford, an elderly man, presumably her father. He was a financial analyst who left her a sizeable fortune at his death, which she parlayed, into an even larger one by adroit investing. She moved to Chicago in the early Nineties and married Robert de Garmeaux in the late Nineties then moved to Minnesota, where they bought their restaurant and settled into society life.

I couldn't find much information about her prior to the Nineties, which was somewhat surprising since Saul Bedford was apparently well known in his community. Perhaps he kept his family isolated from the media.

I looked at the bookshelf above my computer laden with abused paperbacks, hoping for a glimmer of murder motivation in those dusty pages. "Why would someone kill the chef in a restaurant?" I asked

Houdi, who occupied the corner of my door-on-crates desk, peering out the small window to the Big Outside. His ears flickered but otherwise he showed no interest in my question.

I went back to the living room and picked up the instruction manual to the Starship Enterprise sitting in my driveway. My close encounter with Lake Minnetonka tonight made me determined to become proficient. I was happy Livvie volunteered to let me use the car and I didn't want to repay the favor by driving it off into a ditch. I skimmed through the Dynamic Cruise Control, which meant the car would adjust its speed to pace another vehicle. Since I normally passed everyone on the road, I doubted I would need it. The next feature was useful, though. I could program the car to my garage door so I wouldn't have to carry around an opener. I had an almost-close-encounter with a stalker in the spring and my remote control almost got me into trouble. I looked forward to not using one. The phone rang as I was reading about how to program the Enterprise.

"Hey, how did it go?" Sam's cheery voice competed with the background noise of clattering and banging. I recognized those unique sounds. He was in the greenhouse at the landscape center and probably working on the watering system, which was notoriously cranky. "I worry every time you and Richie Rich get together. I'm sure he won't let you go."

"Well, if he doesn't, you can just rescue me." I flipped through the manual to "Bluetooth" and peered at the illustrations.

"I'll do that."

I blinked in surprise. He sounded almost serious. "The cops released T.J. Livvie thinks it was a break-in that went bad."

"I'm glad for Livvie's sake they released him.

Livvie's good people. How long was the chef guy dead?"

"The police said a day. Why?"

"I've been thinking about it. Hold on." I heard a banging noise then Sam came back on the line. "Was he bloated?"

"What?"

"You know—if a body is lying around, wouldn't it be, you know—bloated?"

I hadn't considered that. I tried to remember details from the many mysteries I read but wasn't sure if bloating was mentioned. "I don't know."

"I'm surprised no one missed him. I mean, he was gone for a day. And weren't there people around? If it was under construction, you'd think there would be workers around." I heard some more banging. "Why would someone break into a restaurant that's under construction?"

"Copper pipes? I heard those fetch a good price on the market."

"Yeah, you're right. Maybe that's what it was. Listen, I was thinking. Did you want to take our party clothes with us to the wedding and we can change when we get to the party? The wedding's on that side of town, too. That way we won't have to come back here and change."

His thought made sense. "That sounds good. Oh, hey, Livvie and T.J. are going to get married. They asked me to sing at their wedding."

There was a long pause and I heard more wheezing noises in the background. "How long has she known him?"

I calculated. "About five or six months."

"Wow. I guess they know what they want." His voice was thoughtful.

"And listen, Livvie wants to buy Grandy Theo's house. She's going to sell her house and she wants Grandy's house for her and T.J."

"Do you want to sell the house to her?"

"Sure. It's a nice place but not where I want to live. If Livvie wants it as her honeymoon home, I'm happy to let her have it. She said she'd give me two million for it."

"Two million bucks?" He whistled. "Are you going to finally quit your job?"

"Why? Do you want me to? Has someone given you grief about me sleeping with you?"

"Nope. But that's a nice chunk of change."

Sam was right but I hadn't thought that far ahead. When I was named the beneficiary of Grandy's estate earlier in the year, I decided to set up a charitable trust with part of the money and reserve part for myself. Those plans were put on hold when John filed his suit, but if I sold the house, that money could be spent how I wanted, right now. "I'll think about it," I said. "I enjoy working. Besides, I don't have the cash yet. I need the job."

"I'm holding you to the two-week notice thing." Sam's words were teasing but his tone wasn't as light as I thought it should be. Was he worried about how the money would affect us? That was a topic we had never really discussed, despite Charlie's suspicions to the contrary.

"We'll see what happens," I hedged.

"Okay. Do you mind having some company tonight?"

I smiled, leaning back on the couch. "I'd love some company."

"Great. I'll go home and shower then come by."

"Why shower?" I laughed softly. "You'll just have to shower again later."

"I like the sound of that. See you in a half-hour or so."

I flicked on the TV to catch the weather forecast for the next day in order to determine my clothing choice. Sunny and a high in the mid-forties. Not bad for late October in Minnesota. I went in the bedroom to consult my closet. This was my first outing with Sam to meet his entire extended family and I wanted to make a reasonably good impression. I settled on a pastel patchwork cardigan with brown pants then I checked my costume for the Fifties party. The poodle skirt I sewed together looked passable as did the bobby socks, sneakers, and argyle sweater found at a local thrift store. I was set.

It was as I was carefully folding the skirt to put into a travel bag that I realized why Sam sounded so odd when he asked about Livvie and T.J. He and I started seeing each other six-and-a-half months ago. I sagged down on the bed and snatched my handbag from the floor, extracting a picture of Sam and me taken at a picnic during the summer. Sam had his arm around my shoulders and our heads touched, his short thick white hair somewhat flyaway around his square, tanned face. His gray-rimmed eyeglasses framed his dark eyes and he looked solid and muscular in his T-shirt and shorts. I touched the face in the picture, remembering the dimples that flashed when he grinned and the way his eyes took on a hazy, intense darkness when he kissed me.

Sam was the total opposite of Charlie. Sam was stocky, muscular, white-haired, blue-collar and blunt to the point of pain. In the seven months we had been...paramours, we had fun together, spending a lot of time initially engaging in high-octane sex at my townhouse or Sam's apartment. Our relationship had soon settled into evenings together several nights a week, sex when we felt like it, and snuggling the rest of the time. We never discussed the future or commitment or love.

And, to be fair, was I ready to talk about it now? I enjoyed being with Sam, but I didn't want to think about the future. I was content to let things chug along the way they were. If it ain't broke, why fix it?

I pushed the thoughts aside. Just because Livvie and T.J. were ready to take the plunge, it didn't mean I had to. I went back to my den and found a notepad so I could jot down the questions Sam asked:

Why didn't anyone miss Robert for a day?

Where were the construction workers on Friday? Why wasn't his body discovered earlier?

The body: bloating? Decay?

That last question made me add another one:

Heating system in the restaurant? Freezer?

I peered up at my bookshelf, reaching for a John Sandford novel. If anybody talked about bloating, it would probably be Sandford. I hesitated when headlights shone into the den, signaling someone turning into the drive.

I grabbed Houdini, circumventing his dash for the outside by stuffing him in the bedroom and closing the door. I jerked open the front door, prepared to greet Sam with a hug and a kiss.

Instead I found Sheila Peavey, Sam's ex-wife and the woman I suspected of murdering her husband six months earlier.

Chapter 5

"Nice car," Sheila said. "You've come up in the world."

She looked just like I remembered her although she was thinner. *Jail time will do that,* I thought. *Of course, on her lost weight looks good.* She was about five inches taller than me with an oval face and killer fashion sense as evidenced by her coordinated 'fall-theme' clothes. The brown slacks and brown sweater with swirly leaves on it contrasted beautifully with her thick blonde hair and ice blue eyes. At first glance she looked like a perky cheerleader-mom type until you saw the calculating and hard look behind the mascara and eye shadow.

I took a step back. "What are you doing here?" I heard the telltale sound of cat claws pulling at a door and I changed my mind, moving forward to block the doorway.

"Why don't I come in?" she said coolly, brushing past me.

I didn't have time to argue. A yellow furry bundle was racing across the living room. I stepped back inside the house and slammed the door just in time. Houdi skidded to a stop on the tile foyer floor then shot me a disgusted look. With a flick of his tail he sauntered into the kitchen.

"What was that all about?" Sheila asked with a disdainful smile on her perfectly lipsticked lips.

"What do you want?" I shifted position so I blocked her further entry into my home.

She moved in response, going to the doorway that led to my den, located immediately off the entryway. She glanced inside, giving my makeshift desk a critical assessment then she turned her attention back to me. "I'm looking for Sam. I've heard you and he are a hot item."

"What could you hear? You've been in jail." As soon as I saw her reaction, I longed to retract the words. I wanted the woman to leave, not stay and argue.

"I was only detained for a week," she spat, dark patches of color flaring on her cheeks. "I don't know why anyone would think I wanted to kill Mike."

This time I *did* manage to restrain my tongue. I could think of several excellent motives, most attributed to her, for the murder of Michael Peavey. "Sam isn't here. He's at work."

"I stopped there. They said he was coming here."

I opened my arms in a *look around* gesture. "Not here."

"I'm surprised no one's filed a lawsuit about your relationship with Sam." She peered past me, probably assessing my furniture and design choices, or lack thereof. "After all, you're sleeping with the boss. That's favoritism."

I didn't allow my insecurity to show. I was worried about that, too, but I had a talk with the other full-time employees earlier in the year and was assured that 'we're all grown-ups' and 'we aren't worried.' *I* worried, though, and did everything I could to make sure they knew I wasn't getting any preferential treatment. "We've had employee meetings about it and—wait a minute, that's none of your business."

"Of course it is. What happens to Barlow's Nursery and Landscaping is my business. If they go *out* of business, I stand to make a lot of money."

"It must really stick in your craw that you can't sell the land out from underneath Sam." I crossed my arms and resolutely ignored the damp feeling on my back where a cold sweat had broken out. I hated confrontation, but I would gladly make an exception for Sheila Peavey. "I guess you didn't know how your father felt when he made that arrangement with Sam's father."

She stiffened and her mouth narrowed into a thin, inflexible line. "My father had no business sense. When he signed that agreement with Sam's father, this part of the county was just farmland. He never imagined suburbs would come out this far."

"No one did," I countered. "We're almost thirty miles from Minneapolis. Back then no one could have imagined freeways or urban sprawl or exurbs."

"My mother did." Sheila's voice was low and venomous and I swear her eyes almost spit flame. "They argued about his land deals constantly. My father deeded away just about everything he owned. We once controlled almost half of this county but he ceded some to the city and some to fools like Josh Barlow and sold the rest for half of what it was worth." She stopped suddenly and got a hooded, secretive look. "Why do you think I married Sam in the first place? My father nagged me about it constantly. *Sam Barlow's a good boy, his father and I are old friends.*" Her voice took on a mimicking, singsong quality. "*You should pay attention to Sam. He's going to go somewhere.* My father was wrong about Sam just like he was wrong about everything else."

"Wait a minute. You met Sam while you were in college." I tried to remember what Sam told me about his relationship with his ex, but all the facts were jumbled up with the murder that occurred the previous spring. "I didn't think you knew him before then."

"Of course I did. There weren't that many families in the county. Everybody knew Sam. He went off to join the Marines and went overseas. He sent back postcards and letters from foreign countries." Sheila wrinkled her nose in disgust. "Sam seemed so mature when I saw him again in college."

"So why do you need to see him now?" I demanded.

"That's between me and Sam." She smiled smugly. "I've been trying to get in touch with him but he never answers my calls. So I thought I'd come over here and see him for myself. He and I need to talk."

The way she hesitated before the word 'talk' made me wonder if she was implying something more than 'talk'. I smiled slowly. "I don't think Sam will want to talk. You may as well leave now."

She turned as headlights shone into the foyer's side windows. "Let's just see for ourselves. I think that must be him, right?"

I grabbed Houdini, who had innocently sauntered out of hiding when he heard Sam's SUV outside. The big cat squirmed in my arms, but I successfully wedged him into the den before opening the front door.

Sam's black and white flannel shirt was rolled up at the sleeves, revealing his thick forearms and his black denims had damp spots on them where the sprinkler system probably went awry. His salt-and-pepper hair was longer than usual and a bit flyaway, wisping around his ears in soft curls. "Sorry I'm late. Is that the car Livvie let you borrow? Nice wheels. I think we'll have to take it tomorrow. I had to haul some trees in mine and it's—" Then he saw Sheila standing in my foyer. "What the hell are you doing here?"

Sheila smoothed a strand of hair back behind her ear. "Hi, Sam. I needed to talk to you and I've heard this is the place to find you."

Sam came into the house, closing the door firmly behind him. The color combination of his clothes highlighted his craggy face and dark, almost black eyes. He glanced at me and for an instant I saw humor in their depths. "You can let His Majesty out now."

I nodded and opened the den door before it got clawed to pieces. Houdi sped out, glared at the closed front door then did a carom shot off the wall into the living room and from there into the bedroom. Sheila jumped back, knocking into the wall. "What's wrong with him?"

"He's pissed off and so am I. What the hell are you doing, bothering Cassie?" Sam put his arm around me and I leaned into his solid warmth. Unlike Charlie, Sam didn't tower over me. I fit snugly against his side, my head level with his shoulder.

Sheila's face stiffened and I could see her trying out different expressions in her mind. She settled on cool indifference. "We need to talk to her about this land dispute. If we play our cards right, we can all benefit."

I stayed very still, feeling the tenseness in Sam's solid, muscular arm. "The only way you could benefit is if my business fails," he said levelly. "And that's not going to happen no matter how many dead mice you drop around or how many vandals you hire to damage my property."

She blinked in surprise but didn't protest fast enough to make her words believable. "I'd never do something like that."

"Yeah. Right." Sam's arm tightened around my shoulders. "I told you, Sheila. You can leave Cassie out of this."

"Out of what?" I asked, twisting my neck to look at him.

"She can buy the land, Sam. That way we both get what we want."

A shiver raced over me as soon as I understood what she was saying. "I beg your pardon?" I managed to ask.

"You're inheriting all that money. You can buy the land, give Sam the property, and I get my money." Sheila looked from me to Sam, her eyes evaluating our reaction. "It's a win-win situation."

I pulled slowly away from Sam. "Have you two discussed this?"

"We did," Sheila said.

"Sheila did," Sam countered. He eyed me warily. "I didn't agree to it."

"You're crazy, Sam. It's a perfect solution." Sheila smiled at me but it didn't soften the calculating look in her blue eyes.

"I think you should leave," I said, keeping my voice steady with an effort.

Sheila looked at Sam, puzzlement plain on her face. "I thought you were going to discuss this with her?"

"Why don't you leave, Sheila? Then Sam and I can talk about it." I tried to smile but I'm sure it came out as a grimace.

She nodded as though that made perfectly good sense. "Sam, you'll let me know what happens, won't you? I'd like to get this settled as soon as I can. My legal fees are adding up and I can't get Joe Swenson to return my calls."

I almost gagged. Joe Swenson had been in business with Sheila's late husband. Joe's son, Aaron...I couldn't complete the thought or I'd hit her.

Sam saw incipient violence in my eyes. "You'd better go, Sheila." He moved to one side as Sheila put her hand on the door knob. "Grab the cat," he said to me with a brief smile.

I walked across the length of the living and went into the bedroom where Houdi was stretched out on the bed. I closed the door behind me, blocking him— and me—in. I heard a murmur of voices then the front door opened and closed. Next, I heard Sam's footsteps outside in the hall.

"Cassie? We need to talk."

I was suddenly exhausted. My earlier argument with Charlie, getting lost, T.J's near-arrest, the confrontation with Sheila...I felt like they were all ganging up on me, draining me. I opened the door and walked out, brushing by Sam and going to the end table near the couch where my wine glass still sat. I tilted it up and swallowed fast.

"When Sheila came to me with the idea, I wasn't going to even suggest it to you." Sam took the glass out of my hand and gently pushed me onto the couch, sinking down to sit next to me. "I would never ask you to do something like that."

All I could remember was Charlie's voice when he said, 'you're not accustomed to what can happen when people find out you're loaded. It awakens the oddest emotions in people.' I was sure of one emotion it awakened in me—worry. I looked into Sam's dark, concerned eyes. "How bad is it, Sam?"

His eyebrows drew together as he frowned. "How bad is what?"

"Your debt load." I thought of Charlie's background research on Sam. "How was business this year? You've probably wrapped up the books, haven't you?"

"Not as good as I hoped," he admitted. "The greenhouse damage in the spring set us back and the hailstorm in July damaged a lot of shrubs. That was a big loss."

I decided to make my lawyer, Janelle, my

scapegoat. "Janelle and I were talking about investing some of my money. Do you need financial help?"

Sam drew away from me. "That sounds like something Richie Rich would say. What did he say? Did he do a check on me? He did, didn't he? That jerk."

"Charlie is just worried about—" I shut up but not fast enough.

"Oh, I see. You're getting some money and I'm a gold digger, right?" Sam's tanned face flushed a darker brown. "And I suppose Sheila's little act tonight only reinforces it, doesn't it? Damn it, Cassie. I didn't agree to her idea. She came over here without my knowledge." He got to his feet, moving restlessly toward the front door then back to me, his hands jammed into his jeans pockets.

"It happened to Livvie once and Charlie doesn't want to see it happen to me. You don't know how bad Livvie's marriage was. Her husband was a tyrant. Luckily her money was tied up in such a way he couldn't spend it all, but he sure tried. And when he couldn't, he took his frustration out on Livvie." I remembered those terrible years with aching clarity. That was when Livvie crawled into drink as a means to block out what was going on. I also remembered my own mother who was abused by my father and what happened when she tried to get away from him. "I can't escape my past, Sam. You know that as well as I do. Charlie and the others just want what's best for us." Then basic honesty forced me to amend that statement. "They want what's best for me."

Sam sighed heavily. "I know that, Cassie. But this isn't your mother and father, and it's not Livvie and her husband. It's me. What do you think?" He sank back down on the couch and held me still when I would have looked away. "Tell me, Cassie. What do you think?"

I didn't want to face this question or him. I wanted to go back to being Cassie Whittington, semi-retired garden center worker. I didn't want to be an heiress and worry about who was my friend for Real and who was my friend for Money.

I forced myself to look into his eyes. Sam was good at hiding his emotions, but I saw a flicker of worry and anger lurking in their dark depths. "What did you say to him?" he asked in a low voice. "What did you tell Richie Rich?"

I hesitated and that was my undoing. Sam released me so fast my head started spinning. It was either that or the anger I felt radiating off of him in waves. He jumped to his feet. "Damn it, Cassie. What do I have to do to prove to you the money doesn't matter?"

"I'm sorry, Sam. I wish..." What did I wish? A hundred conflicting thoughts seemed to rush through my brain. The one that percolated to the forefront was *I wish I didn't have to deal with this.*

He stared at me, waiting for me to continue. As always, it was impossible to read his emotion on his face. His dark eyes hid any sign of what he felt. Only his hands, clenched tightly at his sides, showed me his anger. Then his face relaxed and I thought I saw a wistful look in his eyes before he looked away. "I wish you'd trust me."

"I do," I said immediately but it sounded wishy-washy, even to me.

"But...?" he prompted. His voice was cool, dispassionate but his body was tense as he resumed his pacing. "But you want to have your cake and eat it, too? You want Charlie and you want me? I don't get it. What do you need me for? Charlie's got it all, doesn't he?"

"Now just a minute." I was in no mood to put up with Sam's bullshit, not after the day I had. Good Lord, I started the day with a funeral where I almost had a fistfight with John Whittington. Then I had that verbal sparring match with Charlie at his condo. Then I meet Livvie's new guy, only to get roped into his involvement in a murder. I spent hours at a police station, almost drove into the lake, then Sheila came over and implied...It was all too much. "You have no right to gripe about my relationship with Charlie," I snapped. "Charlie's been a part of my entire life. He's been an important part of my life."

"And I'm just temporary, is that it?" Sam glared at me from across the room.

I got to my feet, snatched my wine glass, and stalked into the kitchen. "I don't feel like dealing with your crap, Sam. It's not a crime that Charlie is smart, handsome, and rich. I'm not comparing you to him. You're two different people. I wish you'd get that through your head and quit being so jealous."

Sam followed me, pausing in the doorway to watch as I refilled my glass. "I suppose Sheila doesn't bother you, does she?" he demanded.

I shot him a suspicious glare. "What do you mean?"

"Don't tell me you've never felt a bit insecure because of Sheila."

"Oh, for cryin' out loud. You're divorced. Just like Charlie and I are divorced," I was quick to point out.

"So? I've seen the way you look at her. You and she are totally different. Don't tell me you haven't wondered..." His voice trailed away when he saw me turn slowly to glare at him.

"What the hell are you talking about, Sam? Are you comparing me to Sheila? Is that what you're trying to say?"

He held up his hands. "Not at all. No."

I was suddenly so angry I could barely talk. "Okay, let's do a little comparison, me to Sheila. I'm older, I'm shorter, I'm not as pretty. Is that what you want me to say? Should we compare you to Charlie now?" I took a big gulp of wine and almost drowned myself.

His face stilled into a hard mark. "You're being hysterical." He wheeled and headed back the way he came. "I'll call you later when you've calmed down."

"Whoa, wait a minute. Don't you want to play this game anymore?" I followed him to the living room and watched as he paused at the front door.

"It's not a game." His voice was so cold I shivered involuntarily. "At least it isn't a game with me. I think you need to decide what it is for you, though." He jerked open the front door and was gone before I could answer.

"That son of a bitch," I muttered, striding to the door. I was prepared to jerk it open and give him a good piece of my mind, but I was afraid of what I might say. Too many emotions were boiling around inside my brain. God knows what might have spilled out.

My hesitation probably saved me from a world of grief. By the time I peeked out the side window, Sam's SUV was pulling out of the driveway. I watched as he drove away, unspoken insults rattling around in my brain. I went in to the den, thinking I would write down all of the thoughts and emotions that boiled in me. But when I stared at my desk I saw a booklet Livvie gave me months before. "Read it," she urged when she pressed it on me. "It's about letting go of the past. It's about letting go of attachments."

I had tossed it on the desk and promptly forgot about it but now it resurfaced like a bad penny, staring me in the face. I opened the small booklet. *When you hold on to what's familiar, you limit your experience in the present.* I flipped the page. *Don't allow your life to be governed by 'should', 'must', or 'need'. Let your path be set by 'want', 'desire', and 'allow'.*

I snorted in derision. "Facile bullshit," I muttered. I took the little pamphlet and wandered back to the kitchen, topped up my wine glass, and grabbed a box of crackers. Then I sank down on the couch in the nearby family room and turned on the TV, flipping channels until I got to something on the History Channel, my tried-and-true source for quiet entertainment. I mechanically shoveled saltines into my mouth, washing them town with sips of wine. I peered at another page in the booklet in the light of the TV screen.

Be worthwhile now. Don't fret about the past. Don't focus on the future. Enjoy the moment of now. It truly is all there is…for now. Allow yourself to let go, let the details go. Feel the now.

"Oh, for heaven's sake." I tossed the booklet on the coffee table and glared at the TV. Here I was, the woman who avoided confrontation like the plague, and I had three rip-roaring ones all in the course of a day. From John, to Sheila, to Sam—all combined to leave me feeling drained, exhausted, and curiously empty. I struggled to remember all that had been said that day, but the gentle drone of a documentary and the effects of three glasses of wine all combined to make me collapse on the couch and drag the afghan over my legs.

At some point during the night I woke and stumbled into bed. I awoke the next morning to the sound of the phone ringing. I grabbed for the portable unit by my bedside but only succeeded in knocking it off the night table. I heard the murmur of my answering machine in the living room as it kicked on, answering whoever it was who had interrupted my beauty sleep.

I peered foggily at my alarm clock. Holy crap, it was almost nine in the morning. When was the last time I slept that late? I yawned, considered getting up, then turned over and snuggled with Houdini, who was curled up against my stomach. The air in the room was chill from the window I left cracked open the night before where I heard the soft patter of rain. The sound combined with my evening's consumption of wine to make me need to use the bathroom. I gave up on more sleep and stumbled out of bed to face the day.

Thirty minutes later, freshly showered and with my first cup of coffee in hand, I felt human enough to inspect my answering machine. I pressed the 'play' button, not sure I wanted to listen to the message but knowing I had to. Sam's voice seemed muted, as though he was speaking very close to the receiver.

"Can you drive today? My truck is dirty and I don't know if I'll have time to get it cleaned before we have to leave for Leon's wedding. I'll drive over to your place and leave the truck there and we can leave from your house. Call me if that won't work." There was a brief hesitation. "Please."

Well, apparently we were still going to the wedding together today. Last night was the first time Sam and I had a real argument and I suddenly realized that I had no idea how to face him today. Pretend nothing happened? Pretend that certain things hadn't been said?

I sat down to savor my coffee in the family room, snatching up the little booklet from the coffee table and checking it for any pearls of morning wisdom. *Fill your pockets with time doing what you want to do. Decide what matters to you and indulge it. Don't wait but do it now.*

"Easy for them to say," I muttered. Of course, now that I would have Money with a capital M, I probably could indulge a few whims. I had kept such thoughts at bay while Grandy's estate was being contested, but now and again I allowed a daydream to sneak over me.

What if I could do anything I wanted to do? I never really considered my future in those terms. I always thought in terms of 'what could I avoid doing', not 'what would I like to do.' It was a somewhat sobering thought. Maybe there was more to this affirmation stuff than I knew. I tossed it back toward the coffee table but it slid off, landing on the floor next to the afghan I had shed the night before.

The night before...that reminded me. I re-evaluated last night's words. I hated to admit it, but Sam was right. Perhaps, subconsciously, I was worried about Sheila and whether she still had a hold on his mind, if not his heart. And I could understand Sam's feelings where Charlie was concerned. Charlie and I did have an odd, yet wonderful, relationship.

"Why do I have to give up Charlie in order to have Sam?" I muttered to Houdini, who was sitting on the little booklet as though I had placed it there just for his buns.

Houdi yawned and a flash of understanding made me blink. Cats understood the 'living in the now' thing perfectly. Every look out of a window was a new view, regardless of how many times they stared at the same thing, day after day. Perhaps I needed to cultivate such an attitude. Maybe I needed to let go of worry and just enjoy what I had. It was up to Sam to deal with his insecurities and anger. They weren't my problem.

I kept that thought in the forefront of my brain as I went about my Saturday errands and prepped for the family wedding with Sam. Charlie was a part of my life, and that's just how it was. Sam had to learn to live with it.

Unfortunately, it wasn't something he learned to live with during the brief time we were apart. When I picked him up, he was polite but distant, answering my cheery questions with monosyllabic replies and directing me to the church where the wedding was to be held with the fewest possible words. My good mood began to vanish but I resolved to remain upbeat and act as though nothing had happened. If he had a beef, he was going to have to air it.

Sam's off-handed behavior lasted through the wedding, where I was introduced to various relatives with almost absent-minded formality. As we drove to the reception, I tried to prod him for answers.

"Are you still upset about what we said last night?" I asked bluntly as I drove Livvie's Lexus through narrow streets. I wasn't familiar with this part of town and I followed other wedding-goers in front of us, praying they knew the route.

He didn't say anything for almost a block and when he did answer, I had to strain to hear. "I've just had a lot to think about lately, that's all. I guess I'm starting to wonder..." He tapped the door handle impatiently. "I'm starting to wonder where we're going."

My stomach twisted at the words. I considered a flip reply: *we're going to the reception, silly.* I bit my tongue in time when I saw his somber expression. "Where do you want us to go?" I hazarded a glance away from the crowded streets and was dismayed to find him watching me, his dark eyes perplexed.

"I don't know." He smiled briefly but it was a sad, almost wistful, smile. "I don't think you do, either. And that has me wondering just what the hell we're doing." He leaned forward and peered through the foggy mist that surrounded the car. "You can park in the lot across the street. It's probably easier."

I managed to get the car into a parking space without dinging it, which was a minor miracle given the fact my hands were trembling. Sam didn't elaborate on his words as we got out of the car and I didn't want to try to answer them.

After all, I really had no answer, did I?

*****

"I don't know this song," I said hesitantly as Sam led me out to the dance floor. I had long since shed my cardigan due to the energetic polkas, waltzes, and line dances Sam's family favored. My sweater and Sam's suit coat were keeping company on a chair at a nearby table.

He leaned closer to me, his breath warm and beery. "Come on. It's easy." Sam appeared to be taking advantage of my designated driver status. I wasn't really counting, but I think he had downed at least four beers from the keg in the corner. "Just watch me."

I eyed him warily as he insinuated himself into the lopsided circle of wedding revelers. We hadn't really spoken to each other since the parking lot and he spent most of his time at the reception chatting with relatives with me nearby, smiling and feeling left out. I consoled myself with the thought that he would soon feel the same way himself, once we got to our second party of the day, but I was starting to feel miffed at his cool act.

I watched as people made 'beaks', flapped 'wings', wiggled 'tail feathers', then clapped. Sam grinned at me as I joined in the fun, fumbling the process only once. Then some gliding music played. Sam and the man next to me grabbed my hands and we all went in a circle then reversed direction, circling again. The 'chicken' music started to play again and we repeated the whole thing.

By the third time, I was laughing so hard I almost fell over and did a spread eagle rather than a chicken at the 'tail feather' portion. Luckily, the dance soon ended and I tottered off the dance floor, dropping into a chair next to a table covered with a once white paper tablecloth. Sam said something about 'bratwurst' and vanished into the crowd swarming the dance floor for Chubby Checker's *The Twist*, spun by Darrell Dobbs, the Dancing D.J.

I sipped the ginger ale I had left at the table and fanned myself with a discarded wedding program as I looked around the V.F.W. hall. The place was jammed with Sam's cousins, aunts, uncles, sister, brother-in-law and other people whom I met in a blur of introductions.

"Oh, it's so nice to see Sammy happy." A rotund woman with red hair of a color not found in Nature beamed at me as she sank into the chair on my left.

"He deserves a good woman," a big-boned woman with wispy white hair said as she pulled out the chair on my right. "That Sheila led him on a terrible dance."

"Of course, you can't completely blame Sheila," the white-haired woman said. She took a sip of her beer. "I'm Sam's Aunt Darlene."

"I'm his Aunt Marge. Sheila was raised to be a hard woman," the round little woman said. "Her father didn't have any boys and he made sure Sheila was tough as nails."

"That doesn't excuse her running off and cheating on Sam." Darlene huddled close to me and Marge did the same, wedging me between the two women so we looked like a three-headed monster. "Thank goodness they didn't have children. I hate to think what a child of Sheila's would turn out like."

I had a pang at that thought. Did Sam miss having kids? Had he wanted children? It was a topic that never came up for discussion between us. Was that a regret he was feeling? I shelved the thought for later consideration, when I didn't have to handle the Relatives.

"I was surprised when the police let her go." Marge almost quivered with indignation. "Sam said

71

he was sure she killed her husband."

Two pairs of alert, elderly eyes regarded me with unblinking curiosity. "I thought so, too," I admitted in a low voice. "I was as shocked as anyone when she got out."

They both sat back and nodded. "She'll get what she deserves." Darlene said it with the surety reserved for those who had a firm foothold in religion. "No bad deed goes unpunished."

"I hope you're right." My cell phone, buried in my slacks pocket, thumped on my thigh. Livvie still hadn't gotten in touch with me and I was worried about her. She was supposed to call me and update me on her situation. "I'm sorry." I pulled out the phone and examined the little screen. As I hoped, it was Livvie. "I need to take this call, a dear friend is having some trouble and I need to talk to her."

The two ladies looked up when Sam took a seat at our table, a laden plate of brats and sauerkraut in one hand and a beer stein in the other. "Hey, Aunts," he said, setting everything down. They turned their attention to him as I put the phone to my ear.

"Livvie? Speak up, I can barely hear you." I leaned over and plugged my right ear, pressing the phone to my left ear.

"I said I'm afraid Paul will kill him!" Livvie's voice was a harsh whisper and breathless. She could barely compete with *Cherish*, the obligatory slow dance being played.

"What?"

"Paul and T.J. are in a fight. I'm afraid he'll kill T.J.!"

Chapter 6

"Did Livvie call the police?" Sam asked as we sped away from the wedding.

"She was outside the restaurant when she called. Apparently Michelle and Mike, that other chef guy, were going in to talk to Paul. I don't think anybody called the police." I clutched the wheel of the Starship Enterprise as I turned onto the divided highway. Overcast skies and drizzle combined to make it feel like premature dusk. It was only five in the afternoon but the headlights clicked on automatically. They probably had some kind of sensor. I was surprised the car didn't sprout fins when we hit puddles.

"That's stupid. They should call the police." Sam reached into his gray suit coat pocket for his cell phone.

"Don't do that. I'm not sure what's going on. If we call in the police it might just spook somebody. Check the map. How far do I go?"

Sam picked up the road map I tossed on the console when we got in the car. "Five miles on this road then we go left." He tapped his knee impatiently. "I'm surprised the police let them back in the restaurant. Isn't it a crime scene?" He sounded irritated, not worried. I wondered, fleetingly, if he was peeved at leaving the wedding. Then I decided he was probably just peeved at

73

leaving the beer.

"It's also a place of business," I pointed out. "They can't keep them out forever." I held out my cell phone. "Call Livvie. She's in my contact list. Make sure they didn't go anywhere." I eyed my speedometer and the empty road then I added a bit more speed.

"We're not qualifying for NASCAR," Sam commented as he peered down at my phone.

"I'm only six miles over the speed limit."

"The speed limit is insane on this road." He reached up and started tapping the roof. "Slow down."

"It's fine." I let up slightly on the speed. I saw him glance at the speedometer and shake his head. Then he resumed peering up at the roof. "What are you doing?"

"Looking for the lights. I can't see anything on your phone."

"I don't know where the lights are. Don't touch anything. This car has a brain of its own. You might activate a tracking beam."

"Well, I can't call Livvie unless I can see the damn phone."

"Try pressing some buttons. That should turn on the light on the phone."

He muttered something and I chose to ignore it as I peered out my window at the trees flashing past, interspersed with glimpses of houses set far back from the road. "This is a nice suburb. I didn't see it last night. I was too busy trying to figure out how to drive this car."

Sam ran a hand over the leather seats. "Nice. Are you going to buy it?"

I shrugged. "I doubt it. I need a winter car, something that will go in snow. I don't want to worry about getting stuck."

"It's all-wheel drive."

I glanced at him suspiciously. "How do you know?"

He pointed to an insignia on the dash. "AWD. You're right. This is like a rocket ship or something. Who knew a car needed so many gadgets? I wonder how much it costs."

"A lot. Livvie said she'd give me a deal."

Sam made a 'hmpf' noise. "Yeah, right. That means it'll only cost an arm, not an arm and a leg. Of course, you've got arms and legs to spare, so to speak. Or you will have."

I clenched the steering wheel tightly. "That remains to be seen," I said, struggling to keep my voice level. "John might have something to say about that."

"That asshole..." Sam glared out his window. "So what else did Livvie say? What's going on with T.J. and his son?"

I was glad for the change of subject. "She said they were relaxing at T.J's home and Paul called. He had to go to the police station again. He's afraid he's going to be arrested. She and T.J. drove over to the restaurant and he and Paul got in an argument. T.J. told her to get out. She called Michelle and Mike. Apparently he and Paul are chummy."

"I'll bet that created some tension between them."

"Between Paul and Mike?"

"No, between T.J. and his son. Didn't you say Mike was in line for the head job? If T.J.'s son sided with his competition it must create some bad blood." The phone in Sam's hand chimed *The Boys of Summer*. He opened it but before he could speak, I heard Charlie's voice from the speaker above the dash.

"Cassie, this is Charlie. I'm calling about..."

"What's that?" Sam looked down at the phone in his hand then at the dash.

I had made a mental note about this the night before when I read the manual so I knew which button to press to mute the voice on the car speaker. "It's that Bluetooth stuff. Go ahead, answer it."

Sam warily put the phone to his ear. "Cassie's phone." There was a pause. "Yeah, Charlie, I know. We're on our way there now." Another pause. "Hold on." He turned to me. "Do you want to talk to Richie Rich?"

I shook my head. "I'm not that Bluetooth literate yet and I don't think I can multi-task right now. Tell him to call me back."

"She's driving," Sam said into the phone. "Call her later." He listened for a long time. "Okay, I'll tell her." He folded the phone. "Charlie said he talked to Livvie and he said things were calming down. He said to call him if you think he needs to be there." Sam tilted his head and regarded me. "Remind me again why we're going there if her brother isn't going?"

"Because Livvie is closer than a sister to me and I'm worried she'll fall off the wagon and start drinking again." I glanced at the impound lot as we drove past, relieved to see I was on the correct road. "When she went into rehab all of the family went there for counseling, too. They said stress can trigger a relapse and we need to be there to help her."

"So why isn't Little Lord Fauntleroy there, too?"

I blew out an exasperated breath. "Charlie and the others don't understand addiction. They thought Livvie was just a social drunk." I waved a hand, keeping the other firmly on the steering wheel. The car purred along as though I was unnecessary, which I probably was. "They figured she could just quit drinking and that's all there was to it."

"I suppose they didn't think one of *the* Whittingtons was fallible," Sam said.

I didn't bother to correct his skewed opinion.

"She and I had long talks about how hard it was for her to give up the booze." I glanced at Sam. "I didn't tell you everything her husband did to her. He did a real number on her head. T.J. has done a lot to help her straighten out and if he's in trouble, she's going to be stressed. The others may not take her addiction seriously but I'm not going to be the one who lets her down." I made a right turn at the top of the hill then instead of going straight to the police station, made another right turn, which led us onto the narrow road leading to the restaurant.

Sam grinned. "Let her brother John let her down. He's good at that."

I breathed out a sigh of relief that he wasn't going to argue. "No shit." I drove slowly down the quiet street until I reached the short drive for the restaurant. I turned right into the lot marked "Staff" where a silver BMW sedan was parked, its 'LIV2' license plate a companion to the 'LIV1' plate on the Enterprise.

Further in from the road, nearer the lake, was an SUV that looked like it should morph into a superhero. The thing was so tall only a giant could easily climb into it without a leg up. Next to it was a burgundy Mercedes sports coupe, a car I knew cost at least fifty-thousand because I researched them last spring when I thought I was coming into some Big Cash.

"Expensive wheels," Sam muttered as I parked beside LIV2.

"Cheffing must pay well. After all, Michelle owns the restaurant and it has to be an expensive chunk of land. It's right on the lake, smack in the middle of the pricy part of town." I opened my car door and stepped out but didn't slam it behind me. Sam did the same. We grinned at each other over the top.

"Great minds think alike," he said softly.

A rush of happiness made my stomach flop. I nodded, wondering if we had finally managed to put our angry words behind us. I didn't want to question that now. I wanted to just savor the moment.

I examined the buildings I barely noticed the evening before. The white frame building that housed the kitchen—Hell House—was very narrow, just slightly wider than my townhouse, which was just the width of two bedrooms and a shared bathroom. The house extended the length of the lot with trees on the right overhanging the twelve parking spaces, some of which were now occupied by the Starship Enterprise and the other vehicles. At the front of the property I heard the shushing sound of waves and the cries of sea gulls as they swooped over the lake. The sharp smell of wet vegetation wafted toward us on the westerly breeze.

The dining house—The Feed Bag—was a dark powder blue square building with white shutters around the windows. A narrow drive branched to the left of the structure, presumably leading to patron parking on that side.

I started toward the back door of Hell House and the stoop where I stood yesterday. A remnant of yellow crime scene tape hung off the left side of the door. I heard voices and started to put my hand on the knob.

"Over here." Sam gestured to the narrow walkway between the two houses then peered around the back of Hell House before starting forward. I didn't quibble with him taking the lead. After all, Marine training trumped horticulture training in situations like this.

He turned a corner and stopped. I peeked around his solid bulk. Black antique-looking lamps hung off Hell House at six-foot intervals, creating spotlights in the haze. A screened porch was ahead of us at the front of the Feed Bag. We could see only a corner of it, but it appeared to be full of people, all talking at the same time. "What the hell?" Sam muttered. We walked forward through the spotlights.

A metallic odor created a cloying taste in the back of my throat. "What's that smell?"

"Paint." Sam glanced to our left where the windows were open in the blue restaurant building. I heard the whoosh of fans going inside and when we passed one window a light waft of dry air mixed with the industrial smell touched my face.

I peeked inside. Bright overhead lights illuminated a large empty space with pale yellow walls and wooden floors. Tables and chairs were stacked against one side of the long room. I did a fast count and saw fifteen tables.

"They must be airing the place out," I whispered. "That probably explains why they're on the porch." Our feet, previously noiseless on the grass, made crunching sounds as we stepped onto the gravel around the latticework skirt of the porch. As we came closer to the front of the buildings, I saw the lake. It was spread out before us, a low white fence separating the front of the houses from a rocky drop-off to the equally rocky shore below.

A tall man nearest our side turned to glare at us through the screens of the porch. I recognized him from last night as Paul Watson, T.J's son. He was a hard-looking man, his body rangy and lean. For someone who worked inside, his face was weathered and harsh, with high cheekbones and piercing hazel eyes. He reminded me of that cook on television, the one who'd been a drug addict and now traveled the world and ate weird things. I could see a vague resemblance to T.J. in the suspicious, anxious way Paul stood. But where T.J. looked worn yet unbowed by life, Paul seemed combative, as though he expected the worst from life and was prepared to fight whatever came his way.

"Who are you?" he demanded, his gaze going from Sam to me. His voice was raw and deep, so rasping it made me shiver to hear him.

Sam shifted position slightly, edging his shoulder forward. "Sam Barlow." His voice was conversational but I saw his eyes shift from one person to another through the screens as they paused in their arguing to stare at us. "We're friends of Livvie's."

Michelle glared at us. "This has nothing to do with you. It's a family matter." Her gaze went to Livvie and her lips thinned. "It *should* be just for family."

Sam sauntered forward, glancing up at the light mist coming down. "Thanks for inviting us in. I appreciate it." He started for the front of the porch.

"We didn't invite you." Michelle moved so she almost blocked the doorway. Her black hair hung in a straight line, brushing her chin. The collar of her dark jacket was turned up to frame her face, making her appear ghost-like, as though her pale face floated above her body. Her black slacks completed the effect, helping her blend into the shadows.

"Sorry for your loss," Sam said politely as he pulled open the screen door.

She stepped back, her red lips open in a pout. "What?"

He paused inside the threshold. "Sorry. I thought your husband was murdered."

For an instant surprise registered in her dark green eyes. Then she composed a careful mask of grief. "Thank you."

"No one asked you to join us," a voice said from the crowd.

I followed Sam. The rest of the occupants came into view and I saw the speaker. Mike, the bullet-headed man, regarded us with not-at-all-concealed anger from a spot behind Livvie, who stood opposite the screen door near a door to the restaurant.

"We'll ignore your lack of politeness," Sam said mildly. He nudged Michelle aside and gestured me ahead of him. His gaze settled on T.J., pausing briefly on T.J.'s right arm and the hook. T.J. and Livvie both wore faded denims and denim jackets over matching fisherman's knit turtlenecks. She looked tired, her normally flawless makeup not quite as immaculate today. T.J. appeared flat-out exhausted, the stubble on his cheeks more pronounced and with dark circles under his eyes. They probably spent most of the night talking about the murder and today's argument with Paul was straining them to the limit.

"Cassie said you were in the Navy?" Sam asked, keeping his voice light and polite.

T.J. nodded. "I was discharged in '73."

Sam jammed his hands in the pockets of his black jeans. "I went in after Hanoi. Marines."

"What are you doing here?" Paul's face was barely visible in the shadows on the porch. Like Michelle, he wore a black turtleneck but he wore washed-out jeans that emphasized the lean line of his body. Michelle moved near him. She was almost his height and the way she stood—partially turned toward him, her right side almost touching his arm—made me do a double-take. I did some mental math and realized she was only a couple of years older than Paul.

"Livvie's a friend of mine," Sam said. "What affects her affects me."

"And me," I added. "I'm Cassie Whittington."

"One of that family," Mike muttered.

I straightened indignantly. "Yes, I am." I glimpsed Sam's frown and added, "Kind of." I looked around the porch. Five round wooden table, which would easily seat four people, were pushed to one half of the space. A dark blue reed rug on the floor was rolled up and propped near the tables. Bamboo shades were partially down, giving the whole area a hooded, secretive look. The only light came from two windows on either side of the restaurant door.

"You've never been there for me," Paul said in a low, angry voice. He had obviously decided to ignore us and continue whatever argument they were involved in.

"I know that, Paul and there's nothing I can do to make it up to you." T.J.'s shoulders sagged but when Livvie touched his arm sympathetically, he smiled sadly at her. "I was so hooked into drugs when you were growing up I didn't know what I was doing. There's nothing I can do to change the past."

"You can at least help Paul with his future," Michelle said.

"How?" I blurted. "By telling Paul to lie to the police? That won't help anything."

All eyes swung to me. "What do you mean, lie to the police?" Mike demanded. He leaned forward and I instinctively leaned back.

Then Sam's arm went around me and I relaxed. It was a great feeling, knowing my back was covered. I glanced at him and our eyes met. I savored the feeling for a brief instant then I turned my attention back to the people staring at me. "Paul was already here when T.J. got here. I'm sure the police would like to know how long he was there and if he went into the building."

"I told them I didn't," Paul rasped.

I smiled politely. "But did you?"

"That's really none of your business."

I continued as though I hadn't heard. "Is there a security alarm?"

"What about it?" Mike crossed his massive arms across his equally massive chest, his maroon University of Minnesota sweatshirt doing nothing to disguise his muscle-y physique. He was like one of those no-neck linebackers I occasionally saw on the sports channel. *Now I know where the term 'dick head' comes from*, I thought inanely as light glinted off his bald pate.

"Of course you must have an alarm." I glanced at Sam, who watched Mike the way Houdini watched the neighborhood dog when Buster and his owner were out for a walk: *potential threat but contained. Be alert.* "We talked about that earlier. If you have copper pipes, those are high-ticket theft items. And I'm sure your kitchen has some expensive cookware." I looked up at the menu board over the door leading into the restaurant. "And you've got truffles and escargots and other pricy menu things. Truffles cost a fortune, don't they? You must have a security system."

Mike took a step closer to us, which made him brush against Livvie, pushing her off-balance. I put out a hand to steady her. "We told you," he said with a sneer. "This doesn't have anything to do with strangers. This is family business."

"Then why are you here?" I demanded. "You're not family. You're just a cook."

I was sure he was going to take a swing at me. His mouth flattened into a thin line and his bulbous nose seemed to glow as his face suffused with color. "I'm the sous-chef." He said it the same way someone would say, *I'm the President of the United States.* "That's a bit more important than cook."

"Right." I turned to T.J. "Did the police ask you about the security alarm? Is it one of those security systems that keep a log?" I saw Mike out of the corner of my eye. I thought the top of his head would blow off. He almost vibrated with palpable anger at my dismissive way of handling him.

T.J. frowned. "They asked, but I wasn't sure how it worked. I never have to set it." His eyes went to

Michelle. "Did they ask you about it?"

She bit her lip, her eyes darting from Livvie to me. "They did ask. I told them it was disabled while we had construction going on."

"Was it?" I asked.

Her face turned toward me and she tilted her head so her hair would swing back, out of the way. "It's none of your business."

"Of course it is," I said. "If Livvie's fiancé is in trouble, it matters to me."

"Fiancé?" Michelle whirled to confront T.J., who stood near Livvie now. "You're getting married?"

T.J. nodded. "That's where the funding would come from."

"What funding?" Michelle demanded.

I saw the startled look Livvie shot T.J. She slipped her arm through his, her hand resting near the hook poking out from his denim jacket. "T.J. and I were in talks with Robert to buy the restaurant," she said in a somewhat trembling voice.

"That's impossible," Michelle snapped into the sudden silence. "Robert and I were partners. He couldn't consider an offer unless he consulted with me."

"I overheard him on the phone a day or two ago," Paul said slowly. "I was outside the office and he was talking to someone." His forehead furrowed as he remembered the conversation. "I didn't hear everything because of the noise from construction." He looked up and I imagined an office space above the main dining area. "I heard him say your name then something about the restaurant and profits. He sounded worried. When I came in to talk to him, he had a pile of receipts on the desk and the computer was on. I saw a spreadsheet on the computer screen."

"So?" Mike demanded. "He was the chef-de-cuisine. He was supposed to look over the accounts now and then."

"No, he wasn't," Michelle corrected. "That was my job. Robert hated dealing with the financial side of things. I'm surprised he managed to turn on the computer. It makes no sense that he would consider selling the business."

Livvie looked up at T.J. He appeared uncomfortable, shifting his weight from one foot to the other as he said, "Robert told me..." He stopped, wincing.

Michelle took two strides across the room to confront him. "What?"

"He was filing for divorce." T.J. looked down at her then his glance slid to Paul, who looked stunned. "Because of Paul."

Michelle gasped audibly. I nodded. That explained the proprietary way they acted toward each other. Sam nudged me and I glanced at him. He was staring beyond me, to the side of the porch. "Looks like we have company," he murmured.

I followed his gaze and saw the telltale white-blue reflections of a police light flash in the driveway.

Chapter 7

The police were brisk, efficient, and quick in the serving of their search warrant. Because we weren't part of the restaurant staff, we were asked very politely to leave when the police descended on the house to inspect all the kitchen implements. I overheard one of them telling Paul they were going to 'check the pastry hooks and other mixer attachments.' Then Livvie, Sam, and I were firmly hustled away. We made hasty arrangements to meet T.J. at Grandy's house, just a few miles away on the south side of the bay where the restaurant sat.

"How big is a pastry hook?" I asked Sam as we followed Livvie's BMW to Grandy Theo's old house.

"It must be pretty big. They make a ton of pastry if that menu board was right, not to mention bread. Is a pastry hook the same as a bread hook? I've seen pictures of those and they're wicked." Sam looked around the neighborhood as I steered the Starship Enterprise down the narrow streets. "I thought the houses would be bigger."

"They're big enough." I knew this part of town well because I came out here every week to visit Grandy when she was alive. But it was dark now with more drizzle misting the road ahead and I was still nervous about piloting the Enterprise.

"I thought the widow acted a bit weird," Sam said as I navigated the twisting road leading to

Grandy's house. "Now I know why."

"Yeah, she wasn't exactly in mourning. If she and Paul were having an affair, it explains her lack of emotion. I'm surprised she's not a better actor, though. She looks like the kind of person who knows how to put on a good show."

"What do you mean?"

I glanced at him. "How did she strike you? If you had to sum her up in a couple of words, what would you use?"

He thought about it for a second. "Sexy babe and smart businesswoman."

I rolled my eyes. "What a guy answer."

"Hey. I'm a guy. What do you expect?" He shot me a wary look.

"You thought she was sexy?"

"I'm not going to answer. That's one of those trick questions. No matter what I say, you'll get pissed off."

He was right but I wasn't going to let him go easily. "She's a player," I said confidently. "I've seen her kind all my life. She's a High Society wannabe."

"What do you mean?"

"Compare her to Livvie. Just think about it."

To his credit, Sam did. He was silent for a few minutes as I drove through the park not far from Grandy's house. "Okay, I see what you mean. She's sort of flashy. Livvie is...different."

"Livvie is old money. Michelle is new money." I frowned in thought. "But that news article made it sound like she was old money," I said, thinking out loud.

"What news article?"

"I did some research earlier." Ahead of us, Livvie pulled into the driveway at Grandy's and I parked behind her.

Sam got out, staring up at the two-story white stucco house. "It's not a mansion. It looks just like a big house."

"The land is worth the money." I hurried to the side door leading to the porch off the kitchen. "Look behind us."

Sam got our party bags out of the car then turned to stare at the expanse behind us. "Wow. Is that...?" He hurried after me.

"Yep. It's the lake." The house sat about a hundred yards from the shores of Lake Minnetonka on a tall bluff overlooking Smithtown Bay. "I'm so glad Livvie wants to buy the house. If she buys it, I know it won't be torn down and a McMansion put in its place." I heard Livvie ahead of us, calling out to Betty Burke, the live-in maid who still had her home at Grandy's house. I had called Betty as soon as I knew we were coming so she wouldn't be surprised when company showed up at her door.

When we entered the big kitchen a pot of tea was steeping on the stove and a plate of her special ginger cookies sat in the middle of the round white kitchen table. Betty had Livvie in a hug, her black face as wrinkled as a nut and her strong arms encircling Livvie as though she was a child again, running to Betty for comfort. The sight brought sentimental tears to my eyes as I remembered all the times I spent in this house and the many nights Betty and Grandy comforted me after my father died.

Betty released Livvie and turned to me. "There's the songbird," she said softly, holding open her arms. I went into them, feeling her large, plump breasts push against mine and her talcum-powdered scent envelop me. Betty always smelled of Cashmere Bouquet powder, probably because that was the gift of choice from us kids when we were little. I remembered going to the five-and-dime with three dollars in my pocket to buy Mother's Day presents. I always spent a dollar on each of my 'mothers':

Grandy, Mom, and Betty. And every holiday, each woman would exclaim that a tub of Cashmere Bouquet was just what she needed.

Betty released me with a murmured, "It's so good to see you, child," then she turned her intelligent and shrewd dark eyes on Sam. "And this must be Sam. I've heard so much about you." She held out a hand and Sam took it, giving it a brisk shake.

"All good, I hope," he said.

"Not really, since most of it came from Charlie, but I got the idea." Betty laughed, her layers of flesh jiggling with her. She was almost as round as she was tall and there was a liberal sprinkling of gray in her close-cropped Afro, but she was still as light on her feet as when she used to roller skate with us kids. She was wearing her usual 'uniform': a long dark blue skirt, a white blouse, a blue cardigan sweater and pink-edged tennis socks covered by immaculate white tennis shoes, laced with small charms from her grandchildren in Georgia. "Come on in and sit down a bit." She pulled out one of the wooden chairs and gestured to the table.

I knew it was no good arguing that we needed to get going to the costume party. Betty was a law unto herself and it didn't bother her that we might keep the rest of the family waiting. Her opinion of Charlie's father—C.R. Whittington the Second—was the same as the one Grandy held all her life. According to them, the best thing the Second did was father children and make money. The first accomplishment was the most important.

I sank into a chair and looked around. The room was about as big as my townhouse living room with cabinets lining the walls, broken up by doors leading to the basement, dining room, and the porch near the driveway. The house was updated through the years but never renovated, so it still had the charm of the Twenties, when it was originally built.

"So your man is in trouble, eh, Livvie?" Betty asked as she brought the teapot to the table. "I liked him a lot. I was pleased when you brought him over for lunch that day." She raised an expressive eyebrow in my direction and I knew I was on her Shit List for not bringing Sam around sooner. I made a mental note to schedule a lunch with Betty in the near future.

"Actually, it's T.J.'s son, Paul, who might be in trouble." Livvie took the delicate tea cup Betty handed her. "Paul was having an affair with the restaurant owner's wife."

"You mean the wife of the man who was slashed?" Betty asked, handing me a cup.

I winced at her graphic phrasing. "Robert de Garmeaux," I said, mangling the French accent. "He was the owner and the head chef at the restaurant."

"So T.J's boy was having it on with the head man's wife?" Betty smiled at Sam. "Would you like tea or something stronger? I've got some Heineken in the chiller."

"Beer would be fine, thank you," Sam said with obvious relief as he eyed the fragile cups in front of Livvie and me.

Betty went to the fridge and extracted a bottle of Heineken then plucked a beer mug from the cupboard, setting both down in front of Sam. "Do the police think he did it?"

"They're at the restaurant right now with a search warrant," Livvie said, sipping her tea.

"Why do they need a search warrant?" I asked. "After all, the guy was killed there. Can't they just take all the stuff in the restaurant because it was part of the murder scene?"

We all silently considered that. "I watch that CSI show a lot," Betty finally said. "I don't think they can do that. I think unless they take things away with them right away, they've got to get papers to come back after it later." She regarded Livvie with shrewd assessment. "Do you think T.J.'s boy did it?"

I sat back, surprised at Betty's bluntness. I was even more surprised when Livvie murmured, "I'm not sure. That's what has me scared." She fiddled with her spoon, shifting it this way and that to sparkle in the overhead lighting. When she finally looked up to face us, I saw the haunted look in her eyes. "Paul has anger management issues. When T.J. got out of the Army, he was messed up from drugs. His wife died while he was overseas and Paul was raised by T.J's mother-in-law. They never got along and it wasn't until T.J. started to get straight that he and Paul had any contact." Livvie sipped her tea. "I think Paul blames T.J. for the trouble in his life."

"That's convenient," Betty said wryly. "He sounds like John. He's blamed Charlie for all his troubles when it was really just that John wasn't as good as Charlie at a lot of things." She shrugged one shoulder, light catching on the gold of the cross she wore around her neck. "Life ain't fair sometimes. Not all of us are blessed. Best thing to do is accept it and move on."

"Amen," Sam murmured.

"So tell me about you, Sam Barlow," Betty said, turning her attention to him. "You and our songbird have been stepping out for a while now. You must be a good man. Cassie doesn't stick with men very long."

I almost choked on my tea, smiling weakly when Sam shot me a questioning look. "Betty knows all about me," I managed. "She was with Grandy since...well, since forever, right?"

As I hoped, Betty took the diversionary bait. "I joined Mrs. Theo back when she had that hip surgery, when she was seventy or so. I came as a temporary nurse and somehow I just stayed for almost twenty years. What do you plan to do with the place?" she asked me, her dark eyes flickering from me to Sam. "You folks going to move in?"

Damn. The diversion wasn't as good as I hoped. She was still angling for information about me and Sam. Luckily Livvie came to my rescue.

"Can I tell her?" she asked me. I nodded, and Livvie said, "T.J. and I are going to buy the house from Cassie. It's just across the bay from his restaurant so he'll be able to boat over there in no time. That way Cassie will get some money the way Grandy wanted and I'll get the house. I love this place," she said, looking around the kitchen. Then she smiled at me, a flash of her old impishness dancing in her dark blue eyes. "I get the Nest."

"I got dibs and I've had dibs since summer," I said automatically then we both broke out in giggles. "It was a thing we did when we were kids," I explained to Sam as I wiped away a laugh tear. "There's a cupola on top of the house and we called it the Nest. It's only big enough for one person and it was always so much fun to sleep up there. We used to call dibs on it as soon as we got into the house. Then we started this routine about 'I've had dibs since last time,' which stretched to 'dibs since last week' to..." I shook my head. "Needless to say, it was always a stampede when we got here to see who could get to the Nest first."

"I can't wait until it snows," Livvie said dreamily. "It's so nice to go up there and watch the white caps on the lake before it ices over. I used to haul my old blanket up there and some cocoa in a thermos and sit up there all day with a book and read and watch the lake." She touched my hand. "Thank you, Cassie. I was hoping I could live here."

"Once that gets settled, I'll be able to move on," Betty said with satisfaction.

Livvie looked stricken. "You wouldn't, would you? I was hoping you'd stay."

"No need for me here once you move in," Betty said. "I was here to take care of an old woman. You and your husband won't need that."

"But—" Livvie looked to me for support.

"Maybe Betty wants to retire," I said, taking a cautious sip of the hot tea and thinking fast. "Maybe she wants to hang out in Georgia with the family." I glanced at Betty, who was frowning in thought. "After all, you know how she loves to visit her son and his kids. Isn't that where you'd move? Your other boy is in Chicago, right? He's doing a residency at a hospital there. I suppose you'd rather go to Georgia with Del, though. That's where the grandkids are. Or would you stay here and get a house somewhere?"

Betty tapped the table with one pink-polished nail. "I have to admit, while I love to visit Del and the kids, I'm not sure I'm cut out for life in Georgia. It gets too hot there in the summertime." She looked at the door leading to the dining room and I knew she was visualizing the lake in her mind as it lay outside the front door. "It's so pleasant here in the hot summer months. But I might want to take some long trips in the wintertime, the way Mrs. Theo and I used to do." Her dark complexion darkened even further as she said, "A gentleman I met at the Seniors Night Out—well, he and I have been keeping company. We play bridge together and he was talking about taking a cruise in the wintertime, leaving from Florida and going to some of those islands."

I sat back and stared at her, dumbstruck. "Seriously? You've been a widow for what—forty years?"

She took a sip of her tea and smiled at Sam. "You're never too old for love, that's what I always say. Wouldn't you agree, Sam?"

He looked startled. "Uh, yes, ma'am. Of course." He raised his beer mug and took a long swallow, avoiding my gaze.

I was saved from further embarrassment by my cell phone, which chimed *The Boys of Summer* from Sam's coat pocket. Sam handed it to me with a small smile. "LLF is calling," he murmured.

I snatched the phone out of his hand and got up, walking to the other side of the room to lean against the sink. "Hey, Charlie," I said in a low voice.

"Where are you guys? Are you coming?"

I glanced at the clock over the stove. It was almost seven. We were due at the Hunt Club any minute. "I thought you weren't sure you were going."

"You talked me into it."

I doubted that, but I didn't argue. "We're on our way. We're at Grandy's house now, changing our clothes. I don't think Livvie's coming, but Sam and I will be there."

"What happened at the restaurant?"

"Long story. I'll fill you in later. We need to get moving."

"Good. Dad is getting pissed off. You know how he is about these family things."

I did know, unfortunately. The Second often planned dinners and expected the family to jump to his tune. I'd been out of the inner circle for years but my inheritance had dragged me back into the fold and I was now subjected to the same rules as the rest of the siblings. "We'll be there in a few minutes. All we'll miss is the opening cocktails."

"Janelle is here." He lowered his voice. "She's wearing one hell of a dress."

I smiled. My ploy worked. I suggested to Janelle that she go for the glam side of the Fifties and apparently she took my advice. "She's got the body for it," I said.

"For what? Did you put her up to something?"

"She'd look good in a burlap bag, Charlie. I'd better go. I have to get dressed yet."

"I'll tell him you're on your way. People are just starting to move toward the dining room now, so if you hurry, you won't be late."

I folded the phone. "We need to get changed," I told Sam. "Charlie's Dad is foaming at the mouth." I hurried on when I saw Betty prepared to dismiss this. "I don't want to get Charlie in trouble. I told him we were on our way."

"God forbid we get Charlie in trouble." Sam pushed away from the table and picked up the small bags he brought in. "Lead on. I'm ready to channel my inner James Dean."

"Sure you won't join us, Livvie?" I asked as I headed for the doorway to the dining room and the upstairs beyond.

She shook her head. "I'll wait for T.J. to call. I think we'll just go back to his house tonight. I didn't sleep much last night."

"Okay." I pushed open the swinging door and we passed through the dining room where three sets of china gleamed in the massive display case against the wall.

"All this is yours, hmm?" Sam asked as we walked through the living room full of comfortable but pricy antique furniture.

"Yeah. Grandy left it all to me." I touched the chintz sofa arm. "She and I had tea together every Saturday for years. When I was a kid it was so much fun to come here and pretend to be a grown-up. Later it was nice to come here and feel like a kid." I went to the wide oak staircase and started upstairs. "You can take the boy's room on the left," I said, pointing to the room at the top of the stairs. "I'll take the girl's room."

"Boy's room?" Sam paused at the top.

"There're four bedrooms—Grandy's, the Grown-up Room, the Boy's Room and the Girl's Room. Depending on who stayed overnight, there was a place for them." I made a right turn at the top of the stairs and went into the pink and white room. "See you in a minute, James Dean."

Sam winked and ducked into the blue and white room opposite. I closed the door behind me and looked around. It hadn't changed much, if at all, since I was a child. Despite its overly feminine décor, it was a relaxing room with two twin beds, white dressers and nightstands, and framed family pictures on the walls. I spent a few nostalgic seconds looking at photos of me and the others on the lake then I dumped out my traveling bag and got busy.

Five minutes later, I was presentable in my bobby socks, sneakers, poodle skirt, and sweater. I put my wedding slacks and sweater into the bag and emerged to find Sam lounging against the banister, the epitome of Fifties male studliness. His black T-shirt was tight across his chest and I saw the outline of a pack of cigarettes rolled up in one sleeve. His jeans were rolled up, too, and he wore white socks and loafers. I pirouetted in front of him, twitching my poodle skirt so he could see the design.

He grinned when he saw me. "I can't remember the last time I saw a woman in a skirt who wasn't wearing panty hose." He slipped an arm around me and gave me a quick hug. "Pretty sexy."

"You look pretty sexy yourself." I pulled away with a laugh. "Let's go rock and roll, okay? I feel like dancing."

"I'll race you." He dashed down the stairs and I followed, laughing.

Twenty minutes later, we pulled into the parking lot at the Minnetonka Horse and Hunt Club. "Where's the valet?" I asked rhetorically then I saw the sign. *Valet parking unavailable. Please self-park.*

"Self-park," I laughed as I maneuvered into the already full lot. "Is that even a term?" I found a spot at the far end of the lot near the trees that bordered the pavement. Two empty spots were nearby, giving me a measure of hope the car wouldn't get dinged. A red Mustang, a gray Porsche and a burgundy Benz kept the Enterprise company while it waited for our return.

I grabbed the poodle-shaped felt 'handbag' I made from leftover material and tucked my arm through Sam's. "Let's go deal with the family," I said.

"Oh, boy. Can't wait." He kissed me then shrugged his shoulders, settling his black leather jacket. We walked into the ornate lobby and I handed the invitation to the guard on duty. Seconds later, we were ushered into the large member's room, which was now a dining area where guests were taking seats at one of the dozen or so tables.

C.R. the Second was standing in front of the enormous fireplace where logs crackled and hissed. He had a drink in hand as he talked to a slender woman with her back to us. She wore a black slinky gown, her dark blonde hair slicked back like a movie star's.

I saw Charlie across the room at a window, Janelle Rimes with him. She was stunning in a cobalt blue gown of heavy satin, cut away at the bodice and falling in waves to her feet. Her long black hair was twisted up into an elaborate hair-do, held by sparkling clips. Matching earrings dangled from her lobes and a similar necklace glittered around her throat.

"Who's the swanky babe with Charlie?" Sam muttered.

"My lawyer."

"Wow. She's a looker."

I nodded. "And she's in love with Charlie." *But*

who wouldn't be? I thought. He wore a dinner jacket, white shirt, and white tie, looking like Cary Grant to her Ingrid Bergmann, George Clooney to her Angelina Jolie (minus the puffy lips). Charlie waved when he saw us then gestured to his father, frowning.

I shook my head, not understanding the message being passed. Sam and I started forward into the room. "Where do we sit?" he muttered as we walked by a table almost full of guests.

"I don't know, I'm guessing...yep, there's name tags things." I nodded to the small holders shaped like music notes, which held names. "Let's find our spots."

I started to approach C.R. to say hello and as I did the woman turned.

Sheila Peavey smiled at us.

Chapter 8

"What the hell is she doing here? I thought this was family only." Sam turned so his back was to the room and his ex-wife, his dark brown eyes almost flashing fire.

I looked around the large hall. At least fifty people were already seated at the white linen-covered tables. I spied John Whittington and his wife Diane. They were pointedly ignoring me from across the room. Becky, John's twin, was seated with her fourth husband at the head table next to Claire, the Second's fourth wife. The older Whittington grandchildren, most in their twenties, were sprinkled around the room. Matthew, John's oldest, paused with upraised wine glass to shoot me a glare.

"It's obviously not just a family affair. The Whittington family isn't that big." I smiled at a few faces I recognized and walked slowly down the aisle, looking at the place names on the tables. "At least we're sitting together," I murmured, stopping at a table in the center of the room. I scanned the other place names at the table, relieved to see a stranger next to me and Janelle next to Sam, with Charlie next to her. I looked over the heads of people in front of me and saw Sheila sitting at a table next to the head table. At least we wouldn't be inflicted with her at our table.

I slipped into my seat and tugged Sam down

next to me. A heavyset man wearing a cardigan sweater, baggy slacks, white shirt and a bowtie took the seat next to me. "Good evening," he intoned. "Parker Shaw and my wife, Lucille." He held out a beefy hand, which I shook. His wife, dressed in a starched blue dress with a white Peter Pan collar and black patent leather belt smiled her greeting at me.

"Cassie Whittington and Sam Barlow," I murmured.

"Ah, yes. You're Charles' ex-wife. I remember that wedding," Lucille said brightly. "So unusual. It's pleasant to see you again. You sang at Theo's funeral, didn't you?"

"Unusual?" Sam murmured. "You had an unusual wedding?"

"Kind of." I turned my attention to Mr. and Mrs. Shaw. "Yes, Charlie and I still sing at family events." I glanced past Sam to my ex-husband, who was holding a chair for Janelle. Sam turned to her, leaving me to deal with Ozzie and Harriet alone.

The other seats at the eight-person table filled with stragglers whom I didn't know. The waiter came over and fussed around us, pouring wine and setting down a plate of snacks.

"What is it?" Sam whispered to me as he stared at the lumpy offerings in front of us on the crystal plate.

"Probably pate, caviar and expensive cheese," I muttered back. "You know, goose liver and fish eggs and that kind of junk."

He narrowed his eyes as he considered his plate. "I may pass."

"Try it," Janelle said in a low voice from his right side. "It's edible." She smiled at me. "You two look perfect. You're the only ones who actually look like you came from the Fifties. The rest of us didn't have the guts to go for the costume."

I shrugged, spreading a bit of caviar onto a slice of bread with the provided spoon. "What the heck, right? It's a chance for grown-ups to play dress-up."

"Why is the spoon plastic?" Sam whispered.

"It's pearl. You can't use metal because it taints the caviar. Go ahead, eat up. The stuff on your plate probably cost fifty bucks."

"No way," he said in disbelief.

"Way." I gobbled up the goodies and washed it down with the wine the waiter poured. When we were growing up, the Second insisted that all the children have exposure to gourmet foods and wines and it had been a long time since I tasted Russian caviar. Of course, he also insisted that we learn how to gut a fish, shoot a rifle from a deer stand, and cross-country ski. I hadn't done those things in a long time, either and didn't plan to do so any time soon.

I made idle chitchat with my left-most dining companion as we sampled the clear mushroom soup and headed into the main course of duck breast in port wine sauce. Sam bravely tried everything put in front of him, his eyes widening in surprise as he tasted how the wines complemented the food. "Maybe there's something to this gourmet stuff after all," he whispered. "We should hit a few restaurants and try some new things."

"If you don't mind paying a hundred dollars a plate, we can."

He grinned at me. "You mean you won't buy?"

I felt a brief quiver of disquiet at his casual mention of my soon-to-be-wealth. Then he said, "Hey, we've got a friend in the restaurant business. I'll bet they can give us a good deal. After all, we'll be going Dutch treat. I don't have that kind of money to throw around." Janelle said something to him and he turned to his right to talk to her. I was surprised how relieved I felt at his cavalier explanation.

"I heard Olivia is considering buying *La Suzette*," the florid man next to me said. "I didn't realize she was a foodie."

"I didn't realize it was common knowledge," I said, surprised.

"I suppose it isn't. She approached my bank about the funding. We manage her trust account. I assumed you knew about it since you're family."

"I knew." But I wasn't sure if the news about her engagement was widespread, so I added, "She has a friend in the business who will help her."

"Well, I hope the friend knows what he or she is doing." The man sipped his wine with satisfaction. "At least the people here know how to set a good table. I was very disappointed at *La Suzette*."

"What was wrong?"

"The duck was overdone," the woman next to him said emphatically. She prodded the fowl on her plate with little delicate stabs of her fork, the juice oozing out of the meat. "It was dry and overly seasoned."

"I had poached salmon with black truffles and it was very poor." Mr. Shaw took a miniscule bite of duck from his plate, patted his lips then continued. "I complained to the waiter. I told him it didn't taste like black truffles at all."

I nodded politely. "There are different kinds of truffles?" I knew there were, of course, but the knowledge was lost twenty years ago when Charlie and I divorced and I went from being one of the Wealthy to being one of the Normals.

"There are four or five premium varieties, then there are the American ones." His lips thinned. Obviously, it pained him to discuss American truffles in the same breath as imported ones. "Suffice it to say, the imported variety are far superior. When I ordered the dish, I was under the impression it was made with imported black truffles.

The *chef de cuisine* was called and tasted the dish himself." The man smiled smugly. "His indignation turned to anger when he tasted it. At least they removed the cost of the dish from our bill."

"Really? That was nice of him."

The wife nodded. "At ninety dollars a plate, they should remove it."

"Ninety dollars?" I made some mental calculations in my head. If the restaurant sat sixty or seventy people, and they charged, on average, fifty dollars a plate, and ...

"Truffles cost over five hundred dollars a pound," her husband said. "This was supposed to be truffle infused, which means it used a great deal of the fungi." He sighed heavily. "I hope Olivia has better luck with her chefs."

Apparently, the news of the murder hadn't yet made its way into the hallowed halls of Minnetonka High Society. "I'm sure she will," I said inanely. "She's a good judge of character."

He shot me a disbelieving look. "Really?" His tone of voice clearly said, *Since when?*

"Oh, look. C.R. is going to talk." I moved to one side for the waiter, who was poised to hand me a cup of coffee. I hid my relief at avoiding the delicate subject of Livvie's questionable instincts about men. Minnetonka was not just a lake, it was a region of the Twin Cities and it was an exclusive region at that. Everyone knew everyone else's secrets and Livvie's disastrous first marriage was probably well-known.

I leaned back in my chair just as Sam leaned toward me. "Janelle is a classy lady," he murmured. "I think Charlie's crazy for not sweeping her off her feet."

I smiled at him. "I keep telling him that. Maybe you could add your opinion."

"I doubt he cares about my opinion."

"Hush," I whispered as the Second got to his feet and moved once again to the center of the room near the fireplace.

"I wanted to express my appreciation to all my friends and family for coming to our little get-together tonight. Thanks to your generous donations, we've raised almost forty thousand dollars for the local food bank, money which is sorely needed in such poor economic times."

Polite applause greeted this announcement. I wondered if anyone in this room had ever come close to poor economic times, but I kept my skepticism off my face. Forty grand was chump change to the Whittington family but it would mean a lot to charity.

"I'd like to thank some of our more generous donors." He gestured to the two tables nearest the fireplace. "Sally Jennison, Sheila Peavey, Mark Doyle—please stand up and take a bow. We wouldn't have been able to donate such a generous amount without your equally generous contribution."

The three named people all stood. I glared at Sheila Peavey, who looked gorgeous in her black sheath gown and pearls. "Where's she getting the money?" I asked Sam out of the side of my mouth.

"The patents," he said in a low, angry voice. "Mike's patents."

"But aren't those in dispute?"

"She was never charged in his murder," Janelle whispered, leaning over Sam's arm to do so. "She inherited his estate. There was probably a stipulation about his business, too."

"That is so not right," I sputtered. "She shouldn't gain from his death. She shouldn't—"

"I think a more pertinent outrage is why the hell my father invited her," Charlie whispered, peering behind Janelle to look at me.

I turned back to the front in time to intercept a

glare from the Second at our rudeness. I lifted my chin and glared back at him.

"And now I hope you'll all stay and enjoy an evening of dancing next door. I believe we have a band who has guaranteed us all a night of nostalgic music." He smiled benignly, his silver hair and old-fashioned black tuxedo giving him the air of a well-dressed Michelangelo's God who stepped down the ceiling to mingle with the little folk.

People began to stand and move toward the far doorway leading into the next room, a meeting room/ballroom/community room often used for hunt training and demonstrations. I leaned into Sam, who put his arm on the back of my chair. "I can't believe she's here," I said, peering over him to talk to Janelle. "That bitch."

Charlie leaned closer to Janelle to talk to us, putting his arm on the back of her chair. We looked like we were in a football huddle. "Father said he was inviting shareholders from one of his companies. I wonder if that's why she came here."

"She's stalking Cassie," Sam muttered. "Last night and now tonight."

"What?" Charlie's voice and eyes were sharp.

I waved it away. "She came to my house last night, looking for Sam." I didn't mention Sheila's little scheme to use my inheritance. I wouldn't give Charlie any ammunition for that argument. "I can't believe—" My words were drowned out by the sounds of *Twist and Shout*, coming from next door.

Charlie rolled his eyes and got to his feet, holding out a hand to Janelle. "Shall we?" he said loudly.

Janelle stood gracefully, the blue gown clinging to her slender body. The color was perfect for her, a lovely contrast for her dark hair and setting off her pale skin and the delicate pink of her cheeks. "Nice dress," I said enviously. I could never pull off a number like that.

She leaned down to speak into my ear. "You were right. I think…" She straightened and I saw Sam's gaze jerk away from her décolletage back to an innocent examination of a painting on the wall. I nudged him with my elbow as Charlie and Janelle walked away.

"What?" he asked as he stood. "Can't a guy look?"

I took his arm and we wandered toward the music in the next room, pausing at the doorway to view the sea of people laughing and dancing in the semi-lit space. I spied a bar at the far side of the room and pantomimed a trip in that direction. Sam nodded. "Lead on," he said over the noise of the band.

I struck out around the perimeter but about halfway I lost Sam in the crowd. I glanced back and saw him talking to Sheila. I debated joining him then decided not to aggravate the situation. He was a big kid and could handle himself. Or could he? As I hesitated the crowd moved and I lost sight of them. A little voice echoed in my head. *Let go of the past. You don't need to know every detail. All you need to know is the now.*

I made my way to the bar, tucked at the back. As I left the dancing area the drop in the noise level was immediate. I signaled to the bartender. "A glass of zinfandel," I said, leaning on the polished oak bar. I looked to my right and saw the Second sitting in semi-darkness, a glass of whiskey near his hand.

He smiled briefly. "How are you doing, Cassandra?"

I eyed him warily. "You've got an interesting mix of people here."

"Yes, it is." He nodded to a man who walked by.

"Of course, you knew Sheila Peavey was Sam's ex-wife." I took the glass the bartender handed me and sampled a healthy swig. I looked out at the crowd, but lost sight of Sheila. She was probably lurking out there, waiting to pounce on me when I least suspected it.

His gaze returned to me. "Who? Mrs. Peavey? She's a new investor in one of my companies. She's actually quite a large investor. I asked some of the new shareholders to join us tonight. All the money goes to charity."

"That's not the point. She's Sam's ex-wife and she was accused of murder in the spring." I was still seething about that little miscarriage of justice.

"Accused is not convicted." His green eyes, so like Charlie's, bore into mine. "As we all know."

I flinched. He seldom mentioned the family tragedy we shared, when my father murdered C.R.'s first wife and the mother of his children. C.R. killed my father that day and was arrested but soon freed when the circumstances of my father's death became known.

"It's odd she's here," I muttered. "I don't understand it."

"Perhaps she's trying to put her past behind her. It doesn't matter. She's his ex-wife." He glanced around the room. "Your ex-husband is here, too."

I followed his gaze and saw Charlie talking to a woman on the far side of the room. Sam had left Sheila and was now chatting with a buxom woman in a cheerleader's outfit. I frowned. She looked pretty damn good in that outfit. I felt like a frump in my poodle skirt and sneakers.

"I see you and your boss are still dating," he commented.

I sipped my wine. "Sam's not my boss. His sister is."

"He co-owns the business, right?"

"Yes."

"Then he's your boss. Did you convince Janelle

to come?"

"Yes, I did. I thought it might be useful to have my lawyer with me when I saw John."

The Second smiled wryly. His face was craggy, lined now but still handsome. *This is what Charlie will look like in twenty years,* I thought. Charlie's father was lean, somewhat stoop-shouldered, but still had that Douglas Fairbanks aristocratic look about him. I compared him to Sam's uncle whom I met earlier that day at the wedding and smiled at the thought. In twenty years, Charlie would look like Richard Gere and Sam would look like Harrison Ford. Two different men, two different personality types.

"It's amusing to see two grown men act like idiots," the Second murmured. I had the eerie feeling he was reading my mind.

I whirled to see what had him so amused. Charlie was staring at Sam across the width of the room and Sam was watching him, covertly, as he talked to the cheerleader. "I don't know what to do," I said, more to myself than to the Second.

"There's nothing you can do, Cassie."

I looked at him in surprise. His expression was sympathetic and I had a sudden memory of that same expression when I was a child. I used to be afraid of him, but he was fair with me and while he never showed me any love, he never showed me animosity, which was a small miracle in itself.

"I love Charlie," I said simply. "I always will. But there's Sam now..." I shook my head, not sure where my thoughts were heading. "I don't know if we can make anything work."

"Charlie's in love with the past," his father said softly. "He loves you but he also loves that time in his life when you and he were together." He took a sip of his whiskey and I saw bitter knowledge in his eyes. "It takes a patient woman to make a man forget his past. Charlie's afraid to try for happiness with someone else because he's afraid it won't measure up."

"That's silly. There are all kinds of happiness in the world."

The Second smiled briefly. "You know that and I know that. I doubt Charlie knows that." He took another swallow of his drink. "It's a terrible business with Olivia's friend, isn't it?"

"He's her fiancé," I corrected.

"Not if he's in jail. It sounds as though that might be a real possibility."

For a fleeting instant I wondered if C.R. would frame T.J. just to get him out of Livvie's life. Then I shook the thought away. The Second was capable of a lot of things, but framing someone for murder probably wasn't within his power. "What if he stays out of jail?"

The Second's eyes closed partly, giving them a hooded, bird-of-prey look. "Perhaps by then she'll come to her senses. A person she met during alcohol rehabilitation is hardly a suitable match." He shook his head. "I can't believe a daughter of mine would marry a cook."

"A chef," I corrected. I thought it was perfectly suitable but kept the idea to myself. I never won arguments with the old man. The best I could hope for was to leave the arena unscathed. "You won't oppose the marriage, will you?"

"She's forty-two. She's somewhat past the age of consent. Olivia can do as she pleases." He smiled fleetingly. "She always has. It's a pity about the restaurant, though."

It took me a minute to figure out what he meant. "T.J.'s restaurant? What about it?"

"The land where it sits is under dispute. I suspect they'll have to close."

"What?"

He nodded. "That part of the bay has been in dispute for years. It was owned by the Donovans, an old and rather unpleasant group of people." His raised eyebrow told me what he thought of that family. "They clung to the land for years, never developing it. Then they finally started selling parcels, but it wasn't zoned properly." He sipped his drink, nodding to some people who bumped past us, dancing to *High School Hop*. "To further complicate matters, when some businesses started building, they had to sign a lease for the land, they didn't purchase it outright. The city finally stepped in and put a lien on further development. The businesses there are embroiled in a lawsuit but I don't think they have the kind of money needed to fight it."

"That doesn't seem fair."

"It's lakeshore property across from some of the most expensive property in the Midwest," C.R. said dryly. "I rather doubt fairness will enter into it." He turned aside to talk to a man and I drifted away, thoughts awhirl. Another land dispute? How weird that T.J. was involved in a land dispute and so was Sam. I wondered who owned the land where the restaurant sat. Could that be a motive for murder?

I looked for Sam in the crowd but he had vanished.

So had Sheila.

I struggled not to be angry about that fact. Surely they were both just…somewhere else, right? It wasn't anything to worry about, right? I sipped my wine and watched Charlie and Janelle dancing together. They looked spectacular, like two people lost in a dream and holding on to each other for stability. I felt a stab of jealousy so sharp I actually rubbed my chest, wondering if I was having a heart attack.

Charlie deserved happiness. He was one of the nicest people I knew. Why couldn't I have that kind of happy? I ordered another glass of wine and allowed the Glooms to settle on me. Why did I have to be in love with a man who...

Wait a minute. Was I in love? I looked for Sam guiltily, as though my momentary doubt about my feelings might smite him dead or something. He was still nowhere to be seen, though. I did spy Sheila talking to two men who appeared to be hanging on her every word. She was so svelte and chic in her gown and jewels. I sipped my wine, watching John's son Matthew as he watched Sheila. Hell, she even had the younger set intrigued. Of course, she was younger than me and she was taller and she was...

"Oh, hell," I muttered. All of the little positive affirmations I read earlier appeared to have flown out of my brain. Worry, anger, and envy flowed in to take their place.

"I wonder how Livvie's getting along?"

I turned on my bar stool and regarded Sam, who had snuck up beside me. "I hope no news is good news." I thought guiltily of Livvie, probably worried and frightened for the man she loved. My guilt doubled when I saw how bored Sam looked.

"I'm ready to go any time you are," he said casually. "I think we've put in enough of an appearance, haven't we?" His eyes moved around the room, pausing when he saw Sheila. He frowned then pursed his lips, as though considering something.

"What is it?" I asked.

"Nothing." He touched my arm. "Can we go?"

I considered finishing my wine but Sam was already moving away. I decided I probably shouldn't drink it anyway, since I was driving. I followed him, edging my way along the perimeter of the dance floor. We escaped the dancing room and entered the lobby.

"That was an interesting dinner," Sam said. "I felt surrounded—your ex-husband, my ex-wife, and a bunch of snobs who feel good about donating money to charity."

My tenuous hold on my temper began to fray. "It was almost as interesting as our lunch this afternoon," I snapped. "Of course, I realize caviar can't compare to bratwurst, but I thought the pressed duck was passable when it was paired with the pinot noir."

The angry look he shot me would have stopped me in my tracks if I hadn't been so pissed off myself. "Well, gee, I guess I should have asked about the vintage on the keg of beer just to be on the safe side, to make sure it was passable." He said the last word with a sneer.

"I don't know why you're so acting like such a—"

"Cassie!"

Sam and I turned simultaneously. John Whittington—my personal nemesis—was striding across the lobby toward us.

Chapter 9

I glared at John. This was all I needed to top off a shitty day.

"We need to talk, Cassie," John said. Like Charlie, John was tall with thick dark hair and hazel eyes. He lacked Charlie's amazing good looks and sunny personality, though, and I think that lack galled him all his life.

I crossed my arms. "Talk to me about what? Talk about how you're going against Grandy's wishes and gypping me out of my money? How you're trying to..."

Sam stepped in front of me. "Talk to her lawyers. They're all back there." He jerked his head toward the ballroom. "Let's go." He put a hand on my sleeve.

"Wait a minute." I jerked my arm away. "What's going on, John? How come you're—"

"Come on, Cassie. He doesn't want to talk to you. He just wants to argue."

"Stay out of this, Barlow," John snarled. "You've got no right to talk for Cassie."

"Yeah," I said. Then I frowned. What the hell was I doing, agreeing with John Whittington? I checked John, to gauge his reaction. He looked as surprised as I felt but he also appeared...tentative, worried. What was going on?

"Excuse me." Sam backed away, his hands up. "I

didn't mean to speak out of turn."

"Damn it, quit being an idiot," I snapped. "You know what I meant."

"No, I don't know what you meant. I just figured you wouldn't want to talk to this crazy bastard, but if you do, don't let me stop you." Sam started to walk away but stopped when John put a hand on his leather-coated arm.

"What's that crack supposed to mean?" he demanded. John's face was twisted with rage, a grotesque mask of anger that made him appear as distorted as a comic-book caricature. What had Sam said that got him so enraged?

"Let me go." Sam's voice was low and level but I recognized the simmering anger in it. I suspect that, like me, Sam's day had just reached the breaking point.

"Let's leave," I said dismissively. "We can talk when John is calmer. It's no use talking to somebody when they're not thinking clearly."

"You rot in hell." John jerked his hand away from Sam as though it was contaminated.

Sam and I hurried away. As we did, I glanced behind me. John was watching us, a bewildered expression on his face alternating with a calculating look that was chilling in its intensity. "That was odd," I said as we got to the Enterprise and settled in.

"He's an asshole. Of course he would try to ruin your night." Sam got into the car and watched as I ignited the Enterprise. "Of course, it wouldn't take much to ruin it, would it?"

"What?" I focused on getting the car on the road.

"You've been in a lousy mood all day. I suppose John is just the capper, isn't he?"

"I've been in a lousy mood?" I shot Sam an amazed look. "You're the one who's acted like I'm a total stranger just tagging along with you."

"Well, in many ways—" He shut up so quickly I looked at him, wondering if he was choking or something.

"What?" I demanded.

"Nothing."

I decided to let it lie. I was tired, I had a headache, and I just didn't want to deal with his prima donna mood. We drove in silence and I was grateful since I needed all my energy to drive a strange car in the dark on an unfamiliar road. A slushy light snow was falling and throwing reflections back at me in the lights, which added to my excitement.

Sam finally spoke when we were almost to my house. "I talked to Charlie tonight." His voice was thoughtful. "It was sort of a man-to-man thing."

I glanced at him. "What?"

"He wanted to know if my intentions were honorable."

"Oh, for heaven's sake." I longed to beat my head on the steering wheel, but since I was driving, I decided it wasn't advisable. "Charlie has this thing about my possible inheritance."

"Well, he's right to be worried," Sam said. "It's a lot of money."

"Everybody keeps telling me that," I snapped. "I haven't seen any yet. So I'm not too worried about what might happen." I turned into my townhome development then parked the Enterprise in the driveway. I looked at Sam over the top of the car as we both got out. "I understand it's a lot of money. But it's not real yet." I strode to my front door and unlocked it, making a mental note to program the Enterprise to open my garage door remotely.

Sam paused next to me. "I don't know, Cassie. Charlie seemed—" He opened the door and before either of us could stop him, Houdi was out, racing away like a yellow tornado.

"Damn!" Sam sprinted after my disappearing cat. He made a grab for Houdi but missed, almost toppling off the sidewalk and landing in my driveway. The near-miss slowed Sam just enough that Houdini gained momentum, his fat legs churning into the lawn and barely touching the street.

I spent a precious minute tossing our bags into the house and closing the door then I followed them. I caught a glimpse of a yellow butt disappearing into the bushes across the townhouse road. On the other side of the bushes was a small up-hill, which leveled off briefly then led to a steep down-hill leading to a drainage pond. Beyond that was a major boulevard in town. "Catch him, Sam!" I yelled. "The road's over there. He'll be pancaked!"

Sam plunged into the darkness and the shrubbery, pushing his way through bare branches that snagged his coat. With one last thrust he was past them. I wiggled my way after him, branches whapping my bare legs and snagging on the felt of my poodle skirt. One appliqué got tangled on twigs and I heard a tearing sound as I jerked away. I finally got free and worked my way up the hill then teetered on the brink when I got to the top. The street light behind me cast enough light for me to Sam halfway down the other side, pausing at bushes along the way to peer into them. I followed him and did the same, visions dancing in my head of a smirking yellow cat, glaring at me from under a burgundy viburnum or red-twig dogwood.

I took my time crisscrossing the slope and calling Houdi's name, alternating with faint curses I prayed the portly feline didn't hear. This went on for ten minutes or more then it started to rain, a cold drizzly heavy mist that soon saturated my thin sweater. "You need to go back and get warmer clothes," Sam said as we met near the middle of the hill.

I looked at the drainage pond. "What if he fell in? He's not used to being outside. He's just a big dumb indoor cat. What if—"

"Go back and get changed," Sam said. "Bring some flashlights when you come back." I was so relieved he didn't suggest we give up the search that I almost kissed him, but our earlier argument stuck with me. I settled for squeezing his arm tightly. He gave me a little shove toward the hill. "Make us some coffee, too, okay? And if you can find a good raincoat, bring it along."

I nodded mutely, already so cold I could barely move. I turned and scrambled back the way we came, pausing at any likely hiding place that could shelter a rotund, gloating cat. As I passed the Enterprise it glowed, recognizing its companion brain in the keys I carried stuffed in my poodle pocket.

When I got into my townhouse I headed straight for the kitchen to get the coffee started. Then I ran warm water on my frozen hands before stripping out of my clothes, leaving them in a pile on the bedroom floor. I pulled on jeans, sturdy work boots, and a flannel shirt while the coffee perked. Then I grabbed Sam a windbreaker, found two flashlights, and was back out the door dragging on my jacket in ten minutes, a thermos under my arm.

Where could the silly cat be? He knew nothing about the Outdoors. I got him as a kitten from the Humane Society and the closest his paws got to dirt was the litter box. In my old apartment, he would occasionally go out on the balcony and peer down at the world below or let the breeze ruffle his whiskers, but he had never been cold, wet, or lost before. The only wildlife he saw was ladybugs and box elder beetles. He wouldn't have the first idea about how to survive outside. A car would flatten him and he'd sink if he got close to the drainage pond. The thought made me race out the door, tears streaming down my face and mingling with the rain.

The bright beam of the flashlight showed me Sam far down the hill on the other side of the drainage pond near the road. I prayed I wouldn't find a limp cat body by the shoulder when I got there. As I walked up to Sam, a car zoomed past, the headlights blinding me, as though proving to me how precarious the area was. I held my breath, waiting for a screech of tires but when none came, I hurried to Sam.

When he saw my bobbing flashlight beam he came to me, taking the windbreaker and thermos lid of coffee gratefully. I winced when I saw cuts on his red, rain-chapped hands. The bushes were a tangle down here near the pond. "I thought I heard him over there," he said, gesturing with the cup to a clump of thick bushes. "Let's check it out." He gulped the coffee, the steam fogging his rain-smeared eyeglasses. With a muttered curse he took them off, tucking them in his windbreaker pocket.

I approached the brush pile cautiously. My townhome was on the edge of the city, and beyond this pond and the boulevard were farm fields and woods. Foxes, groundhogs, and hawks were regular visitors to my yard and once I spotted a coyote in the distance, running down a deer. I nudged the brush with my foot, prepared to leap back if a snake or a fox came jumping out. Sam added his flashlight beam to mine, creating a confusing mix of light and shadow. I didn't see any yellow cat in there. The pile was big though, at least ten feet long and about six feet wide. "You could hide the entire Humane Society in here," I grumbled, getting down my knees and peering underneath.

Nothing. No laughing cat, nothing. I straightened up and bumped into Sam as I tried to get my balance. His flashlight swung and I caught a glimpse of glowing eyes, staring at us from a few feet away, deep in the wood pile. "He's in there," I said, moving forward.

"Something is in there," Sam corrected, pulling me back. "Hold this." He handed me the coffee and the flashlight and started tackling the brush.

"Be careful," I said, juggling the thermos as I tried to re-cap it. "I've seen foxes around here."

"Foxes nest in the ground if they can," Sam said, pushing his way into the pile. "I hope." He looked at me over his shoulder. "It's a good thing I'm in love with you."

I almost dropped the thermos. It was the first time he ever used the "L" word. "What?"

"You heard me. I wouldn't do this for just anybody." He leaned over. "Give me more light here."

Good Lord. He said it. Should I say it? As soon as I considered it, I discarded the idea. It would sound so stupid to say, *oh, hey, I love you, too* when I honestly wasn't sure if I did. I mean, I loved Sam but was I in love with him? It would sound too wimpy to say that right after he said it. It would sound like—

"Cassie? More light?" He gestured toward the debris on the ground.

I closed my gaping mouth and set the thermos on a somewhat flat piece of ground. Then I edged closer, angling the flashlights to illuminate his way. All of a sudden he ducked out of sight. "Sam!" Visions of him dropping into a fox hole, breaking an ankle, or being bitten zipped through my brain. I started forward, prepared to do what I could for rescue.

"Gotcha," he said as he straightened. "Here." He held out his hand and I jammed one flashlight under my armpit as I took a tiny squirming bundle of black fur.

"What the hell...?" I looked at it quickly. A small

kitten blinked warily at me. I tucked the creature into my jacket as Sam dipped down again, soon emerging with a kicking yellow cat.

"Got him," he said in a triumphant voice. Sam slung Houdini under one arm and wiggled out of his windbreaker, wrapping the jacket around the cat. Houdi didn't protest too much. The rain was coming down in sheets now and it was damn cold. "Let's get back before he escapes again." Sam hugged my cat to his chest and started toward the hill, plucking the flashlight from my armpit as he went. Rain rolled off his black leather jacket and his white hair was plastered to his head. I probably looked just as bedraggled and I wondered if my nose and cheeks were as red as his from the cold.

"Wait a minute. What do I have here?" I turned my flashlight into my jacket to reveal a small black kitten, green eyes looking up at me. As I watched, it yawned, tiny teeth flashing in the light. Its pink tongue darted out, licked my hand, then it settled back against my chest, purring. "Oh, for heaven's sake. Where did Houdini find this? Are there any more?"

Sam was already ahead of me. "I didn't see any. Didn't see a mother, either. I'll bet somebody drove by and tossed it." He gestured with the flashlight toward the road, only yards away. His voice was lost in the wind as we neared the top of the hill. I kept my head down and missed most of what he said, catching only '...assholes in the world who don't think animals...'

We crested the hill and hurried across the road to my house. I almost fumbled the townhouse door, my arms full of squirming kitten, flashlight and thermos, but I managed to get it open just as Houdini leapt from Sam's arms, the kitten leapt from mine, and the thermos hit the ground with a resounding POP.

Sam pushed me inside and closed the door behind us. "Let's not go through this again," he said, leaning against the door.

"Where is it?" I started into the living room but stopped at the sight of Houdini, ambling across the living room toward the kitchen, the kitten following behind like a little shadow. They were both mud splattered and wet, but otherwise appeared as though it was just a typical Saturday night at home.

"That little poop," I muttered, peeling off my wet jacket and letting it drop to the foyer. I looked down at my jeans, then at Sam's. We were both wet from the waist down and he was covered with scratches. I kicked off my boots and headed for the kitchen.

Sam followed, making a beeline for the coffee pot. "You got any whiskey?" he asked, filling a mug and heading for my cupboards.

"Top shelf, near the fridge," I said, peering into my laundry room. Yep. As I suspected. Houdini was watching the kitten who was staring at the kibble, a quizzical expression on its face. I grabbed a saucer, put some kibble in it then dribbled water on the chunks. The dry food immediately puffed and softened. I put it next to Houdini's Big Boy dish and the kitten fell on it with a growl of pleasure. Houdini stepped up to his dish and began to crunch. "It looks like we've adopted a new cat," I said, coming back into the kitchen. I grabbed my broom and dust pan to sweep up the thermos, which had shattered on the foyer floor. Luckily most of it was contained within the thermos body.

When I returned to the kitchen Sam was leaning against the kitchen island, watching the cats. He handed me a mug and I took a long sip of whiskey and coffee, with a little bit of chocolate drifting on top. He'd found my stash of cocoa. I sipped and leaned against him. "Thanks." I pulled his face down to mine. "For everything. I mean it."

He smiled, his dark eyes smoldering and warming me all the way to my toes. "Anything for my girl." He put an arm around my waist as the cats meandered out toward us. "I think we should wipe 'em down," he commented.

I looked at the muddy paw prints on my white-and-gray tile floor and sighed. "Yeah." I got rags out of the cupboard and tossed him one. "Be my guest."

Five minutes later the cats were relatively clean and we were covered with cat hair. Sam tossed our towels toward the laundry room and drew me toward the back of the house. "I suggest a shower." I hesitated, looking at the laundry room where the cats had resumed their chow-down.

"They'll be fine," he murmured, tugging me away. "If they were going to fight, they would have done it by now."

He was right. I decided to forego worry, a simple thing to do once we got undressed and climbed into the warm, steamy shower. In a few minutes, I almost forgot to breathe as Sam knelt in front of me, water cascading over his head. Then it was my turn to reciprocate and by the time we were done, I was tired, happy, sated, and warm, all arguments forgotten and lost animals found. When I felt like that, it was easy to convince myself that all was Happy in the World.

We cocooned ourselves in bathrobes and emerged into the living room to find Houdi and the stranger lying in Houdi's well-furred chair, dozing. "Well, I guess I won't worry about fleas, worms, or other ickies," I said resignedly. "I'll get the kitten to the vet tomorrow and have it checked."

"Sunday? Vet?" Sam asked, dropping onto the couch.

"My vet keeps a few weekend hours for busy pet parents. I'll keep my fingers crossed it didn't bring in any parasites."

Sam reached over and plucked up the kitten, the little critter squirming in indignation at the process. "It looks healthy," he said. "It—" He flipped it over and lifted its tail then let the little beast totter on his thigh, "her eyes are clear, her fur looks good, and she's got energy. I'll bet she wasn't out there long."

The kitten stumbled off his leg and onto mine, collapsing on my arm with a purr. She fit neatly in the crook of my elbow, her fluffy black fur a startling contrast with my white bathrobe. Houdi eyed me suspiciously but when he saw the kitten was sleeping, he let his head drop back on the chair with a sigh. "I wonder if he knew she was out there," I murmured, rubbing the tiny head that relaxed against my left wrist.

"I wouldn't be surprised." Sam yawned and I followed suit. "I've got to open the store tomorrow." He looked at the clock on the DVD player. "Man, it's midnight already. Let's hit the sack."

He helped me up and I tucked the baby in with Houdi, but as soon as I did, she jumped down, following us into the bedroom. I dropped my bathrobe by the side of the bed and the baby clambered into it, poking her little head into the sleeve and purring as she kneaded it with tiny sharp claws. I heard her little *meow* of contentment and I felt like echoing it. Any worries I had about Sam and our relationship vanished as I drifted off to sleep.

****

Sunday started off quietly. Sam and I spent breakfast together, laughing at the kitten and Houdini as they played while I made us chocolate coffee cake in mugs as a treat. Sam left for work at the landscape center, promising to call later and get any updates about Livvie and T.J. I got an appointment with the vet for noon and spent most of the morning kitten-proofing my home. Funny, I thought it *was* cat-proof but a kitten proved me wrong.

At noon, I took Little Critter in for her examination. I took Houdi, too, using the reasoning that whatever cooties the baby had, he had probably picked them up by now, too. Everyone checked out okay, although blood was drawn and the final verdict wouldn't come back for a few days. Until then I decided to hope for the best.

I dropped the cats off at home and went shopping for kitten food, splurging on a few new toys and a cat bed at the same time. Then I came home and by mid-afternoon was sitting in my living room, the Sunday paper moving on the floor as Houdi hid so Little Critter could pounce. I retained my hold on the Arts and Entertainment section, which had a feature story on restaurants in town. Given my new found connection to the culinary world, I read it with interest.

A restaurant east of the Twin Cities was featuring a once-a-month culinary extravaganza, very haute cuisine with haute pricing to match. Seating was limited and every course would feature a signature item, a la *Iron Chef* without the competition between cooks. This month's ingredient was quail and I (and the reviewer) wondered how they'd come up with a quail dessert. Next month's ingredient was truffles and the article featured a write-up on the pricy fungi.

The death of Robert de Garmeaux was also mentioned along with a brief article about his wife, Michelle, paired with speculation about the restaurant's future. On impulse, I went to my computer and spent a few minutes with Google, finally turning to Yahoo and getting some different results. Within twenty minutes, I had a relatively clear timeline on Michelle Bedford's entry into the restaurant business and a good sense of *La Suzette*'s ratings and reviews. My dinner companion from the night before was right. The reviews were mixed, with some raves and some so-so.

I pushed away from my desk and considered it. It was odd that the quality would vary so wildly with the same chefs in place. Perhaps they rotated cooks on different nights? I idly clicked through the four pages of links on my computer screen and leaned forward when one caught my eye on the final page of my Michelle Bedford search, buried within another topic listing.

Alaska beauty finds love in California.

I squinted at the screen. *Michelle Dumbrowski, formerly of Stanton Bay, Alaska, has made her way to California and found love with Saul Bedford. Mr. Bedford, a retired oil executive, met Miss Dumbrowski when...*

I read the article from a small town newspaper in California, dumbfounded. Michelle was from Alaska? A beauty queen from Alaska? There was her picture, complete with crown, parka, and sash. It was a very young Michelle Bedford, but it was her. And that old guy—Saul—wasn't her father. It was her husband.

"Wow, who would have thought?" I muttered to Little Critter who was crawling on my desk, batting at Houdini's tail as the Big Yellow Guy stared, once again, at the Outside. "Here I thought Michelle was some society babe and she was a beauty queen from Nowhere, Alaska." I picked up the newspaper I had set next to the computer as the phone rang.

"Is this Cassie Whittington?" the caller asked.

"Yes, it is." I wiggled my finger under the paper and Little Critter pounced.

"This is Michelle Bedford."

"Wow. Speak of the devil." I looked at my computer screen. "I mean, how did you get my number?"

There was a pause. "There are only two C.R.

Whittingtons in the phone book. I assumed Charles Whittington lived in Orono."

I grinned. Charlie's address was a lot pricier than mine, in Pickaway. I gave Michelle Bedford credit for tact and intelligence. "What can I do for you?"

"I'm looking for Olivia Carlyle. Do you know where she is? We were supposed to meet to discuss some business matters and she hasn't appeared."

I felt a stab of worry. I should have called Livvie to get caught up on what was happening to her but my reconciliation with Sam had taken center stage in my attention. "No, I haven't. Did you try her cell phone? And T.J.?"

"Of course. I thought she might be with the family or..."

I could almost feel the impatience jingling through the phone line. "By business, do you mean the restaurant?" I asked, looking once again at the computer screen. The young beauty queen was smiling at the camera and a big fish—a salmon?—was featured on a flag flying behind her. It looked cold wherever the picture was taken.

"Yes. I wanted to find out about this ridiculous thought she had that Robert was selling the restaurant."

"I've heard good things about your restaurant," I lied. The only things I 'heard' were bad. "Someone mentioned your salmon dish, the one with truffles. I suppose you have connections with you being from Alaska and all."

There was a long silence. "I beg your pardon?"

"You know...salmon? It must be hard to get good salmon here because—" The kitten took that moment to pounce on my keyboard, making the story in front of me disappear. "Oh, damn. Cat, look out, you'll—" The newspaper fluttered to the floor and the picture of raw truffles looked up at me.

126

"Truffles!" What a perfect name for a small black kitten. "That's it!"

"What?" Michelle demanded. "What about truffles?"

"Oh, I'm sorry. It's just an idea I had."

"If you hear from Olivia, please have her call me." The phone went dead in my hand.

"Truffles," I said to the kitten, who peered at me from around the back of my chunky computer monitor. Her green eyes opened wide and she pounced again, this time on my computer mouse.

I plucked the little attacker from the desk and set her on the floor where she tangled with the newspaper article. "Truffles, meet Houdini," I said as the big yellow cat jumped down to join in the journalistic attack. "Houdi, meet Truffles." I laughed out loud at the sound of her name. It was so appropriate. She was small, black, and last night she looked like a little lump of truffles. And given the vet bill I got that morning, she was almost as expensive as the fungi.

My cell phone rang in its charging cradle and Truffles jumped straight up in the air, her tail puffing out. I laughed again as I picked up the phone and looked at the number on the small screen. Panic made my stomach plunge. I put Betty on my speed dial when Grandy got sick. For an instant, I remembered that day when Betty called and said Grandy was in the hospital and I needed to get there, and fast.

I opened the phone and pressed it against my ear. "Betty, what is it?"

"Can you meet Livvie at the police station? T.J's been arrested for murder."

Chapter 10

"What do you mean, he was arrested for murder?"

"He confessed to the murder," Betty said, her voice clipped and matter-of-fact. "The police took him into custody. I thought someone from the family should be with her. I tried calling Charlie but he's not answering his phone."

I remembered how cozy Charlie and Janelle looked at the party the night before. "He might be busy. Why the hell did T.J. confess?"

"I have my suspicions, but I'm not sure. Can you go to the station? I don't like Livvie being there alone."

"Of course I can." I looked at the clock. It was almost five. The landscape center closed at five. Maybe Sam could go with me. I wanted the moral and emotional support. "I'll call Sam and see if we can go."

****

Forty-five minutes later Sam and I entered the by-now-familiar police station. I glimpsed Janelle and Charlie entering ahead of us, both dressed in jeans and sweaters. I wondered fleetingly if they arrived together or if they met there.

When we got inside the waiting area, I saw Paul Watson intercept them. He looked like a coiled, tense spring, wound up and glowering at Charlie. Then I saw Livvie, who sat in the same chair as last night. She looked terrible. Her eyes were red-rimmed from weeping and exhaustion made her shoulders slumped. I remembered her comment about not sleeping the previous night. Did she know then? Did she suspect T.J.?

Mike Johnson and Michelle Bedford were nearby but not with her, standing and talking off to one side. Johnson looked as belligerent as he had the night before and Michelle's eyes widened when she saw Sam and me enter. She edged away from us as though afraid of associating with us.

Livvie caught sight of me and got to her feet, her movements jerky and uncoordinated. "Betty shouldn't have called you but I'm glad she did."

I put my arms around her and held her as she wept. Her tears quickly soaked into my *Yeah, I'm hot but don't blame me for global warming* sweatshirt. I felt so helpless. What could I do or say to mitigate such grief? Then I felt Sam's arms around us both.

"We're here to help, Livvie," he whispered as he bent his head near us.

"Oh, Sam. Thank you." She drew away, sniffling.

Paul Watson left Charlie to talk to Michelle Bedford on the far side of the small space. Charlie came over to us, pulling a handkerchief from his back pocket and handing it to Livvie. "What happened?" His voice was rough but I saw concern in his eyes.

"Why would he do it?" Livvie murmured.

Janelle moved closer, blocking the view of the police counter and the Cooking Bunch, who watched us suspiciously. "Don't say anything." She glanced over her shoulder at two officers who were in the vending machine alcove. "You could incriminate yourself and Tom."

Livvie stared at her blankly. "Why did he confess? It makes no sense. He couldn't have done it.

I know it."

"I suspect the police know it, too," a deep voice said behind me.

I turned to find a necktie on a level with my nose. I raised my gaze to the face of an enormous black man who regarded us all with calm certainty. "I'm sorry. I don't think I know you," I said faintly.

He smiled genially. "Billy Armstrong. I'm Tom's attorney." He nodded to Janelle and Charlie, his dark eyes taking in the Cooking Bunch who huddled on the far side of the room. "Janelle, Charlie—we need to talk." He patted Livvie on the shoulder, his hand as big as my head but surprisingly gentle. "Not to worry. We'll be back in a minute. Excuse us." He nodded to me and Sam then he, Charlie, and Janelle vanished out the front door.

"Why are they going outside?" I whispered.

Sam guided Livvie back to her chair. "Makes sense to me. They're probably afraid of being overheard."

Livvie kept her eyes fixed on the door near the police counter. "Will they release him? If he needs bail, I can do that. How do we find a bail person?"

The front door opened and I turned, expecting to see Charlie re-enter. I almost fell over when the Second walked into the room looking as though he owned the place. As always, he was impeccably dressed in dark slacks and sweater under a charcoal gray suit coat. He glanced at and dismissed the startled police officers then his gaze passed over the Cooking Bunch. In one glance he probably correctly evaluated their net worth, social status, and profession. The Second was good at stuff like that. His gaze moved past them and settled on Livvie. "Hello, children." He smiled at Sam. "Mr. Barlow."

"What are you doing here?" I demanded. "How did you know...?"

"Please. Betty called me. Despite our differences

of opinion, she keeps me in the loop."

"Betty?" I squeaked.

He shot me a reproving look. "Of course. She knows everything about everyone in this family." He sat down to the right of Livvie and to my stunned surprise, put an arm around her shoulders. "We'll straighten it out, Olivia. Don't worry."

Livvie looked up at him with such a terrified look my heart almost broke. "I love him so much, Daddy."

"I know, dear. I know." She rested her head on his shoulder and he looked at me over her tousled brown-blonde hair as though daring me to say anything.

I sank into the other chair, my legs wobbly. What was the world coming to? The Second, acting like a human being? It must be a dream. The outside door opened and Billy Armstrong came back in, trailed by Janelle and Charlie. Armstrong went to the front desk while Charlie and Janelle joined us.

Charlie raised an eyebrow when he saw his father comforting Livvie but he wisely didn't say anything. He stood next to Sam, unconsciously mimicking Sam's posture: hands in jacket pockets, legs planted solidly, and his back to the police, blocking their view of our conversation. For an instant the two men looked like oddly skewed mirror images of each other.

"Armstrong has poked holes in everything the police have on T.J.," Janelle said quietly, looking very preppy in her light blue sweater and stone-washed jeans. Her black hair was tucked into a tidy braid and her woolen jacket's collar framed her face, highlighting her flawless complexion. She didn't look like a hotshot lawyer. She looked like a sorority girl out on a date. "They don't have much except a kitchen implement anyone could have wielded, the fact he was gone last night with no alibi, and no motive."

"There is one motive," Charlie said with a glance at the threesome on the other side of the room who shot us covert glances. "He wants to protect his son, Paul."

As soon as he said it, pieces fell into place. "Of course," I said. "He feels guilty because of Paul's upbringing and he's taking the rap for him."

"Noble but stupid," the Second said. "I hope he doesn't have the same kind of altruistic sense when he's in business." He smiled when he said it but I detected a hint of seriousness behind his words.

Livvie was so focused on Janelle I don't think she heard him. "So he can leave tonight?" she asked. "They won't hold him?"

The Second's arm tightened around her. "Will they consider bail?"

Janelle nodded. "A million dollars. It's a county law in any capital crime case. It's already been set by Judge Avery."

"Fine. Is there a bail bondsman available or should we contact one?"

Sam looked from me to the Second, his eyes wide. I knew what he was thinking. *This guy just volunteered to write a check for one-hundred-thousand dollars. Is he crazy?*

Even Janelle looked startled. "I think we'll be able to work out something."

"Good." The Second stood. "I know Daniel Avery. I'll be happy to sign whatever papers or forms are necessary." He looked past Charlie to Billy Armstrong, who was talking to an equally large police officer near the door. Both men were smiling like old friends. "Can Mr. Armstrong recommend a good investigating agency? I think we should hire someone to do some evidence gathering of our own."

"Rob Renard, another lawyer in my firm, has a sister who's married to a guy who works for a security agency." Charlie moved to one side, pulling out his cell phone. "I'll give Rob a call and get that started."

I followed him. "Is your father really going to front the money for T.J.?" I whispered as Charlie thumbed through his contact list on his phone.

"If he says he will, he will. I don't think the money's in any danger. Let's face it, T.J. won't go anywhere. He's got Livvie and Paul here. He won't flee." Charlie's gaze flickered to the Cooking Bunch who now were deep in conversation with Billy Armstrong. Michelle looked angry and Mike looked ready to blow a fuse. Paul just looked bewildered.

"No, but..." I shook my head. "Why's he being so nice?"

Charlie looked past me to his father, who was talking to Sam. The Second still had his arm around Livvie and he looked every inch the concerned father, glancing from me to Sam. Wait a minute. The Second was looking from me to Sam? Concerned father?

"He and I were talking before Grandy died, last spring. I don't know, it was sort of odd, it was one of those things where we were out on the boat, just relaxing." Charlie looked at me, his green eyes amused. "He said he was starting to understand how Grandy felt about him. He said something like, *the older I get, the more I appreciate grandchildren. You can look at them and think about the mistakes you made with their parents.* Something like that." Charlie found the number he was seeking and put the phone to his ear. "Maybe he's mellowing."

A lifetime of suspicions where C.R. Whittington the Second was concerned made me doubtful, but I kept it to myself. I listened to Charlie's brief one-sided conversation and waited anxiously until he closed the phone. "Handled," he said with satisfaction. "Marcus Sloan will contact me tomorrow and we'll see what we can find."

I remembered my meager research into Michelle Bedford and on impulse I said, "You should check into Michelle Bedford and Mike Johnson, too. They're involved in this." I glanced at the parties in question as I said it. They were still talking to Armstrong. Paul stood apart from them, his narrow face alternating between anger and what I thought was sympathy.

Charlie quirked an eyebrow at me. "Do you know something I don't know?"

"No. Just call it instinct." I hesitated to put my unsubstantiated feelings about Michelle into words. "There's something not right about Michelle Bedford. It's hard to explain."

He held up a hand. "Say no more. I know the importance of a woman's intuition." He smiled, little crinkly lines fanning out around his eyes. "I'll have them checked, too."

"How long will it take for T.J. to get released?" I asked, glancing back to Livvie. Sam was with her, her hand on his arm as she stared at Janelle, Armstrong and the Cooking Bunch. The Second stood nearby, listening in. Livvie looked confused, wrung out, and exhausted. "She should go home. She's beat."

"She won't leave." He smiled wryly. "Would you leave if Sam was in this situation?"

"Of course not," I said automatically. I saw Janelle looking our way. "She's a nice person. She's very smart, too."

"Not you, too."

"Hmm?"

"Everyone seems to want me to notice Janelle."

"Everyone?" I asked innocently.

"My father, Livvie—even Becky mentioned her." Charlie tucked his phone into his jacket pocket. "I know she's nice. I know she's smart. I know she's..."

His voice trailed away.

"She's what?" I prompted. Charlie was looking over my shoulder, and I turned.

The Second was behind me. "Can you make the arrangement for the bail, Charlie? Just call Morganthal, at First Trust."

Charlie nodded. "Do you have his private number?"

The Second handed Charlie a business card. "I'd appreciate it. I'm not sure about the logistics of it all."

Charlie glanced at his watch. "I'll make some calls." He walked away as Sam moved toward us.

"I appreciate you coming over, Cassie," the Second said in a low voice. "Livvie needs all the help she can get."

I looked up at him in surprise. His handsome, patrician face appeared concerned and that surprised me, too. "I'm glad you recognize how vulnerable she is. I wasn't sure if anyone in the family really did." I turned to Sam as he joined us, his face worried.

"I think we all recognized it. Some of us take it a bit more seriously than others. Odd how a person can have five children and have them all grow up to be so different than each other."

"Five?" Sam asked.

The Second's mouth twisted up in a brief smile. "I consider Cassie one of the children. Her mother was a dear friend and a mother to my children when their mother died. Cassie will always be a part of the family, whether she inherits the money or not."

I looked away, unwilling to let him see my tears of gratitude. Livvie said the same thing to me earlier in the spring, but it was different hearing it from him. "Thank you, C.R."

"It's only the truth. Now if Charlie would just accept it, you could both move on with your lives."

He sighed heavily. "Charlie is afraid that by letting go of the past, he'll lose you, too. And you need to understand that you can move on. Charlie will always be there for you no matter what. We all will."

I wasn't sure what to do with such unsolicited advice, so I did nothing except mumble, "Of course." I was saved from any further serious talk by Mike Johnson, who broke away from a low-voiced conversation with Michelle Bedford and approached me.

"Can I talk with you? In private?" He walked back toward Michelle without waiting for my answer.

"I'm being summoned," I murmured. "Be right back." I joined Mike and Michelle, who stood near the little alcove where a vending machine belched and sighed as it cooled soft drinks.

"Michelle was telling me about what you said earlier," he said as I approached them. "What did T.J. tell you?"

I frowned, puzzled. The only time T.J. and I talked about this whole mess was when I drove him and Livvie to the impound lot. "You mean about the restaurant?"

"Yeah. Did he say they were doing an audit?"

Now I was really confused. Audit? Why would they check the books? Then I remembered a stray comment Janelle made when we were talking about investing. Any time a company changed hands a detailed audit was done. "I'm sure they'll do one," I said. "Livvie would insist on it. She's a pretty shrewd investor. I suspect she'll want to see the balance sheets."

He looked so surprised it pissed me off. People always assumed wealth equaled stupid, but Livvie had parlayed her trust fund into a very comfortable fortune and she did it mostly on her own, with just a little guidance from advisors. It was easy to underestimate her savvy. "Trust me, Livvie will make sure this is a sound investment before any agreements are signed." I looked at Michelle, who was following our conversation with little side glances at Livvie and the family. "You said you kept the books for the restaurant?" I asked. "You'll want to make sure everything is in order before you go into negotiations. Livvie's got some fierce legal people on her side."

"But what about—" She looked from Mike to me. "You said—"

"I need to go," Mike said, interrupting her. "Are you going to stay?"

Michelle turned as Paul joined us. "I'll wait with Paul."

Not a smart choice, I thought but didn't say. Paul looked like he wasn't sure whether to strangle someone or cry. I'd never seen anyone who alternated between the two emotions so quickly and so thoroughly. "I'm waiting," Paul snapped. "I want to talk to him."

Not *talk to Dad,* but *him.* I sighed. There was a lot of unhealed scar tissue there.

"Whatever." Mike shoved past me and strode toward the door.

I rejoined Sam. "Not a happy family," I murmured.

"Not all can be as lucky as you," he said then smiled at the Second as he joined us.

"When do you lock up shop for the year?" the Second asked Sam.

"After Christmas. We do a good business in trees and wreaths. Then we close it up until March. I'm hoping to talk Cassie into a trip to Florida then."

"Wise idea." The Second turned to me. "You need to see the house in Naples that Grandy left you. You should assess it before it goes on the market. That is, if you're going to put it on the market. Are Priscilla and Emil still the resident caretakers there?"

I nodded. "I get regular weekly updates from them. I can't wait to meet them. They sound fascinating."

The Second made a 'hmpfh' noise. "That's one way to phrase it."

"Of course, that's assuming I'll get to keep the house," I reminded him. "After all, John has a lien against the property pending the outcome of the hearing."

"John's an idiot. He can't win and he knows it. He's just doing it to be aggravating." The Second glanced at his watch then at Charlie, who finished his phone call and came toward us. "I assume the bail is set. Do you two need to get back? Do you have to work tomorrow?"

Sam and I both nodded. "I'm on at noon," I said.

"I'm opening." Sam glanced at his watch.

Charlie pocketed his phone. "I guess Livvie can't have too many lawyers on hand so Janelle and I will stay until T.J. gets released."

I slugged him in the arm. "You old romantic, you. Way to woo a girl." I went to Livvie before he could reply, slipping into the seat next to her. "Sam and I are going to take off but Charlie and Janelle are going to stay," I said softly. I glanced behind me. "And your father, I think. Color me surprised."

Livvie nodded miserably, dabbing at her face with Charlie's hankie. "I'm glad you came, but I wish you didn't have to."

"I understand. Sam and I were glad to come. And you know we'll do anything we can to help. You just have to call. You know that, don't you?"

"I know. Cassie..."

"Hmm?"

"I know he didn't do it. I'm absolutely sure of it." I nodded but she saw my uncertainty. "That's something we learned in rehab. You have to learn to totally trust someone. That's part of it all. One reason I got addicted was because I was afraid to trust, afraid to open up to someone completely. It's a part of the process to learn to trust again." Her dark eyes, rimmed with red from crying, implored me to believe her. "I trust him completely. He couldn't have done it."

I felt a brief spasm of guilt. Had I ever learned to trust anyone so completely? Had I ever learned to put my trust in a person like that? I looked up as Sam moved in to talk to Livvie. Did I trust Sam that much?

"We're there when you need us, okay?" he said, leaning down to brush a kiss on Livvie's cheek. "You just call." He grinned at her. "Call Cassie and you get stuck with me, too."

Livvie laughed shakily. "Good to know. Thanks, Sam. I appreciate it."

We started to leave, but the Second stopped us near the door. "Thank you for being there for Livvie. She and I both appreciate the help."

I thought that was a bit pompous of him, but I kept the idea to myself. "Let us know if we can do anything to help," I said as Sam pulled open the door.

"I will. And Cassie?" He leaned closer. "Take care. Sheila Peavey is an angry woman. I don't know her well at all, but even I could see that last night."

I nodded automatically, distracted by the sight of snow falling and twinkling in the streetlight's glow. "Thanks for the tip."

Sam and I hurried out to the lot and the Enterprise greeted us, lighting up like a Christmas tree when the key in my hand came near it. I took a minute to re-familiarize myself with the controls then I started out cautiously on the damp roads, once again on a dark unfamiliar street in bad weather. I decided to take the main road I knew back to my house rather than a shorter route on an unfamiliar road. I figured it was better to deal the devil you know than the one you don't.

"Your father—or step-father or ex-father-in-law or whatever he is—we were talking. He said that Sheila requested an invitation to the party last night. She was talking to his secretary about the party and the secretary mentioned it to the old man."

"I suppose she read about in the society pages." I made a snorty laugh. "I think that kind of crap comes out on Friday in the neighborhood edition." We entered the vast city park south of Lake Minnetonka and northwest of my suburb. The highway skirted the northern edge of the park, but a smaller county road led right through the park, cutting miles off the drive. I took the right turn onto that road and darkness closed around us.

"Why would she care about a party like that?" Sam mused. "She was never into that sort of thing."

"Maybe she's changed. It's been ten years since you were married." I slowed down as the road wound out of sight ahead of us. The headlights swiveled like a pair of eyes, maintaining a straight-ahead view, but I found that disorienting. I was accustomed to old-fashioned, point-ahead lights that left perimeters of darkness around me.

"I suppose she had to do stuff like that when she was married. Mike needed venture capital to get his company going. I suppose they went to parties like that, or had to woo investors and stuff. Watch out up there. Deer are running at this time of year."

"It's too late for deer. They're out at dusk."

"They're out all the time," he countered.

He was right, so I slowed the car. I glanced down and sighed. "The donut light is on again," I muttered. "Damn."

"Donut?" Sam leaned over the console to look for himself. "Tires?"

Trust a guy to know right away what it meant. "Yeah, it happened the other night, too. I had to stop and get air in the tires." I didn't tell him about my near-run-in with Lake Minnetonka. The nagging little beep started just as I spoke.

"Pull over. I'll check it."

"It's pitch black out, Sam. You can't even see the tires much less check the tire pressure. I doubt there's a tire thingy in the glove compartment."

"These cars come with everything." He opened the glove compartment and started to rummage. "I'll bet—"

The car lurched, the wheel almost jerking out of my hands. "What the hell?" I looked down at the light, which had turned from amber to red. "I wonder if it's a flat."

The car lurched again. I took my foot off the gas and was contemplating the brakes when all hell broke loose. The car staggered as though hit and I heard the crunch of metal. On the right side I saw a tree looming up but it was odd. All I saw was the top part of the tree.

Then I realized we were tipping toward a ditch, the front passenger side of the car veering toward the edge of the road. I jerked the wheel to the left and the donut light started flashing faster, the beeps louder and more insistent.

We stopped suddenly and I was thrown forward then back. A BANG erupted and something hit me in the face. I gasped at the fumes that enveloped me. From overhead, I heard a faint voice.

"Mrs. Carlyle? This is OnStar. There's an indication your airbag went off. Are you all right? Mrs. Carlyle?"

The voice faded...

Chapter 11

Lights.

Camera.

Action.

I peered upward groggily. Lights passed overhead. A voice said, "You're at the hospital. It's going to be okay."

I didn't believe them. No one could hurt as much as I did and be okay.

"It'll be..."

****

"The doctor said it was normal."

"It's been a day. That can't be normal."

The two voices spoke quietly but I heard them clearly. One was Becky, Charlie's sister.

"She had a concussion. Not to mention the broken arm and the cracked ribs. The nurse said the best thing she can do is rest."

I recognized that voice. It was Diane, John Whittington's wife. What the hell would Diane be doing near me? She hated my guts. I pried my eyes open, wincing when bright light seemed to connect directly with my brain.

Becky sat on my right side, talking to Diane, seated next to her. Becky's chin-length thick brown hair was burnished and her plump, matronly body was settled back in the chair, her knitting on her lap. Diane, however, was perched on the edge of the chair as though she feared cooties from the fabric under her. She was thin to the point of pain and the picture of haute couture in a long-sleeved dress with matching navy pumps. *Beauty and the beast.* They were seated lower than me and...

Ah, shit. I was in a hospital bed. "Hey," I mumbled.

Becky jumped to her feet, tucking her knitting into a bag on the floor. "Did we wake you?" She leaned over me, concern evident in her hazel eyes. "You're in the hospital."

"Yeah. I guessed." I smacked my lips. "I'm dry."

Diane nudged a tray holding a water glass toward me as she also stood. "How are you feeling?" She tilted her head to one side. "You took some bruising."

"What happened?" I sipped carefully at a straw as Becky held a glass for me. The water tasted like the finest wine, soothing my throat and alleviating the persistent itchy feeling.

"You went off the road into a ditch and hit a tree," Diane said, sitting carefully on the edge of my bed. "You've got a broken arm and two fractured ribs."

I looked down, startled to see she was right. My left arm was encased in plastic and bound tightly against my body. When I tried to take a deep breath, I couldn't. Something was constricting my rib cage. "Shit. I'll owe Livvie a new car. Did we hit a deer? I don't remember anything about it."

"You kept drifting in and out," Becky said, moving the water out of the way and leaning closer to the bed. "You talked to the doctor some of the time, but he said you were out of it."

"The police said somebody did it on purpose," Diane said, her sharp gray eyes scrutinizing me. "Somebody messed with your tires."

"What?" I looked at Becky, who confirmed this

with a sad little nod. "How do they know? Don't they have to do tests and stuff?"

"You've been out for a day," Becky said, putting a hand on my right arm where it stuck out of the sheet. "Cassie..."

Her tone of voice alerted me. Something terrible was on my horizon. "Where's Sam?" I tried to sit up but only succeeded in mashing the pillows around behind me. "Where's Sam? What happened to him?" Becky looked so sympathetic I panicked. "Where is he? I want to see him. Where is he?"

Diane murmured something about 'doctor' and slipped off the bed, hurrying out of the room. "I don't want a doctor, I want to see Sam." I struggled to sit up. "Help me out of bed, Becky. I have to see him."

"He's recovering from surgery." Her calm, dispassionate voice stopped me in my tracks. I lay on the bed like a beached whale, unable to move with shock.

"What? Surgery? It wasn't that bad. I wasn't going that fast. What happened?"

Becky touched the controls for the bed and it slowly pushed me upright. "A rib punctured his lung. They had to do surgery then he developed pneumonia. He's in intensive care. And his leg..." She took my good hand and held it, her eyes moist. "His right leg got all screwed up when the car came up against the tree. They had to cut him out of his side of the car. He's going to need more surgery. Some of the bones got messed up. He..."

"What?" I whispered when she didn't continue.

"They'll have to put pins in for sure. It may have to be amputated. The doctors aren't sure yet." She glanced at Diane, who was entering the room. "We've been taking turns sitting with you and with Sam. His sister is here."

The words didn't make sense. "It wasn't that bad," I whispered. "We weren't going fast. It was dark and I was worried about the roads, so I didn't drive fast. Was it a deer? He was worried we'd hit a deer."

A man came in wearing a white coat and started talking to me. I answered automatically, my mind in a fog. As soon as he paused for breath, I said, "I want to see Sam."

He looked up from the gadget he was reading, attached to my arm. "He's in intensive care and sedated."

"I just want to *see* him," I insisted, tears dribbling down my cheeks. "I want to see him."

He gave me a considering look. "I'll get a wheelchair. But just for a minute. Let me finish my exam first. I think the police want to talk to you, too. I'll let them know you're awake."

"After I see Sam," I pleaded. "Please."

"We'll see."

I patiently answered his questions, identified how many fingers, and took the pills offered to me in a little plastic cup then Becky came in with a wheelchair. We rolled down the hall to the elevator, where Diane left us. "I'm going to call Charlie and C.R.," she said. "They asked to be told when you woke up."

Becky punched the UP button. "She's been a champ," she said quietly. "Amazing. All this time I thought she was a bitch and it turns out she's not so bad."

"Don't believe it," I said. "She was probably waiting to see if I died so they could drop the damn probate objection." I caught a glimpse of Becky's disapproving look. "Sorry. It's hard to believe the leopard changed its spots." We rolled into the elevator and Becky pressed the '7' button. "Where are we? What hospital? Hell, for that matter, *when* are we? What day?"

"It's Tuesday October the eighteenth. About…"

145

She consulted her watch. "Ten in the morning. You're at St. Francis, in Burnsville. It was closer to the accident site."

Burnsville was south of Minnetonka and west of Pickaway, where Sam and I lived. I tried to remember our location before the accident, but I just had a hazy memory of the city park. "What happened? All I remember is the donut light coming on."

"Donut light?" The elevator dinged and the door zipped open. Becky rolled me out.

"The tire light. It started blinking."

She headed to the right toward a set of doors with "ICU" next to it in big white letters on the pale brown walls. "I don't think we're supposed to tell you anything. The police want to talk to you."

"But why won't..." My words died in my throat when I saw my reflection in a mirrored hall sign. My face was puffy and bruised and with two black eyes, I looked more like a raccoon than a human. My hair was matted and tangled and my neck and shoulders were livid with yellow and purpled bruising. "Wow. I look like the bride of Frankenstein."

"Nah. Your hair isn't frizzy like the Bride's." Becky pushed open the doors and we entered an open space with rooms all along the perimeter. A big desk in the middle bustled with nurses, equipment and doctors. "You just look like death warmed over."

I craned my neck to look up at Becky who regarded me with amusement. "Thanks."

"That's what sisters are for." She rolled me toward the left side of the space.

"Hey, if a day's passed—who's taking care of the cats?" Panic made my stomach tumble. "What about Houdi? And Truffles?"

"Truffles? Is that the little maniac kitten?" Becky chuckled. "Great name."

"How do you know about her?" I peered up at

her.

"Livvie and I got your keys from the police. We went over and checked on the critters. They're fine." She pushed me forward a bit more until my chair was in a doorway. "We're here."

I leaned forward. Sam lay still, his hands outside the sheets. He was so pale it looked like he blended in, his white and gray hair the same shade as the white pillow. His cheeks were sunken and his closed eyes twitched in time to his fingers, which jerked on the bed with little spasms. "Sam," I whispered. I urged Becky forward, putting my right hand on the wheel and trying to move it. "I want to be closer. Please."

"I'm not sure if we should." Becky looked behind us and gestured to one of the nurses. "Can we go in? She wants to see him."

"It's okay. He's sedated."

Becky wheeled me near the bed and I put my right hand over Sam's left hand. It stilled immediately, his index finger curling around mine. "Sam, I'm here," I said softly, leaning forward as much as I could given the equipment surrounding him and the wheelchair confining me. "Sam, it's Cassie. I'm here, Sam. It's okay." Tears rolled off my face and fell on his hand, making damp splotches on the sheet.

"He's in a lot of pain," the nurse said from the doorway. "We've got the pneumonia under control though, so he's breathing better."

"His leg...what happened to his leg?" I looked at the tented area on the right side of the bed.

"We're keeping an eye on it," she said. "The bones were badly broken. As soon as we're sure the pneumonia is licked, they'll probably want to do more surgery."

"But if they wait, won't it be harder for the bones to heal?" I looked back at her awkwardly, almost tipping out of the wheelchair to do so.

"We'll see." She smiled with false brightness and left.

"I know what that means," I said gloomily. I turned back to Sam. He seemed more relaxed, as though he sensed me there.

"We need to go back to your room," Becky said gently. "The doctor said just a few minutes." When I started to protest she said, "We'll come back as soon as the doctor says we can. If Sam gets out of ICU maybe you can stay in the same room with him. We'll see what we can do."

I nodded, bending to kiss Sam's left hand. "I'll be back," I whispered around my tears. "Hang in there, Sam. I'll be right back."

Becky wheeled me back the way we came. I kept my eyes closed, willing the fear and the nausea to stay at bay until we got to my room on the floor below. A uniformed police officer was waiting for us along with another plains-clothes detective who introduced himself as Dave Madison with the Mound Police Department. He looked like every cop I've ever seen on *Law & Order*—stocky, impassive and grim. He even held a small green memo notebook with a pen. "We don't technically have jurisdiction but Burnsville, where the accident occurred, passed the case to us since we're wondering if it's connected to the murder."

I took the business card he offered and let it drop onto the table next to my hospital bed as I settled back against the sheets. "Murder?" Then I remembered. "T.J.! Becky, is he okay? What happened? Is he out on bail?"

She put a restraining hand on my right arm. "We'll fill you in later."

"We need to get your statement about what happened," Madison said as Becky fluffed my pillows behind me.

"Not until her lawyer arrives," Diane said, coming into the room. "He's on the way."

"My lawyer?" I asked, gesturing toward the water glass.

Becky fetched it and held it for me as Diane said, "Billy Armstrong. He's on his way." She regarded the detective with cool hauteur. "He's our family attorney."

I almost choked on the water. The only reason we would need a criminal defense lawyer was if we were a bunch of felons. I saw Becky hiding a smile at Diane's faux pas.

Madison blinked at this bald-faced lie. "Really? Well, we'll just wait for him." He looked at me, his pale blue eyes sympathetic. "How are you feeling?"

"Don't answer that," Diane said.

"Fine," I said. "Just tired. I want to be with Sam. And I want to know what happened."

"So do we," Madison said.

"And now that I'm here, maybe we can figure it out." Billy Armstrong filled the room with his presence, dwarfing the police and Charlie, who came in behind Armstrong. They both wore what I thought of as 'business uniforms': suits, ties, and wingtip shoes. Then I belatedly remembered it was Tuesday, a work day.

The big black attorney came to the left side of my bed. "How are you feeling? Are you up to some questions?"

I nodded tearily. "I want to be with Sam, though," I whispered. "He's hurt bad."

"I know. But first you have to answer questions." Armstrong turned to Madison. "My client is ready when you are." He looked down at me, his dark eyes sympathetic but cautious. "Tell us what happened, Cassie."

Madison looked pointedly at Becky and Diane. "We'd like some privacy, please." His gaze shifted to

Charlie. "It won't take long."

"I'm her attorney," Charlie snapped. "I stay."

Madison's eyebrows rose. "Two attorneys. Wow." He glanced at the officer then at Becky and Diane. "Officer Denton will escort you ladies outside."

"But we should stay in case we're needed," Diane said with assurance.

Becky tugged on Diane's arm. "Come on." She smiled at me. "Hang in there, kid. We'll be right outside."

Charlie took Becky's place on the right side of the bed. He looked haggard, with dark circles under his eyes and his thick hair rough-looking, not his usual well-combed style. I smiled tentatively and he nodded. "Tell us what happened," he said quietly.

I started to describe the trip home but Madison stopped me. "Back up a step. Your car was in the parking lot at the police station on Sunday night, right?"

I nodded.

"And the night before that—you said you were at a party at the Hunt Club?"

I nodded again. "The lot was almost full. I wanted to park away from other cars because, well, it's not my car. I was afraid someone would ding it." I thought of what Becky said. If they had to cut Sam out of the car then it was beyond dinged right now. I sighed.

"Did you see anyone near the car?" Madison asked. "Either at the club or at the police station?"

"It was snowing. I was worried about that and Livvie. I didn't notice much of anything. How is she? Is she okay?"

"She's fine," Charlie said. "She was here last night and she'll be coming back later. We're taking turns."

"Okay, so you got into the car at the police station," Madison said, jerking my attention back to the discussion. "What happened then?"

I described my choice of route, the twisting road and the tire light. "The light was on a couple nights ago, too." I thought back, trying to get the timeline in my head. "I had to stop and get air in the tire, so I figured it was the same thing."

"Which night?" he prompted.

"Friday night," I amended. I couldn't get used to the fact I had missed a day, like a big hole in the middle of my personal mental calendar. I described my close encounter with the lake and the tire alarm. "But on Friday the car drove fine. Tonight—I mean, Sunday—the car was lurchy."

"Lurchy," he mumbled, jotting a note in his memo book.

"You know what I mean...it didn't drive smoothly." I plucked at the covers anxiously.

"What did your investigation turn up?" Armstrong asked, his deep voice echoing in the room. "I assume you've checked the accident scene as well as the vehicle."

Madison closed the memo book and tucked it into a suit coat pocket. "Lug nuts."

I stared at him blankly. "Lug nuts? Those screw things that hold the tires on?"

Madison nodded.

"Those are hard to get off. I had a flat once and I couldn't budge them. I had to call triple-A to come out and change the tire."

"They were loosened," Madison said.

"Who could do that?" I asked no one in particular. "And when? I mean, you don't just walk up to a car and start fiddling with it." I remembered the dark parking lot at the Hunt Club, the cold weather, and the snow. Maybe someone could ...I yawned, suddenly tired.

"I think my client has answered enough questions now," Armstrong said immediately. "Her

151

doctor indicated she needs rest so if you can keep any questions until a later time, we'd appreciate it." His tone of voice indicated this wasn't a request, but a command.

"But who would want to..." I yawned again, almost unable to keep my eyes open. "I think I've been drugged." I looked at Charlie. "I'm worried about Sam. He's in pain, Charlie. Can't I be with him?"

"His sister is here. She was probably just taking a break." He squeezed my good hand gently. "You rest for a bit and when you wake, we'll see if you can visit him again."

"But I want to..." I peered at him groggily, vaguely aware that the other men were murmuring softly and moving toward the door. "Wait, I..."

Chapter 12

It was dark when I awoke. The only light came from a lamp by the side of the bed. I had a moment of disorientation then I remembered: hospital, Sam, accident.

A remote control box was near my right hand and I managed to use it to maneuver my upper body upright. As I did a thin three-ring binder slid down the bed, almost cascading to the floor. I managed to catch it before it fell, pulling it onto my lap. I examined the bed controls, finally finding one that appeared to lower me. After some experimental gyrations, I started drifting downward.

I shoved the notebook under the covers and swung my legs over the side. I was just preparing to attempt a standing position when the rectangle of light to my left got larger. Janelle Rimes came in, paper coffee cup in hand. "Wow, those doctors are good," she said, hurrying to my side and setting her cup down on the rolling tray thing over my bed. "They said the drugs would be wearing off about now. Where do you think you're going?"

"Gotta pee," I muttered.

"There's a bed pan." She nodded when she saw my disbelieving look. "Yeah, I agree. Come on." She came around to my right side and put a hand under my good arm. With much maneuvering and shuffling we made it across the room to the bathroom door near the entrance. "Can you manage?" she asked as she parked me near the stool.

I nodded. "I'm underwear-less, thank God. I'll yell if I need help."

She helped me lift the gown and got me positioned then she left, leaving the door cracked open behind her.

"I owe you for this, Janelle," I called out as I did my business. "This is above and beyond your lawyerly duties."

"I'll bill you," she laughed. "After all, it comes out of the estate. I think you're good for it. Livvie told me about the house deal you and she worked out. I've got the papers all drawn up and ready for you to sign. In a few weeks you'll be a rich woman."

"You'd better deduct the cost of a car," I said as I flushed.

The door opened and Janelle came in, holding a bottle of gel disinfectant. "Don't attempt the sink. Here." She squirted some goop on my hands and I gratefully managed to clean them with only minimal disarranging of my sling. I could see that the one-handed thing was going to be awkward as we shuffled back to the bed.

I sat on the edge and caught my breath. "What time is it?"

"It's a little after five. You're due for dinner soon. They want to keep you overnight to make sure all parts are working correctly."

I edged back carefully into the bed, my hospital gown making the action awkward. Janelle once again came to my rescue, helping me get my legs under the covers without exposing my fifty-year-old butt to the world. "Can I see Sam?"

"Charlie's with him now." Janelle dragged a chair closer to the bed and picked up her coffee cup. "Sam's sister is there, too. The doctors are going to do surgery tomorrow on his leg. They're hoping to put pins in to stabilize it." She grimaced. "I didn't realize the pins would be on the outside of his body. For some reason when people said 'pins' I thought they'd replace bones with metal."

I grimaced, too. A high school friend had a bad arm fracture once and had to have stabilizing pins put in. I remembered how grotesque it looked. "I can't believe it's so bad. We weren't going that fast."

"You went off a ten foot embankment and rolled partially. Sam's side got crushed the worst. Physiology isn't my strongest subject, but from what they said, the bones got messed up in his shin. They need to hold it all together until it heals. You're lucky it's been so dry lately. Otherwise there would have been water in the car. And you're lucky there was OnStar."

"No kidding. If we were driving my Jeep, we'd still be out there." I made a mental note to make sure I had OnStar in the next Cassie-mobile. "Can I see Sam tonight? I want to see him before the surgery."

Janelle settled back in the chair and crossed her legs. Her pale blue jeans, bulky red sweater and glossy black hair in a French braid made her look like a college student, not a thirty-something corporate attorney. She propped one foot up on the bed rail and her white sneakers made the picture complete. "You can go stay with him after you eat," she said. "The doctors agreed you can be in the room with him until lights out. And if you want to be there in the morning, that's okay, too."

I relaxed back on my pillows, one worry solved. As I did, I nudged the notebook I found earlier. "What's this?"

"Charlie left that for you. That detective guy your father-in-law hired did some research. Charlie thought you might like to read a copy."

"Ex-father-in-law," I said absently as I opened

the notebook. Double-spaced typewritten pages all blurred in front of my vision. "I'll look at it later."

"Yeah. I keep forgetting you're divorced."

I rolled my eyes. "Not you, too. Charlie and I aren't an item anymore, you know?"

"Oh, not you." She sipped her coffee. "Charlie."

"Charlie needs to…" I didn't continue. We all knew what Charlie needed to do. Grow up. Move on. Get over it. Put his life in perspective. "The police think somebody did this on purpose. Why? And when?"

"That's a puzzler. As it turns out, that amber tire light you saw indicates more than just tire pressure."

"Really?" I tried to visualize the instruction manual in my head but I skimmed past the part about tires because I thought I knew what it would say. Dumb me.

"Oh, good, you're up," a chipper voice said from the doorway.

Janelle moved to one side as a woman in a pink uniform came in and bustled around me, positioning my pillows, my roller tray and setting down a dinner tray once I was aligned correctly. She removed plate covers with a flourish. I surveyed my feast skeptically, as did Janelle when the pink person left.

She peered down at it then straightened, sipping her coffee. "What is it?"

"Red jell-o, chicken and green beans…I think." I took an experimental bite. "Not bad." My stomach rumbled and I decided beggars couldn't be choosers. Janelle talked while I gobbled the food. I eyed the chocolate pudding in a disposable cup perched on the edge of my tray. My reward awaited me enticingly.

"The police checked your car and confirmed it with the car company. Apparently when that light comes on, it means the tires need to be inspected. One of the things that might be wrong is tire pressure, so it didn't hurt to do that. But it can also be an indicator of something else wrong."

"So someone could have fiddled with the tires as long ago as Friday," I said as I polished off the soggy green beans. "That's when I first saw the light."

"It's possible. The police are going back through your schedule, such as it is." She flashed me a wry smile. "They're trying to piece together when the car was exposed."

I gave it some thought as I chewed some tough but edible fowl, washing it down with milk from a carton. "It sat outside my house on Friday night," I mused as I masticated. "Then there was the wedding on Saturday and the Hunt Club on Saturday night. We were at the restaurant on Saturday before the party and..." I gave up and took a final bite of chicken before snagging my dessert reward and peeling back the foil top.

"Exactly," Janelle said, wiggling her sneakers. "The car was alone a lot."

"But it's hard to get lug nuts off," I said around a mouthful of chocolate creaminess. "Those suckers don't just pop off. Somebody would have to work at it."

"Unless they had a ratchet thing." She said this uncertainly, as though not sure of her facts.

"A what?"

"I heard Charlie and Billy Armstrong talking about it," she admitted. "There's some kind of power tool thing that you can put on a wheel and it just zaps the lug things right off."

We both considered it as I finished my meal. "I didn't know that," I finally said.

"Neither did I. But apparently they use them in tire stores and places like that. And there are home models you can buy anywhere, like at Sears or wherever."

I pushed my tray away and it rolled gently to

the foot of the bed. "So anybody could have done it?"

"Anybody who knew about lug nut zappers." She watched as I opened the thin notebook. "Have you gone over that?"

"I just found it." I peered at the double-spaced typewritten pages.

"The guy C.R. Two hired is getting a lot done."

I ducked my head to hide my smile at her designation for the Second. "That was fast. It's only been a day since he was hired."

Janelle held up two fingers. "Two days."

"Okay, two days since I mentioned it to Charlie." I leafed through the pages, pausing when I got to a one-page summary of Michael Johnson. "He has a criminal history."

"Who?" She peered at the page. "Oh, yeah. The cook."

"Sous-chef," I corrected. "He's like the head cook."

Janelle shrugged. "As long as he knows how to fry fish, I don't care what you call him."

"Fish." A stray fact started rattling around my brain. "Oh, that's right. Salmon. Michelle."

Janelle laughed. "I agree she's a cold fish, but a salmon?"

"No, it's something else I read." I flipped through the remaining pages, finding a one-page summary for Michelle Bedford. "It's not mentioned here. Ha. I did better research than a detective guy." I let the notebook drop to my lap, jerking when it hit my broken arm. "Damn. That hurts."

"It's broken," Janelle pointed out.

I tried to ignore the insistent throbbing somewhere near my wrist. "I did a Yahoo search and turned up more details than that."

"Don't tell that to Father, he'll get peeved at what he's paying," Charlie said from the doorway. He was still in his lawyer uniform but he seemed more relaxed than he had earlier. "You look a lot better than you did this morning."

"Did the bruises go away?" I asked hopefully.

"Nope. You're still Rocky Raccoon. But at least you're mobile."

Janelle got up and moved to one side. "Take my seat, Charlie."

"Nobody sit down," I said grumpily. "I want to go see Sam. I ate my meal like a good kid, so now I get to see him, right?" I started to push the covers aside and the notebook slid off my lap to the floor.

Charlie picked it up, straightening the pages. "Did you look through this?"

"Just a bit. Your private eye missed one key piece of info about Michelle. Help me up, Janelle, okay?" I swung my legs toward the side of the bed and she steadied me. "Be useful, Charlie. Get the wheelchair."

"Now I know you're better. You're bossy." Charlie smiled when he said it, grabbing the wheelchair and angling it near me. "Your wheels." He dropped the notebook on my rolling over-the-bed stand. "The guy just got started with his research. Give him time."

"Time, schmine. I found it during a Yahoo search. We'll see if the hotshot detective guy finds it." I gestured to the faded cotton robe folded at the foot of the bed. "Let's wrap up my buns, okay?" Janelle helped me into the shabby blue garment decorated with tiny yellow diamonds then helped me get settled in the chair.

"Whoa." Janelle put an arm on Charlie's as he pushed me near the door. She snagged a thin blanket from the closet and tucked it around my legs. "You're not going to survive a car wreck just to get pneumonia."

Pneumonia. I shivered at the thought. Poor Sam, all banged up and with pneumonia on top of it.

I tapped the arm of my chair. "Lead on, Scout. Speaking of wheels, I'll need to get a car," I fretted as Charlie rolled me out of the room, Janelle following. "I'll need something big enough to haul Sam around."

Charlie paused. "Sam?"

"He can't go home with a bunch of pins in his leg. Someone will have to take care of him. His apartment is on the second floor and there's no elevator. He can't go back there. My townhouse is all on one floor. So he'll have to stay with me. I'll need a car with a big enough back seat so he can stretch out."

Janelle pushed the UP button at the elevator, glancing above me at Charlie. "You've given this some thought," she said.

"Not really. It's just obvious, that's all." I dropped my head back and looked up at Charlie. His eyes were narrowed as he considered what I said. "Right, Charlie?"

"I suppose." He wheeled me into the elevator.

"Sam can't go home alone."

"Why don't you wait and see what Sam wants to do?" Charlie suggested. "He may not want to have you fussing over him."

"Mary can't take care of him," I argued. "She has to run the business with him being laid up. And there's no one else in town who can care for him."

"Charlie's right," Janelle said softly. "Let's wait and see what the doctors say."

I heard and heeded the cautionary note in her voice. "Sure. But I'll still need a car. Janelle, you said we can move on with the house sale?"

"Yes, you just need to sign some papers."

"Do you have them with you?"

She held the door for us as Charlie maneuvered me out of the elevator car. "They're back in your room."

"Let's get 'em signed and done with."

"Why the sudden greed?" Charlie asked lightly.

I leaned forward as we neared the ICU, anxious to see Sam. "I'm tired of being poor, Charlie," I said over my shoulder. "I'd like to be able to buy a car if I need one."

"I'll buy you a car, Cassie."

I slammed my hand down on the arm of the wheelchair, startling him into releasing it. "No, you won't, Charlie. I'm going to buy my own damn car and live my own damn life, okay? Believe me when I say that I appreciate the help I've gotten from your family. But I'm not a Whittington anymore and it's time we all remembered that."

Two nurses at the desk in the middle eyed us warily. "Everything okay?" one called over.

"Just fine," I called back. "We're visiting Sam Barlow."

"Charlie." Janelle's voice was calm and gentle. "Let's go see Sam."

My chair started moving again. "I didn't realize you felt that way, Cassie," Charlie said in a low voice.

I wanted to weep with frustration and anger. "Charlie, I have ties to you and the family that can never be severed. But I have my own life, too. And right now, the most important thing in that life is Sam." I looked up at Charlie, surprising a look of sadness in his dark green eyes.

He smiled but I could tell it was forced. "I understand."

He didn't, but I wasn't going to correct him. We entered Sam's room and Mary Hannon, Sam's sister, got up from her seat on the far side of Sam's bed. "Cassie, I wanted to come see you but I got so busy." Mary bent over and enfolded me in a gentle hug. "Joe and I are taking turns at the stores and between that and Sam..." She straightened and I saw tears in her light brown eyes. Her chin-length brown hair hung in a straight line to her somewhat double chin. Mary was a big-boned, stocky woman in her mid-forties. She had worked in landscaping all her life, managing the Pickaway store and its employees in a fair and equitable fashion. She still wore her *Barlow's Nursery and Landscaping* blue sweatshirt, the standard uniform for all employees. I had three like it in my closet at home in various colors.

"I wanted to be with Sam," I said, peering past her. "The doctor said I can stay." I took her hand and gave it a squeeze. It was chapped and work-roughened, much like my own. Between hauling plants, sorting stock, and transplanting or moving trees, a woman's hands took a real beating at a landscape center.

Charlie carefully edged my chair closer to the left side of Sam's bed as Mary resumed her seat on the right side. "Thanks, Charlie," I murmured as I took Sam's hand.

"We'll go get something to eat and come back later," Janelle said, leaning over. "I'll make sure to get those papers to you tonight so we can do that."

"Thanks, I appreciate it." I turned my attention to Sam who was lying in a halo of light from the lamp positioned over his right shoulder.

Charlie leaned over and brushed a kiss against my cheek. "Hang in there, C.R."

I nodded, barely able to speak around the sudden lump in my throat. "I will, C.R.," I managed.

I heard them leave but my focus was already on Sam. "He looks better tonight," I whispered to Mary. "He doesn't look as tense."

She smiled at me from among the tubing, bottles, and machines on her side of the bed. "I think the pain medication is finally kicking in." The indirect lighting kept most of her face in shadow except for her face. "How are you doing?"

I touched my face, wincing when I encountered tenderness. "Whatever drugs they're giving me are working. So far it's not too awful. But my arm hurts like crazy." I took a deep breath but stopped when a sharp pain stabbed me. "And my ribs." I touched Sam's hand. "But I'm okay compared to him. I'm so sorry, Mary. This shouldn't have happened."

"It's not your fault. There was nothing you could have done to prevent it. I'm just thankful it wasn't worse than this."

I silently blessed her for her understanding, but my guilt wouldn't go away that easily. "It is my fault," I insisted. "Somebody has it in for me. At least, that's what the police said."

She straightened in surprise. "They told me it was done on purpose, but the officer I talked to said they weren't sure if it was you or your sister-in-law who was the target."

Now it was my turn to straighten. "Livvie?"

Mary nodded. "It is *her* car."

I didn't consider that. What if someone had a grudge against Livvie and got us instead? As soon as I thought it, I tried to dismiss it. Who would have a beef with Livvie? And why?

"Michelle," I muttered. "Mike?"

"What?" Mary leaned forward and as she did, Sam stirred, twitching restlessly. His head turned toward me.

"I'm here, Sam," I said, tilting forward as far as I was able. I ran my hand up his arm, feeling the sinewy hardness of his muscles. Sam worked out every day at the local health club, lifting weights or running. He was proud of the fact he weighed the same as he did when he was in the Marines and was almost as physically fit. I knew how hard such a battle was because I had achieved a significant weight loss victory in the past year and still struggled with my weight.

He'll bounce back, I told myself. *Don't worry.* It was hard to convince myself of that but I tried. What was it Livvie's little booklet said? *Don't focus on the future. Enjoy the moment of now.* Sam was alive and he *had* a future. I had to focus on that. We would just have to take it one day at a time from here on in.

His eyelids flickered and opened partially. I saw a glimmer of recognition in his eyes, which looked almost black with the dilated pupils. His lips moved in a parody of a smile then his eyes closed again.

"I'm here," I repeated.

Chapter 13

"I'm here, Sam," I murmured, leaning over his bed.

His eyes opened and he smiled. In the two days since his surgery he had progressed a lot, but he was still as weak as Truffles the kitten. "Hey, pretty lady," he whispered, his throat raw from the breathing tube they inserted during the two-and-a-half hour surgery.

Pretty lady my butt, I thought. My two black eyes remained, but the psychedelic colors of purple and yellow were fading fast. "I'm checking in for bedside duty," I said, sitting carefully on the side of his bed. "I just got here."

"Lucky you. I wish I could get out and not come back."

I took his hand in mine. "You will soon. I've got Becky and Livvie helping me get things organized, then you can come home with me. Another day or two and you'll be free."

"Becky and Livvie?" He coughed carefully, his body stiff as he struggled to keep his leg still. The cast encasing it moved slightly on the bed and he gasped as his hand tightened on mine. "I thought they were mortal enemies.

"They are." I rushed my words, anxious to divert him from his pain. "But they've agreed to set differences aside for a few days. I've also got them researching a new car for me."

He smiled shakily. "Really? What kind?"

"I gave them my checklist." I released his hand and ticked the points off on my left fingers, wiggling slightly in my cast. "It must have OnStar. I'm totally sold on that. Must have that Bluetooth stuff, has to be all-wheel drive, has to get good gas mileage and has to have a good sound system. Oh, and has to be able to accommodate a guy with a cast on his leg."

Sam frowned. "That shouldn't be an issue. You can't be waiting on me hand and foot. Anyway, we can use my SUV if you've got to haul me around. Have the police figured out who messed with the car and why?"

"No, but they've narrowed down the tool used. Unfortunately it's a model used by just about every garage in town and most car enthusiasts." I eyed his lunch tray. Almost all of the food remained on his plate with just a few bites taken from a sandwich.

"How's it going with T.J. and that murder?"

"The police are still investigating." I sank into the chair by his bed. Sam looked thin and taut, but he appeared that way every day since the surgery. The pain was intense. A titanium nail was inserted into his tibia and screws held it in place. The nail would remain in his body although the screws were supposed to be removed in four or five weeks, when he was told he could put weight on the leg again. The doctors were optimistic he would have almost a full recovery, but it was going to require more surgery and months of rehabilitative therapy before we'd know for sure.

Sam didn't complain but I saw what the pain, inactivity and boredom were costing him. I hoped when he got to my house he'd perk up and be less restless. The doctor said that was essential for his healing. No matter what Sam wanted, he had to be relatively immobile for two months. But knowing

Sam the way I did, that wasn't going to happen.

I held up the notebook Charlie gave me on Tuesday. It was slightly fatter now with more reports coming in from the detective the Second hired. "I thought you might want to read through this." I put it next to a small bouquet from Barlow's employees which had pride of place on the rolling bed tray. The bigger bouquets from other friends and business acquaintances were arrayed on the credenza across the room. Once Sam got out of ICU and into a private room, the flowers started arriving.

"Yeah, I might look through it. I get bored at night. I can't always sleep."

"Don't they give you something?"

"I don't want to get used to the drugs."

I started to protest then I remembered T.J. and the problems he had. I nodded my understanding.

"I'm starting physical therapy this afternoon and getting my crutches. I have to learn to get around with this leg."

"Don't get around too much," I warned him. "You know what the doctors said."

"I can't lie in bed for two months," he grumbled. "And there's no way in hell I'm using a bedpan for two months."

"I'm happy to hear you say that," I joked. I changed the subject when I saw the defiant tilt to his chin. "As soon as you get a bit more mobile, we're having a party at the restaurant. They haven't finalized the sale yet, but Michelle wants to go ahead with it. Livvie said there's a problem with the accounts. I guess the police aren't done going through them."

"The police?"

"I suppose when somebody is murdered they go through all the financial stuff, looking for motives." I frowned in thought. "Didn't they do that when Mike Peavey died last spring?"

"I don't remember." He shifted again on the bed, trying to scoot further upward. I resisted the impulse to help him. The doctors told me he needed to start managing things for himself and I knew they were right. It hurt to watch him, though.

"Once they get the accounts, Livvie is prepared to put in an offer on the place. She's certain Michelle wants out. Apparently she's talked about moving back to California. T.J is already planning the menu for your Hospital Freedom meal."

"I'm glad they didn't keep him in jail."

"I'm sure the bail helped convince the cops he was legit," I said wryly. "T.J. isn't out of the woods yet. He's still a 'person of interest,' but I think everybody connected with the restaurant is of interest, so..." I shrugged but stopped when my bound arm zinged me. "Ouch."

"You're pretty banged up yourself." He touched my hand, sitting on the bed. "You shouldn't be talking about taking care of me."

"I'll have you in my clutches. What a great chance for me to take advantage of you."

"I'm serious, Cassie. You shouldn't do it just because you feel responsible."

"I'm not doing it because of that." I wasn't sure if I was lying or not. I *did* feel responsible but was that why I was doing it? *Focus on now,* I repeated silently. *Sam needs me now.* "You need a place to stay and my place fills the bill. I can't go back to work, anyway, not with this broken arm. And now that Livvie and I have settled on the house, I'm good for cash so I can afford to quit my job—temporarily, of course." I jiggled his hand lightly. "I told Mary I'll come back if needed, but things are winding down for the season, so it'll be fine. By next spring both of us will be back in action."

"You don't have to keep working there. Maybe you'll want to do some traveling or something else.

You don't need the money now."

I leaned over and pressed a finger against his lips. "Shut up. I'll think about that when we both get healthier." I touched the notebook he set aside. "Maybe you can help us solve the mystery. You've got some time to think about it"

His dark brown eyes searched my face as I straightened. "If you ever don't want to be saddled with a broken up old man, you let me know," he whispered.

I smoothed his thick gray-and-white hair back from his forehead. It was longer than usual, straight and fine but matted from lying so long in bed. "Don't worry. It's not going to happen. But if—" I held up an admonishing finger to silence his interruption. "If it occurs, you'll know." I tapped the notebook and it echoed hollowly. "Now back to this. The detective the Second hired was pretty thorough but I was the one who first saw through Michelle."

"The Second?"

"My affectionate term for the old tyrant."

"Affectionate. Right." He smiled. "You were suspicious, hmm?"

"Yeah, she wasn't what she seemed. Go to the red tab in the notebook."

He did as I directed and read the report. "Beauty queen?"

I settled back in my chair. "Yeah, Miss Sockeye Salmon or something like that."

He snorted with laughter as he continued reading. "She was married?"

"It looks like it was a shotgun wedding when she was a teenager. She had four kids in about seven years." I looked outside where the noon sun was starting to angle into the room. Sam's recovery room was on the fourth floor and he had a good view of the small lake and the woods beyond. The autumn foliage was at its peak with reds and yellows predominating. "I wonder if she sees any of them since she left Alaska."

"When was she divorced?" Sam asked, turning the page and reading about Mike Johnson.

"It doesn't say, but probably right about the time she came to California, I would guess." I made a note of it in my head: *Michelle: divorce date.*

"The boxer cook has a record," he noted.

"Quite an extensive one." I recited what I read earlier. "Assault. Embezzlement. False identity."

"How the hell did he get hired at a high-class restaurant like *La Suzette?*"

"A question Livvie is asking right now. If she's going to own the place, she wants good people working there. I'm not saying someone can't reform, but I think she's uncomfortable with him there and I don't blame her. After all, he and T.J. were in line for the same job. Although maybe T.J. will want to keep him as head cook since T.J. will become the Big Head Cook or whatever it's called. Anyway, Livvie said they were going to require background checks of all employees, right down to the dishwasher. Which reminds me—the dishwasher vanished."

"What?" Sam flipped through the notebook. "I don't see anything here about it."

"That detective guy is working on it. The kid—the dishwasher—was there when they started construction and now he's gone. They were supposed to reopen next week, but with the murder and the sale pending, they've decided to wait until after Thanksgiving. Apparently there's a big market for pricy restaurant meals during the holidays. Who knew?" I almost shrugged again but remembered my bum arm in time.

"Are the police looking for him?"

"Who, the dishwasher? I think so. From what I've heard, admittedly second and third hand, they checked the address he gave on his personnel record.

It was an apartment not far from the restaurant. The landlord said he moved in at the start of summer and had a six month sublease. He didn't renew the lease and left. The landlord didn't think anything of it."

"Wow. Maybe he did it." Sam moved carefully to one side, reaching for his water glass. I started to get it for him but stopped. I waited with bated breath as he got the glass and brought the straw to his lips, tilting his head forward so far it hurt my neck just to watch. When he set the glass back down, I could tell the small movement exhausted him.

"I suppose it's possible the dishwasher guy did it," I said, thinking out loud. "The pastry hook was in the dishwasher machine. Those things get really hot during all the cycles. T.J. said it's a state regulation. So any evidence on it is long gone now."

"Can't they do that CSI junk you see on TV?" Sam asked. He carefully slid himself up in the bed an inch at a time. "You know, go through the drain and look for blood and whatever?"

"I don't think fingerprints wash away intact down a drain," I said with a grin as I visualized a thin film of black smudges slipping through the pipes. "From what T.J.'s attorney said, they matched the pastry hook to the wound but other than that, they've got nothing to go on. No one saw anything and there's no log from the security company. The security alarm was off because of the construction. I think Paul is on the hot seat. He had motive, means, and opportunity."

"So did a bunch of other people," Sam reasonably pointed out. "Michelle and he were having an affair. Maybe her husband wouldn't give her a divorce. You said the head chef was mad about some of the food being served. Maybe Mike took exception to that. Wasn't he in charge of the day-to-day operations?"

"I'm not sure. I think so." I got up and went to the credenza to look at the four bouquets sitting there. "You're a popular guy." I examined a small planter with a vine and flowering plant, checking the card. I turned to Sam in surprise. "Sheila?"

"She called, too." He looked annoyed. "She's after me about the patents."

"What patents? Oh, you mean the azalea plants?" Sam and Sheila's late husband developed a new species of azalea plants but Mike neglected to share the profits with Sam, which once made Sam a key suspect in Mike's death. Sam was now suing the estate for a piece of the lucrative hybrid azalea pie. "What does she want now?"

"She wants me to settle."

"Like hell," I snapped. "You deserve more than a pittance. You did all the initial major research on it."

"Mike put money into the development, though," Sam countered.

"Develop it? There wouldn't have been anything to develop without you." I shoved Sheila's planter with the philodendron behind a bouquet from the Whittington family.

"She offered me half-a-million to drop the suit."

I whirled. "What? Where's she getting that kind of money?"

"I think she's got backing. After all, didn't your father-in-law say she invested in one of his companies?"

"Ex-father-in-law. He did say that." I considered the conundrum: where was Sheila getting her money? "Is there a sugar daddy in the wings?" Sam looked doubtful and I pressed my point. "Remember last spring? She used sex to get what she wanted then."

"Yeah, there might be a sugar daddy." He plucked at the sheets covering him. "I'm considering her offer."

"Sam, you can't. If you win the lawsuit you'll get a piece of the patent rights. Those can be worth a lot more than half-a-million over the years."

"Maybe. But I need the money now." He met my gaze directly. "This accident is going to cost me a lot of money even with health insurance covering most of it. That means my premiums for the landscape business are going to go up. You know how close to the edge we operate."

I sank back into the seat at his side. Sam and his sister Mary were co-owners of two landscape retail outlets as well as a seedling-growing facility in southern Minnesota. I designed the inventory software they used, so I was aware how close their margins were. He was right. A catastrophic accident like this would put a huge dent into their meager profit, most of which was funneled back into the business year after year.

"Livvie's car insurance will kick in on some of the costs," I said, thinking out loud. "And you know I'm willing to invest in the business. I'll have money from the house sale soon."

"No."

I expected that response so I ignored it and barreled on. "Janelle and I agreed I should invest some money in business stuff like stocks and bonds. I'm going to let her do that, but I'm also going to invest in things that interest me, like alternative energy technology and horticulture and—"

"No."

"I was going to ask her to talk to Joe Swenson."

That stopped him, like I knew it would. "What do you mean?"

"Joe needs a new partner. You and I both know he's not rich. I want to invest in something related to horticulture. It seems like a perfect fit. He's got a company doing research into adaptive plants for changing environments. I have money to invest." I saw the sparkle of interest in Sam's eyes. Botanical research was his first love. He only went into the landscape trade because it was a family business and his father needed his help. "Janelle looked into it, but the business partnership is all goofed up because Mike was murdered and the paperwork hasn't been filed yet." I was starting to get the glimmer of A Plan. I pushed the idea to the back of my brain so my excitement wouldn't show. "I wonder how long it will take to sort it out."

"How long did the police say they needed for Livvie's restaurant thing? It's almost the same kind of deal."

"You're right. I'll check with her when she picks me up." I tapped my cast, already gaily decorated with illustrations and signatures. "I see the doctor later on today. If I get the okay, I can start driving again. I need to have you autograph this, too."

"Later." He yawned. "I guess whenever you're here I really relax."

I saw the empty pill cup next to his plate and figured it was probably a miracle of modern science and not my calming personality, but I decided not to mention that.

"You don't have to hang around while I sleep." He yawned again.

I yawned, too. "Maybe I'll join you."

He patted the side of the bed. "Be my guest. I'm afraid I'm not good for much of anything but a snuggle."

He wasn't good for that, either, given the fact we couldn't jostle the bed. "I need to get some lunch then I'll come back. When you wake up you might have a busted up old lady in your bed if you're not careful." I leaned over carefully and brushed a kiss against his forehead. "Sweet dreams." I turned to leave.

"Cassie?"

I paused by the foot of the bed. "Do you need me to get you something?"

"No. Just...thanks."

"For what?"

"For being here. I appreciate it."

"There's no place I'd rather be, Sam." I smiled at him, hoping he didn't see the lie in my eyes. A hospital was one of the last places I wanted to be, but I knew he needed the company and I had to be there. It was that simple.

He tried to smile back, but he was already drifting off to sleep. *Thank you Big Drug Company, whoever you are,* I thought as I tiptoed out of the room. I headed for the cafeteria two floors down, not far from the main lobby. As I emerged from the elevator I saw the distinctive silhouette of Charles Richard Whittington the Second at the front desk. "C.R.," I called out as I neared him.

He turned, saying something to the receptionist as he did so. "Cassandra, I'm glad I found you. I wanted to speak with you outside of Mr. Barlow's hearing."

"You came all the way over here to talk to me? How did you know I was here?" I started ambling toward the cafeteria as the smells of cooking wafted toward us.

"Livvie mentioned she dropped you off. Are you busy? Do you have time?"

"I was going to get some lunch, if that's okay."

"Certainly. Lead the way." He fell into step beside me and we joined the queue of hospital workers, doctors, and visitors at the cafeteria. The Second stood out like a sore thumb in his natty business suit while everyone around him wore hospital scrubs and blue jeans.

"What do you want, C.R.?" I asked as I grabbed a blue plastic tray, silverware, and napkin. "I'm buying."

He smiled wryly. "What would you recommend? You appear to be familiar with this dining establishment."

"Their tuna salad is excellent as are the loose meat sandwiches, which are offered on Tuesday and Thursday. Stay away from the egg salad," I advised.

"Loose meat?" He regarded the cafeteria worker in front of us, her scoop poised over a tray of crumbled hamburger.

"Sometimes called Sloppy Joe, sometimes called Maid-rites." I pointed to the tray. "I'll have that and some chips." I'd have to eat it with a fork due to my one-limbedness, but I wasn't going to pass up an excellent LMS because of that.

"Make that two," the Second said. "I'm always willing to venture out of my culinary habitat," he said when he saw my astonished look. "I draw the line at a carbonated beverage, though. Coffee for me." He took our plates from the server and put them on the tray, nudging it forward on the runner toward the beverage station. "I wanted to talk to you about your investments now that the sale of the house is going through."

I wrestled with the Pepsi machine, managing to get most of the drink in the cup as he drew coffee from the giant urn. "Janelle and I talked a bit about investing." I hesitated by the dessert display. The Second made my mind up for me when he took two slices of chocolate cream pie and put them on the tray.

"I believe you like this kind of pie," he murmured as we joined the others in line for the checkout.

"I do," I admitted. "I'm surprised you remembered."

"Not only was your mother an excellent nanny for the children, she made exceptional pie. I miss her apple pie and her chocolate pies." He sighed. "I don't often feel old, but sometimes when I look back, it's hard not to."

The cashier rang up our meals and I dug my zip purse out of my sling where I kept it, fumbling out a twenty dollar bill. "Thank you, Cassie," the Second said as I pocketed the change.

"I'm happy to have someone to eat with," I confessed. "It gets boring sitting down here alone all the time."

"You've been here a lot." It wasn't a question but a statement.

"As much as I can. I hate asking someone to drive me, so I usually stay all day. I don't tell Sam that. He thinks I come and go. He'd get mad if he knew I was dozing down in the library or napping in the chapel." I flashed the Second a grin as we sat down at a small table. "Don't tell the priest I said that."

"My lips are sealed." He set my plate and my drink in front of me and I covered my cast with several napkins, extracted from the black holder on the table.

He carefully sampled the messy burger. "You were right, this is very good."

I pulled off the top bun and dug into the sandwich with my plastic fork, managing to get most of the bite in my mouth and not on my sweatshirt. "You said you wanted to ask about my investing ideas?" I prompted as I nibbled on a salty chip.

"As you know, Mr. Barlow's ex-wife is an investor in one of my companies."

"Sam," I mumbled around another bite of burger. "You can call him Sam."

He ignored this magnanimous gesture on my part and continued as though I hadn't spoken. "One of my aides was speaking with her over lunch the other day. Mrs. Peavey mentioned she plans to sell some land in Pickaway." The Second saw my startled look. "Apparently this land is coming available soon for sale. She wanted to know if Marlene—my aide—could help her find a good broker."

"She can't sell Sam's land," I sputtered. "Not while the company is in business."

He held up a hand. "She said she plans to do whatever is necessary to get that land sold." His dark green eyes were troubled. "I believe her, Cassie. You and Sam are in danger."

Chapter 14

I waved a potato chip as though it was a magic wand, able to disperse bad karma. "Sheila's been making veiled threats since I met her."

"Charlie mentioned all the vandalism at the landscape center last spring." The Second nibbled his messy burger, finally abandoning it and using a fork.

I was impressed. He managed to eat half of the sandwich before resorting to civilized behavior. "There was some vandalism, but we haven't had any trouble this summer."

"Sheila implied you would have more this fall. Sam needs to get a security guard out there to patrol the grounds when no one is there." He sipped his coffee. "And you need to make sure you don't work there at any time when you're alone. I think some of Sheila's anger might be personal and it might be directed at you."

"That's weird, since I barely know her. Well, I've already quit temporarily, so that's not a problem," I said, my mind churning with what he said. He was right. A security guard made sense. "I don't know if they can afford a guard. Money's tight now."

The Second took a last bite and pushed his plate away. "A very satisfying meal. That brings me to my next point. I plan to invest in Barlow Nursery and Landscaping, Incorporated."

I gulped down the bite in my mouth. "What? It's not incorporated." I thought furiously. "Is it?"

"No, but it will be soon. Charlie has been in discussions with Mary Hannon about the problems they're facing with Sam being injured and the hospital bills. He's convinced her to accept funding outside the family." The Second smiled fleetingly. "Of course, if you and Sam marry, the money is technically in the family, but you don't appear to be anxious to tie the knot soon. Consequently, an infusion from an outside source is needed."

I decided not to acknowledge the M word. Neither Sam nor I ever mentioned it and I wasn't going to be the one to bring it up, certainly not with Sam all banged up and *certainly* not around the Second. "I wanted to invest but Sam wouldn't let me."

The Second nodded. "To be expected from a man like him."

"That's not what Charlie said," I muttered.

"Charlie is an idiot sometimes," his father said imperturbably. "It comes from being raised with wealth. He has a cynical and yet naïve outlook on life. He tends to suspect the worst in people while not realizing how difficult life can be sometimes." The Second leaned forward, steepling his fingers and regarding me over their tips. "I plan to invest some cash in the operation."

"Why?" I reached for my glass with my right hand, wincing when my left elbow made contact with the chair. The whole sling thing was annoying. "No offense, but you're not a horticulture kind of guy."

"That's a fair question." The Second looked thoughtfully past me, his eyes flickering over the motley assortment of people gathered in the cafeteria. When his gaze returned to me, I saw memories in his eyes. "Do you remember Gloria?"

"Charlie's mother? Of course." I smiled, as

always saddened and heartened by the thought. "She was beautiful. And she was so kind and giving."

"I loved Gloria," he said softly. "I've loved the other women I married, and I love Claire, my current wife, deeply. But Gloria was the first woman I ever loved whom I wanted to spend my life with. She was..." He hesitated, staring down at his plate then looking back at me. "When Charlie was born, it was the happiest day of my life, to know that Gloria and I were starting a family together. All of the children were a joy to me because they were a part of Gloria. When she died I wasn't sure how I could continue without her."

I closed my eyes as though I could erase the memory of my father, drunk and angry, a gun in his hand. He kicked ten-year-old Charlie in the face and left him to drown in Lake Minnetonka. My father then shot Gloria, who turned her back to him to protect Olivia, the baby in her arms. Next my father turned the gun on my mother. The Second shot him before he could pull the trigger.

I saw the whole thing, as did Charlie and the twins, John and Becky. I still had nightmares about my father's face exploding into bloody fragments as I lay in the water, trying to rescue Charlie, whom I adored even then.

"I have made it a point to always look at events from Gloria's point of view." The Second's cool, brisk voice made me open my eyes, startled to be in the here and now. "This is something Gloria would approve of." He smiled, his handsome face softening. "I'm seventy-seven years old. In a few years, I'll be joining Gloria. I don't want to disappoint her."

My mouth sagged open in surprise. "I didn't realize you felt that way."

"Of course you didn't. I don't advertise it. I suggest you prepare Sam for the knowledge his company will now have partners. It's the only way they can stay in business." He dabbed his lips with his paper napkin and shoved a slice of pie my way. "I'm also looking forward to putting a wrench in Mrs. Peavey's plans. She's a somewhat unpleasant woman."

My brain was spinning with the implications of what financing would mean for Barlow's Nursery and Landscaping. If Sam didn't feel obligated to put all his time and effort into the business, maybe I could talk him into going back to botanical research. And if I could infuse some money into the research company, Sam would have a steady income—income he was going to need because his days of hauling trees, lifting fifty-pound bags of fertilizer, and schlepping carts of plants were going to be behind him. A fifty-six year old man couldn't recover from major surgery without slowing down at least a little.

I dug into the pie with gusto. "You go, C.R.," I said around a bite of creamy goodness.

****

"Everything okay?" I asked Sam a week later as we drove Bilbo, my new SUV, to the *La Suzette* restaurant. Bilbo was so-named because its color was "Brandywine" and that word association led to another and to another and finally to *The Hobbit*.

Bilbo had entered my life four days earlier via Livvie and Becky. I was still getting accustomed to driving a Lexus RX 350 and driving with one arm. Luckily, like the Starship Enterprise before it, this Lexus almost drove itself. I spent one afternoon getting away from Sam and familiarizing myself with the controls including the Bluetooth functionality and Sync feature, which let me use my phone via voice control once plugged into the adapter. It was so much fun I programmed speed dial for just about everybody I knew.

Sam was released from the hospital on the previous Tuesday, six days after his surgery. He used a wheelchair for the first few days but here we were on Saturday and he was managing a credible imitation of walking on his crutches.

"It's great to get out." He moved carefully onto the passenger seat, his right leg in the puffy boot-thing barely fitting into the foot well. "No offense, but I was getting sick of your townhouse."

"No offense taken." He didn't say it, but I suspect he was getting sick of seeing me day in and day out, too. The social worker who met with me prior to Sam's release had talked about the home arrangements we would need and the stress of being a 'care-giver,' compounded by my awkwardness with a broken arm. I knew that my townhome would need some work before it could accommodate a man on crutches. The problem was, I didn't have the faintest idea how I could get it done before he was released.

I shouldn't have worried. I forgot all about the Whittington secret weapon: Betty.

She swept into my home two days before Sam was released from the hospital bringing an elderly black gentleman with her. Between the two of them, they made my home handicapped-accessible. Then Betty proceeded to fill my refrigerator and freezer with enough food to last me at least a week with an admonition to call her if Sam got to be too much of a handful. "Albert will come over and help out," she said, slipping her arm through the old man's. "He used to work at the V.A. hospital and he knows a thing or two about male patients."

And sure enough, two days after Sam got home Betty came over and swooped me away to lunch and a movie, leaving her boyfriend Albert in charge. When we returned four hours later, Sam was bathed, freshly shaved and his hair trimmed. He and Albert were on the last beers of a six-pack, with the remains of a pizza littering the coffee table and each man with a cat on his lap. They were arguing heatedly about Civil War battles, a hobby I didn't realize Sam enjoyed. When Albert left, he promised to return soon with battle simulator software, a promise that had Sam examining my computer with a critical frown.

Tonight was our first outing together since Sam's release from the hospital and I was looking forward to it. I didn't count the trips to doctors or physical therapy. Those outings were certainly nothing to anticipate. But tonight's event promised to be different. Tonight Livvie was going to sign the purchase papers for *La Suzette*, which would mark a turning point for her and for T.J.

"Livvie said the detective in charge of the case called her. They're going to make an arrest soon. That's why they were able to release the papers for the restaurant." I turned onto the main road leading to the restaurant. The harvest moon hung in the sky like a fat, benign sun, casting reflections off the lake on our left.

"Did she say who they're going to arrest? Do they have an idea? Is T.J. still worried about his son in the hot seat?"

"I don't think Paul is high on the list any more. Apparently he and Michelle have cooled off their relationship." I grinned as I remembered Livvie's tart comment about that change. *The boy finally saw through that slut.* "T.J. pointed out that once a cheater, always a cheater, which I guess Paul hadn't considered."

"Do you think that's true?" Sam asked.

"I do," I said thoughtfully. "I think some people just aren't cut out for long-term relationships. Let's face it. Infidelity is a simple way to split up a couple. That way nobody has to think about emotion and feelings and all that."

"I never thought of it that way. Infidelity as an excuse." He was quiet for another block. "How do you feel about long-term relationships?"

I didn't really want to get into such serious talk so I did what I always did. I joked about it. "If you're worried about being kicked out before your leg heals, don't worry. I wouldn't do that to you."

He laughed ruefully. "Yeah, I guess there is the pity factor, isn't there?"

"That's not what I meant, Sam." I saw with relief that the restaurant was in sight. "I don't really know how I feel about long-term relationships. I haven't had a lot in my life. Hell, Charlie and I were in a long-term relationship and that only lasted seven years." I turned carefully into the drive for the restaurant, edging the SUV to the left and the restaurant side of the two-house layout. Several cars were parked on the right, near Hell House.

"Who all is coming tonight?" Sam asked.

"Oh, just family," I said dismissively. "Just Livvie and T.J. And of course, Charlie will be there."

"Of course," he said grumpily.

I ignored the innuendo in his tone of voice. "After all, he's Livvie's contract attorney. He's got all the paperwork for the sale."

"Oh. Sure."

I glanced at Sam, who looked subdued. "He and Janelle have been keeping company, as Betty would say."

"Really?" He unfastened his seat belt after I tucked Bilbo into a handicapped parking space near the front porch of the restaurant. "Albert is serious about Betty, you know."

He sounded so smug I didn't have the heart to say *Any idiot could see that, even a man.* "Really? Do you think his intentions are honorable?"

Sam pushed open his door. "Now you sound like Richie Rich."

"Oh, for heaven's sake, Sam. It's a joke." I got out and came around to the back seat, pulling out his crutches. I handed them to him as he gingerly slid his leg out of the front seat.

"Sorry," he muttered. "I just don't—" He maneuvered himself onto the crutches and faced the gently sloping ramp that led up into the restaurant. "You know."

I slammed the car door. "Yeah. I know." I went ahead of him, struggling to keep my anger in check. *Typical of him,* I thought. *Bring up a serious subject just as we're getting ready to meet a bunch of people and can't talk about it. That's so Sam. He drops these little nuggets on me and then—*

"Cassie."

His quiet voice stopped me in my tracks. I turned back to help him. "Can you make it? It's really not that steep."

He stumped up to me on his crutches. I was above him on the ramp so we were even with each other although separated by several feet. "I care about you, Cassie. But now that I'm hurt, I'm not sure where we stand."

I looked around us. The birch trees nearby were silvery in the moonlight and the air had the crisp, wood-scented aroma of autumn. I repressed the quick *We're in Minnetonka, that's where we stand* that came to mind. I walked down the ramp until I was near him. "I'm not sure, either, Sam. Let's just take it a day at a time."

He frowned and I thought I glimpsed surprise in his eyes. What did he expect? I really didn't know how I felt anymore. Despite my assurances to the contrary, living with a handicapped man had awakened my eyes to the reality of, well, of aging. The last week had not been fun and if the future held more of it, I wasn't sure what I would do. What if Sam didn't get his full mobility back? What if he had to retire?

There were too many what-ifs for me to be

confident of the future, so I kept my mouth shut and gave him a supportive arm as he moved slowly up the incline. I left him at the top of the ramp and went ahead to the porch door leading into the restaurant. I peered inside and, as I expected, no one was visible. I opened the door and went in, glimpsing Livvie at the far end of the space as she ducked inside the partitioned area at the back that led to the walkway, which led in turn to Hell House.

"What's going on?" Sam asked as he came into the room. He looked at the fifteen tables, all set out with china. "Why so many tables?"

"I think they're doing a practice run for opening after all the painting and construction." I sniffed the air. "There's no paint smell, so that's good. Livvie said they added that wall back there and T.J. said something about making sure the waiters had a chance to practice with the new layout." I was making up the story as I went, but it sounded plausible.

"Where is everybody?" Sam managed to pull out a chair and sank down carefully.

"Livvie told me they'd be over in the kitchen building," I lied glibly. "I just had to let her know when we got here. I'll go tell them we're here."

I wove between the tables then slipped through the door leading into the back room or 'staging area' where the meals were brought in from Hell House. As I expected, the place was jammed with friends, family, and workers from Barlow's. I glimpsed Betty, Albert, Becky Whittington and her husband, Janelle, Mary Hannon—just about everybody who knew Sam or me. Even Joe Swenson and his wife were there. I smiled at them, happy they came.

"Okay, he's sitting down," I whispered, peeking back the way I came. "Are we ready?"

T.J. gestured to a large table where a huge cake sat. "Paul outdid himself."

He was right. The cake was a miniature of the hospital complete with little white ambulances near the Emergency portal, patients in wheelchairs outside under trees, and a small man on crutches who looked very like Sam standing at a curb, waiting to get into a burgundy SUV. A woman next to him had her arm in a bright red sling. Above it was a banner that read, "Congratulations on a successful hospital escape." I'd never seen anything like it except on HGTV and one of those cake contest shows.

"It's fabulous." I beamed at Paul, who looked pleased with himself.

"Here's the other one." Paul held out a much smaller sheet cake shaped like a contract lying on a dark blue background. The words "La Suzette", "T.J.", and "Olivia" were piped on it in red lettering. "We'll cut into this one when they sign the papers."

"Wow. That's cool." I grinned at him then at T.J., who looked so proud of his son I thought he might sprout several extra hands to pat himself and Paul on the back.

I peeked out the door again. Sam was seated at the table, his back to us, looking up at the menu on the wall. "Okay, let's do it."

I pushed open the door and came out. "Hey, Sam!"

"What?" He looked back over his shoulder at me.

"Surprise!"

****

An hour later, I watched as Sam cut into the hospital cake. "Where's Michelle?" I asked Livvie as we relaxed near Sam at the table nearest the front door, drinks in hand.

"Over there." Livvie nodded toward the back of the room, where Paul and Michelle were deep in conversation. Neither of them appeared happy. Michelle looked even more china-doll pretty than the first time I saw her. The precise black line of her hair brushed her chin and her complexion was porcelain smooth with just a hint of blush on her cheeks. Her clothing helped, too. Her tailored plum-colored tweed blazer, darker plum turtleneck, and black pants made her look like an L.L. Bean ad for 'the active outdoor woman,' probably one who had a home in the Hamptons and had servants to handle the mundane problems of day-to-day living.

"I didn't see her earlier," I said, wondering if my envy at her stylishness showed. I was in jeans and my *Am I getting older or is the supermarket playing great music?* sweatshirt with the left arm cut off. I once again admired T.J. who looked spiffy in his chef whites and pressed slacks. I could barely zip myself up with one hand, much less look ironed. How did he do it?

Livvie smiled at T.J., who was accepting compliments on the fine meal he had orchestrated. "Michelle showed up halfway through the fish course," she murmured. "She slipped in the side door."

I raised my glass to Livvie. "And what a fish course it was. T.J. is a great cook."

"Chef," she corrected automatically. "I think he'll have a chance to shine now. I'm glad T.J. let Mike go. I never trusted him. There was just something about him that bothered me."

"Always go with your gut instinct," I agreed. "So T.J. will be *chef de cuisine* and they'll find another sous-chef? What about Paul? Does he want the job?"

"I hope not. He's a great pastry chef. We've already had some people express interest in the position. Robert had a good reputation and I think that will spill over."

Sam gestured to the cake. "Care for some?" he asked.

"You bet." I sipped my watered-down wine. This

designated driver thing was a drag as was the one-armed clumsiness. I had a new appreciation for the graceful way T.J. handled his handicap. I barely noticed he was one-handed. Of course, he had years of practice and I only had a few days.

"Where's Richie Rich?" Sam asked as I leaned forward to take the cake from him.

"I don't know. He should be here. We can't cut the contract cake until he shows up." I looked at the other cake, still waiting on the table next to the somewhat dismembered hospital cake. "Where's your brother?" I asked Livvie, savoring the rich chocolate cake with gooey white frosting. I smiled as Sam carefully moved the little marzipan figurines to one side lest they be toppled by his enthusiastic slicing.

"I don't know. He called earlier and said he was coming and bringing a guest. When I mentioned it to Janelle, she said something came up when they were preparing the contract and he needed to bring someone with him to discuss it." The glare of headlights briefly shone into the room. "I'll bet that's him now." She got up and moved toward the door leading to the porch, pausing to chat with people along the way.

"Looks like we'll get to cut into the cake soon," I said to T.J. as he walked past.

"I'll be glad to have that contract signed," he said in a low voice. "It's been weird lately. Michelle has been acting so anxious about getting the place sold and then Mike was such a jerk."

"How so?" I glimpsed Michelle, still talking to Paul as they headed for the porch door where Livvie stood.

"He made a scene when I told him he had to go." T.J. looked pained, his plain face contorting briefly. "I didn't want to do it, but with his record I felt I had to. And there were complaints about the food sometimes, so, well, I had no choice."

"Yeah, I heard about that." I looked around as Livvie opened the door to the new arrivals. Charlie came into the room bringing with him a brief scent of fallen leaves and crisp October air. Paul and Michelle paused near the door as it opened again and another man stepped into the room. He was heavily built, stocky and muscular with a weathered face and the look of a man who spent a lot of time outdoors. His thick dark hair was rough cut and he was attractive in a Marlboro man sort of way. His faded denims, pea coat, and bulky beige turtleneck added to his outdoorsy image.

He paused inside the door, his dark gray eyes sweeping around the room. Michelle was just a few feet from him. She stopped as though someone had a leash around her neck and they jerked her chain. Her mouth opened as she gaped at the man, then her glass slipped from her fingers, crashing to the floor with a splash of red wine and shards of splintered glass.

The man smiled at her. "Hi, Mick. How's it going?"

"Who's that?" I asked Charlie who had walked over to stand near Sam and me.

"That's Michelle's husband."

"What? Her husband is dead." I said this in a low voice, looking around to see if anyone else was paying attention. I didn't need to worry. Everyone was busy laughing, talking, and gobbling down yummy cake. The little domestic scene being played out wasn't on any radar screens.

"Sorry. That's her other husband. He's her first husband." Charlie looked at the man, who stared at Michelle, waiting for her to acknowledge him.

She took a step back, shock turning her already pale face deathly white. "Jim. What—how—where did you come from?"

The man smiled again. "I'll bet you never thought you'd see me again."

"Her first husband?" I asked.

Charlie shot me a wry look. "He's the one she forgot to divorce thirteen years ago."

Chapter 15

"How did you get here?" Michelle demanded.

Jim-the-stranger looked amused. "I came by airplane then car. The same as most people travel." He looked around the room. "Sorry. Charlie mentioned there was a party. I guess we're crashing it." His eyes once again searched through the assembled people, pausing at me then moving on to Sam, who was eating his cake while watching Michelle and her not-ex-husband spar. "Where's Mickey?" Jim asked.

"Mickey?" I murmured.

"Mickey?" Michelle's voice was shrill. "What do you mean?" Her ultra-pale face was now pink, clashing with her plum-colored jacket.

"This is fun," I said to Charlie. "It's like watching a soap opera in real time. Who's Mickey? Where did Jim come from?"

Michelle must have heard me. She whirled to confront me. "This is none of your business."

I swallowed the bite of cake in my mouth. "Au contraire," I said in my best mangled French. "You're airing your linen in front of us all."

"Mickey is our son." Jim edged his way past Michelle to stand near Charlie by my table. I peered up at him. He looked uncertain and a bit wary, like a deer caught in the headlights and not sure of his next move.

193

"Is he in town?" I asked, stabbing another bite of cake.

My conversational tone seemed to calm him. He nodded, his eyes flickering between Michelle and me. "He came here to find Mick."

"Mick?" I mumbled around cake.

"Michelle." Jim stared at Michelle, his gaze defiant. "My wife. The mother of our four children."

The room started to quiet as the other guests realized a Jerry Springer Moment was happening. I looked at Livvie, who appeared bemused. "Why don't we go over to Hell House and chat?" I suggested.

"Hell House?" Jim asked. "You don't know hell. Try living with four kids under the age of ten and no mother there to help raise them."

I shot him a sympathetic look. "It boggles the mind." I stood as Livvie and T.J. headed for the back of the room. Michelle was rooted to the spot and looked unable to move. "Let's find some privacy. Follow them." I nodded toward Livvie then turned to Sam. "Do you want in on this Oprah event?"

"I wouldn't miss it for the world." He maneuvered himself upright and got his crutches settled. He started stumping toward the back of the room, Jim beside him.

"What happened?" I heard Jim ask.

"Car accident."

"Bummer. I broke my leg in a snowmobile accident six years ago." Their voices faded as they followed the others out of the room.

I looked at Michelle. "Coming?"

She drew in a long, shuddering breath then nodded. "I suppose I have to face it." She stalked past me.

Betty materialized at my side. "Problems?"

I looked at the group going into the back room. "I don't think so. Keep the natives happy, okay? I hope we won't be long." I considered grabbing my wine glass but decided I didn't want to hamper my one good hand. I headed for the back of the room.

"Not a problem." Betty went to the hospital cake and picked up the knife Sam set down. "Who needs another slice?"

I hurried after Michelle. She was already in the back room and heading for the walkway. Sam was having trouble manipulating the crutches, but Jim was helping him, pointing out the lip in the doorway, the uneven pavement and holding the door so Sam could get into the kitchen of Hell House.

Michelle crowded in behind them so quickly I was afraid she would knock Sam over. I was going to chew her out for that when Jim put a hand on her arm and drew her back. "Hold on. Give him a chance to get by." She shot him a look so filled with venom I'm surprised he didn't drop to the floor and start twitching. He met her look stoically. "You always were too impatient," he said softly.

Michelle jerked her arm away from him. "And you were always an idiot." She stalked past him to stand across the room, on the far side of the entryway.

I winced as I edged my way around Sam to enter the kitchen. It was the first time I'd ever been in the place and I looked around curiously. We were in a large open space, almost the entire ground floor of the rectangular house. The floors were gray and white linoleum tile and the walls were institutional white. Every inch of wall space contained a cooking implement of some kind: three huge stoves, a flat top grill, sinks, and a contraption that had to be a dishwasher tucked into one corner. In the center of the entire room ran a stainless steel kitchen island with sinks, cutting boards, work surfaces and pots hanging overhead. I had the impression that there was a place for everything and everything was in its place.

To the right of the door where we entered was a wall with a small hallway bisecting the back one-third of the house. A walk-in refrigerator was on the left of that hall and the pantry where I glimpsed the body the other night was on the right. I stood near Sam with my back to the door that led outside, to the parking lot and the road beyond.

T.J. looked comfortable and at home, leaning against the kitchen island, his gaze going from Charlie to Jim. Livvie was next to him, her arms crossed as she regarded Michelle with narrow-eyed suspicion. Paul was behind T.J. on the other side of the kitchen island. I didn't see him leave The Feed Bag, but he must have slipped out ahead of Sam. Jim moved to stand next to Charlie, who stopped just inside the kitchen area itself, looking around uncertainly as though uncomfortable being around so many gadgets and implements. I knew how he felt. I was afraid to touch anything lest a flame ignite or a machine whirr to life.

Michelle stalked into the kitchen past Sam and me, her gaze intent on Charlie. "What's this all about?"

"Good question," Livvie asked quietly. "Charlie, is there a problem with the sale? Is that why you said you weren't sure if we could sign tonight?"

The back door near Sam opened and Janelle entered the room. Like Michelle, she wore a wool blazer in hunter green, dark slacks, and a pale green blouse, but on Janelle it looked just like casual clothes, not like some chic fashion statement. She went to Charlie's side and handed him the papers in her hand. "You were right. Sloan called and confirmed."

Charlie looked down at the stapled documents then at Jim. "We had a detective investigate the people involved in the death of the head chef here."

"You did what?" Michelle demanded, her voice

loud in the quiet room. "How dare you?" I snorted with laughter and she whirled on me. "Who do you think you are?"

"A soon-to-be-member of our family was under suspicion for murder," I shot back. "What did you think we'd do?"

"Our family?" Sam murmured.

I glared at him. "Don't split hairs."

He leaned back and almost overbalanced before remembering he was using crutches. His eyes grew cold. "God forbid. Not me."

I struggled to repress the snappish retort that came to mind. And it was a struggle, believe me, as all of Sam's grouchy behavior in the past week seemed to rise up in front of me like a foggy ghost to haunt me. Charlie waited patiently for us to shut up, a little smile playing at the corners of his mouth. It was that smile that made me realize how much I missed his teasing and jokes. At other times in our past together I would call him and complain about the man in my life and he would do the same about the woman he was seeing. We had lost that easy camaraderie now, though. I didn't dare complain about Sam and if he had any concerns about Janelle, he never shared them with me. A jolting feeling of loss made my stomach twist when he turned toward Janelle, his green eyes intent on her.

I sensed Sam next to me, watching us. I felt like I was teetering on some cliff and a step in the wrong direction would pitch me toward him or away from him. Either way I would plummet into an unknown future with a man I barely knew. For a second I swayed, physically dizzy as I contemplated life without Charlie, life without my best friend.

The sensation passed when Janelle handed him a piece of paper and Charlie turned to face me again. He twitched one eyebrow and I knew by the wry pursing of his lips that he had more bombs to drop.

Although he wore casual clothes—dark slacks and a brown sweater under a leather jacket—he still somehow looked like a lawyer. It was odd to see him in the kitchen among the other men. All of them— Paul, T.J., Jim, and Sam—were rough looking, outdoorsy types. Charlie was like a cultivated flower next to a bunch of sturdy native plants. I shook away the horticultural analogies dancing in my brain to focus on his next words.

"I did a title search on the property sold to Robert de Garmeaux and Michelle Bedford and of course, I verified their marriage because the contract was worded very precisely with 'Michelle Bedford, wife.'"

"Wife?" Jim asked in disbelief.

Charlie held up his hand. "I made sure there was a license of marriage on file and because Michelle was married previously, in California, I checked on the divorce decree there. I found her husband there died, leaving her a considerable amount of money."

"Saul Bedford," I said in a low voice to Sam. "I remember that."

Michelle shot me one of those deadly looks, but I was immune. I had years of experience deflecting poisonous stares from John Whittington and his wife Diane. They were Poisonous Look Experts. I glared back at her.

"Well, one thing led to another," Charlie said, holding up the three stapled sheets of papers. "I asked Marcus Sloan, the detective we hired, to research Michelle, T.J., Robert, Paul, and Michael Johnson, all of whom were affiliated with the restaurant. I wanted to make sure there was no impediment to transferring ownership of the property."

"And is there?" Michelle asked.

"I think you know the answer to that." Charlie's

dark green eyes were accusing as he stared unflinchingly at her. "Do you want to tell them or should I?"

"Tell us what?" I asked eagerly.

She rounded on me. "You're enjoying this, aren't you?"

I hesitated, wondering how honest I should be. Charlie saved me from a lie by saying, "This isn't about Cassie or anyone else. This is about you and your husband." He looked at Jim. "James Tolliver."

"Husband?" Paul asked in a choked voice. I felt sorry for the guy. Here was a woman he was involved with and she was showing a whole new side to her personality. Not only had he cheated with her on the husband he knew. He had cheated with her on a guy he didn't know about at all. Paul probably wondered if he had fallen through a rabbit hole or something.

"Michelle and I were married when we were barely out of high school," Jim said. He looked embarrassed and I think I knew the reason why.

"You were out of high school." Michelle's voice was low but I heard the hate-filled emotion that made it vibrate with anger. "I was a senior in school." She looked at Charlie, her eyes defiant. "I got pregnant and we had to get married."

I started to speak but she just glared at me so I shut up. No one 'had' to get married in this world, just like no one 'got accidentally pregnant.' A person could bow to social pressure or neglect to investigate birth control options, but it always pissed me off when people acted like pregnancy was some startling accident beyond their control.

She must have sensed my skepticism. "My mother was the mayor in town and a right-wing Christian. I had no choices."

I kept my opinion to myself with difficulty.

"I couldn't get an abortion and in that town

there was no way I could have a child and give it up for adoption."

"I loved you," Jim said softly. "I would have done anything for you."

"All you wanted to do was work on the pipeline and screw," she spat. "I couldn't get birth control because you and my damn mother convinced me it was a sin. I had four children in ten years and all that was ahead of me was a life in a mini-van, driving kids to hockey practice and school. I hated it. I was dying of boredom. I was stuck in a suburb of a two-bit city in a place where the greatest accomplishment is learning to shoot a gun and where parents pray their kids will get hockey scholarships in order to get out."

"Wow," I murmured to Sam. "A slow death."

"No kidding," he whispered.

"I told you I'd help," Jim said. "You didn't have to run away. You could have gone to school. There were online classes. I told you I'd do what I could."

"Jim, you were gone two weeks at a time to work on the pipeline. I had four kids!" Michelle ran a trembling hand along the line of her black hair, gently moving it away from her chin. I recognized that nervous gesture. I did it a lot when my hair was too long and it bugged me. "The biggest thing I could hope to do was run for the P.T.A. I wanted out. I wanted to experience life. I couldn't do that with four kids in tow."

"So you ran away," Charlie said.

Michelle nodded. "I saved up money and bought a bus ticket. I told my mother I was leaving and she had to take the kids. Jim was on the line, up north and wouldn't be back for days. My mother was mad but I was desperate. I told her if she didn't help me, I'd expose her."

"Expose her?" Charlie leafed through the papers in his hand.

Jim looked uncomfortable. "No need to bring that up, Mick."

"She was mayor and she was on the take." Michelle's voice shook with anger. "She put all her friends in city jobs and got kickbacks from them. The only thing my mother ever wanted was more power. The last I heard she was going to make a run at senator. God help Alaska and the lower forty-eight if she's elected." Michelle took a deep breath, as though willing calmness into her tense body. "She gave me a thousand dollars and told me to get out. I took it and ran."

I watched Jim as she recited these events. He didn't look surprised, just sad. "You knew?" I asked.

He nodded. "Her mother told me when I got home. We put it out that Mick was in the lower states, helping an aunt through an illness. After a week or two, we fabricated a car accident and let it out that Mick was dead." He glared at his wife, anger smoldering in his gray eyes. "It was the only thing I could do for the kids. They missed you."

Poor kids, I thought. *I'll bet it was tough for them.*

"Bullshit," Michelle snapped. "My mother always wanted to get her hands on them. It was her chance to mold them into perfect little rednecks. She sends me updates now and again. She said Brittany got pregnant and had to drop out of school and get married." Michelle laughed, a bitter and brittle sound. "Like mother like daughter, I guess."

"That's really not the point," Charlie said, his voice rising to drown out any rebuttal Jim might make. "We're here to discuss the contract for sale of the restaurant. You and your wife can talk over your problems without our help."

"Spoilsport," I muttered.

Charlie shot me a long-suffering look. "I had to consult the senior partners in my law firm and eventually we ended up talking to a judge about the ramifications of the contract." He looked at Livvie. "Janice Morton."

"I remember her," I said. "She had a crush on you in high school."

Charlie's cheeks darkened. "*Judge* Morton agreed that despite the legal ramifications of the nullification of Michelle Bedford's previous marriage, the purchase of the restaurant was valid. Therefore, it can be sold without contest."

"Nullification?" Jim asked. "You mean you're just canceling our marriage?"

"Not yours," Charlie corrected. "Michelle's marriage to Saul Bedford." He turned his attention to Michelle, who looked ready to scream. "Because you were married when you supposedly married Bedford, that marriage is null and void. I suspect Bedford's children will be anxious to contest your inheritance of his estate."

"What?" Michelle's voice was so shrill I expected the glassware around us to crack.

"Your marriage to Robert de Garmeaux is also null and void, but the contract was drawn up to include you as a partner. Since you signed the bill of purchase and the bill of sale, the sale of the restaurant to Olivia and T.J. can proceed." Charlie handed Livvie the papers he held. "This is confirmation of that. You'll have to keep this in a safe place."

"Great. Let's sign the papers and cut the cake." I smiled brightly at Michelle, who paled so dramatically I expected to see her drop over in a faint.

"Now just a minute," Jim said. "What about Mickey?"

"Mickey?" Michelle looked stunned by all that had just transpired. I felt the tiniest bit sorry for her. She had gone from femme fatale to hockey mom in the space of a half-hour. And she lost her inheritance, her high society status, and her pretensions. Then I saw the predatory look in her eye as she gazed at Paul, who looked as stunned as her. *Witch*, I thought.

"Mickey came here to find you," Jim said. "He ran away from home when he found out you were still alive."

"I never saw him."

"Mickey?" T.J. asked suddenly. "Mick Tolliver?"

Jim swung around to face T.J. "Yes. Twenty-year-old, big kid with dark brown hair and freckles?"

Paul moved forward to stand next to T.J. "Wasn't that the dishwasher? His name was Mick, wasn't it? I remember it was confusing because we had Mike and Mick."

T.J. nodded slowly. "Yeah. That was Mick." He and Livvie exchanged stricken looks.

"My God," Livvie breathed, her hand covering her mouth. "Oh, no."

"What is it?" Jim demanded. "Has something happened?"

"The police were looking for him," T.J. said. He put his good hand on Tolliver's shoulder. "He ran way after the murder." T.J. looked at Charlie beseechingly but Charlie looked as confused as I felt. "The police suspected him because he ran and...there was a car chase. The boy was running away from the police and..."

"I'm sorry," Livvie said softly, glancing from Jim to Michelle.

"What is it?" Michelle took a step forward and I thought she might shake Livvie.

"He's badly injured. The police aren't sure he'll live."

Chapter 16

"Oh my God." Michelle took a step back as though she'd been struck. "No."

"I'm sorry," Livvie repeated. "We just got word from the police about it before the party started. He lied on his application form. Or maybe it wasn't a lie. Dumbrowski? Is that your family name? He put down Barbara Dumbrowski as his next of kin. I believe the police were trying to get in touch with her."

"That's my mother. He listed her..." Now Michelle did sway. She leaned against the wall behind her, obviously not noticing it was the walk-in fridge and probably icy cold. "I don't understand," she whispered. "Mickey?"

Jim looked equally shaken. He sagged and seemed to age in front of my eyes, his face taking on a haggard, stricken look. "Where is he? When did it happen?"

"This afternoon. They contacted T.J. about the accident." Livvie put a consoling arm on Jim's, tugging him with her toward the door. "We'll call the police. They left a phone number and I wrote it down in the office." They started to walk to the back exit where we had all entered.

Michelle followed. Jim stopped and glared at her. "Leave us alone."

His voice was so low and so angry I shivered,

moving away from him to crowd against Sam near the doorway. Michelle looked like she'd been hit. "I care, Jim. You can't deny me."

"You abandoned them," Charlie said behind her. "He can deny you."

She turned to argue with him and Livvie took advantage of the moment to usher Jim out the door to the Feed Bag and the office upstairs.

"It wasn't that I didn't care," Michelle whispered. "I just couldn't stay there. I couldn't stand to be trapped."

Paul and T.J. walked past. Paul glanced once at her then left with his father. "Olivia and T.J. will sign the contract and we'll see to it you receive a copy," Charlie said, his voice frosty. "As we discussed, the money will be deposited in the business account you shared with your husband—that is, with Mr. de Garmeaux. You can expect the funds to clear in three business days." He gestured Janelle ahead of him and they started out the door.

Michelle reminded me of a lost child who just found out that not only was no one going to help her, nobody even cared about her. A part of me thought she deserved it, but another part sympathized with her. After all, what would I do if I was stuck with a bunch of kids in a dead-end life and no sign of a change on the horizon? "I'll find out the hospital where he was taken," I said impulsively. "Do you have a phone number?"

Michelle looked startled, as though unaware Sam and I still remained. She regarded me warily. I realized her eyes were a different color today. A week ago they were green but today they were a bright sky blue. *Contacts*, I thought. *She must change 'em to suit her mood.* That little bit of vanity almost made me change my mind about helping her. "Why?" she demanded.

"Why what?"

"Why help me? Don't you blame me, too?"

I blew out an exasperated sigh. "Look, I've made mistakes in my life, too. I got married for the wrong reasons but I was lucky. Charlie and I knew we made a mistake before life took over. I was able to get out and still stay friends with him."

"Charlie?" She looked at the doorway where my ex and my lawyer disappeared. "He's your ex-husband?"

"Surprising, isn't it?" Sam asked wryly.

She looked at him and I could see the calculation going on behind her stylish make-up. *Why is she with this guy when she had a chance with that hunk?* Sam's salt-and-pepper hair and weathered appearance made him seem older than his age and his recent accident didn't help. He had lost weight, looking almost shrunken compared to the husky, muscular guy I met the previous spring.

I stared into Michelle's eyes, daring her to say it. To her credit, she didn't. "You're luckier than most people," she whispered.

"No, I made good choices," I corrected her. "I hate it when people attribute intelligence to luck. I made hard choices and I stuck by them." I shrugged. "You didn't. There but for the grace of God, I guess. Do you want me to find out where the boy was taken?"

Her pale cheeks reddened. "My son? Yes, thank you." She started to rattle off a phone number but I shook my head.

"Hold on. I need some paper." I looked around the immediate vicinity but didn't see anything that would suffice. I ducked into the pantry and spied a sheaf of papers on a small table with a pen. They all looked like receipts or packing lists. I would jot the number then copy it once I got back in the Feed Bag. "Okay, go ahead," I said, pen poised. I held down the paper with my cast as she recited the number, looking at me then at the door where Jim disappeared as though wondering if she should follow.

"I'll call you as soon as I find out anything," I said. "I don't know if you should go there or not but maybe you can get information or..." Or what? I wasn't sure what she was entitled to or what the authorities at the hospital would do if she showed up. It wasn't my problem, though. I would do my good deed and let her cope with the consequences.

Michelle nodded, her face pinched and bleak. I knew she was struggling not to cry. "Thank you." She closed her eyes for an instant then tugged her purse higher on her shoulder. "I think I'll leave. I can see Jim at the hospital or...I don't know. I can't face him now."

"Maybe use this door," Sam suggested, nodding toward the hallway between the pantry and the fridge. "That might be better for everyone." He carefully shifted his crutches, edging toward the door that led to the Feed Bag. "I'm going to head back, Cassie. I need to sit down."

He looked and sounded exhausted. I realized this was the longest he had been on his feet since the accident. "Can you get back okay?"

"I'll be fine. You lock up." He began a slow shuffle out the door leading to the nearby dining house.

"I'll be right there." I followed Michelle to the door to the Hell House parking lot, pocketing the slip of paper and phone number. "I'll call you as soon as I know anything," I said as she paused on the threshold.

Michelle fumbled with the lock and I moved out of the way of the hall light to help illuminate her way. "Why did he come to look for me?" she whispered.

"Your husband? I suppose because Charlie got in

touch with him."

"No. My son." She shuddered and like a contagious yawn, it made me shudder, too. Icy cold suddenly gripped me and I shuddered again. It was probably the effect of the nearby walk-in refrigerator. "Mickey hasn't seen me since he was nine years old. Why would he look for me?"

I thought of my family—my abusive and drunken father, my frightened but resolute mother. "He probably just wanted to see you and ask why you did it," I said without thinking. It was what I wanted to do sometimes. If I could face my father today, I would ask him why. *Why did you kill Gloria? Why did you hate my mother so much? Why did you abuse her and try to abuse me? Why did you ruin our lives?*

"I don't know if I have a good enough answer. I suppose I need to figure one out, though." Michelle jerked the door open and a fresh breeze smelling of October leaves and lake vegetation wafted into the space. She stepped outside and I closed the door behind her. I started to lock it when I heard an angry voice.

"You bitch. You told them."

I almost pulled the door open but the voice was so enraged I hesitated. Did I really want to get in the middle of an argument in a dark and deserted parking lot? I hesitated with my hand on the door knob then I heard Michelle.

"You're crazy. I wouldn't do that. Why would I jeopardize what I had? They found out because of the sale, that's all."

I relaxed. She sounded angry, not frightened. I reached behind me and turned off the hall light. There were no windows in the door or at this end of the building. I pulled open the door slightly and held my ear to the crack.

"If you didn't tell them, why did the police come

looking for me?"

I widened the crack slightly and hazarded a peek. I recognized the bullet headed ex-sous-chef Mike Johnson, his hands clenched into fists and his back to the stoop. Michelle was in front of him, standing with her side to the steps as she stared at the Feed Bag where I heard people, their voices faint on the clear autumn air.

"Why should I know what the police are doing? Maybe T.J. told them you threatened him when he fired you."

"That bastard." His voice was so thick with hate I could barely understand the words. "If it wasn't for him screwing that rich bitch, I'd have this restaurant."

When I heard that, I almost pulled the door open to give him a piece of my mind. I restrained myself but I was so mad I could barely see straight.

"So now you don't have the restaurant and you don't have a job. You'll be lucky if you don't get sent to prison for what you did."

Holy crap. Is she talking about murder? Is Michelle so tough she could stand in a dark parking lot and talk to a murderer? I peered anxiously through the crack, afraid to leave lest I make noise and afraid to stay, lest I make noise. I decided staying was the more intelligent choice, at least for the moment.

"What are you talking about?" he demanded. "Prison?"

"Fraud is a felony and that means prison time." She sounded smug when she said it. I sneaked a glance and yep, she looked happy at the thought. "So is blackmail."

Ooh. Blackmail. This is juicy. I leaned forward a bit more but my cast made stealth on my part awkward. I tended to clunk when I moved, so I had to be careful. Consequently I missed a portion of his answer.

"...each other, so I don't know if that charge could stick." The volatile Mike now sounded amused *and* pissed off. "As to the other, they'll have to prove it and I have all the paperwork. It would be your word against mine and I think we know how good your word is right now."

"Are you sure you have all the paperwork?" Michelle's voice was fading and I peeked out. She was no longer in sight. Mike turned toward the parking lot on the left by the trees, presumably to face her.

"Of course I do."

"...this afternoon and..."

I strained to hear Michelle but couldn't catch the answer as the breeze shifted, blowing her words away from me. Mike apparently had trouble, too, because he walked away. Their voices were now so low I couldn't hear them.

I closed the door and locked it, wincing when the dead bolt made a clunking noise. As I walked back to the Feed Bag, I considered what I heard. Blackmail? Did Mike find out about Michelle's past and blackmail her? How did he find out?

Wait a minute. I paused just inside the door to the back room of the Feed Bag. The steps leading to the upper level were on my left and I heard Livvie talking. What if Mike made friends with the dishwasher and the kid let it drop who he was looking for? That was possible, I suppose. But why didn't the kid approach Michelle?

I went back into the main dining area, still crowded with people, most of them oblivious to the personal drama played out so near. Sam sat with Becky Whittington Stark and her husband. Although Sam looked tired, he smiled at something Carlton Stark was saying and I could tell Sam was interested in whatever the conversation was about. I crossed the room to Paul, who stood near the narrow bar that ran half the width of the building at the back.

"Are you okay?" I asked softly, noticing the glass of amber liquid near his hand. I shook my head negatively when the bartender looked inquiringly at me.

"I don't know," Paul admitted, his voice raspy and rough. "I thought I knew her."

"How long were you two..." I waggled my eyebrows. "You know."

"Most of the summer." He took a swallow of the whisky, grimacing as the liquor slid down his throat. "She said Robert was old and she was lonely." Paul looked away from me.

"Yeah, I've heard that before," I said wryly. I looked at Becky's husband, who was in his early sixties. Carlton was athletic and fit, the picture of a robust senior moving actively into retirement. I think after three husbands for her, this fourth one was a keeper. Becky certainly seemed happy with him. "Don't always believe it."

"I deluded myself," Paul said. "It doesn't excuse what we did, but at least I can see it now. I should never have hurt Robert."

"He knew?" I asked, surprised.

"I'm sure he guessed." Paul swirled the liquid in his glass. "Do you remember when I mentioned coming in and hearing him on the phone?"

I tried to think back to the night Sam and I came to the restaurant, before the Whittington party. It was so long ago and so much had happened since then. Paul said something then about Robert and restaurant profits. The head chef was going through receipts...I touched the phone number in my pocket, written on just such a receipt. "He was going through the accounts and he said something about profit?"

"He was very cold to me that day. Robert normally wasn't like that. He was very outgoing and friendly. But that day he almost snapped my head off. He was obviously upset. I saw a page from a ledger on the computer screen and it looked like he was adding up figures on a scratch pad nearby. He mentioned Michelle by name and said something like, 'This is what I get for being trusting.' I was so embarrassed." Paul took another swallow of his drink. "I think that was when I knew I had to break it off with Michelle. Robert was a decent man. What we were doing was wrong."

"I'm glad you feel that way. It makes you less of a shithead."

Paul gaped at me for a second then he grinned. The smile transformed his face, making the grim and somber lines relax into mischievous humor. "Glad to hear it."

"I would hate to think T.J.'s son was such a jerk. He'll be a member of my family, so that means you're stuck with us, too." I saw Livvie slip back into the room from the back. "Excuse me. I need to talk to Livvie about that poor kid."

"I'm sorry to hear what happened. He was a hard worker."

"Do you think he did it?"

"Did what?"

"Killed the chef."

Paul looked so surprised I knew he never even considered it. "No. He was a nice kid. I can't see him doing it. Anyway, why would he?"

Why indeed? I thought as I hurried to intercept Livvie. I huddled near her. "Where is Michelle's son? I told her I'd let her know where he is."

Livvie drew back in surprise. "Why?"

"Come on, Liv. She's worried."

She frowned but relented. "He's at Methodist Hospital, over on highway 169. He's in surgery."

Lowering her voice, she looked around the crowded room. "It wasn't an accident. He was beaten. The accident was staged."

"Wow. Do they know who did it?'

Livvie shook her head. "They didn't confide in me." Her gaze went to Sam. "He looks tired. You'd better get him home. We're not going to do the cake tonight, it just doesn't seem right. T.J. is going to the hospital with Jim Tolliver. We'll celebrate later, with the family."

I looked over my shoulder. She was right. Sam was leaned back in his chair, still smiling at Becky but I could tell by his slumping shoulders he was fading. "Just let us know when. Thanks." I headed for the coat rack and my purse, hanging under my jacket.

Livvie hugged me carefully, working around my sling. "It was a great party while it lasted. I'll call you tomorrow."

"Deal." I wandered over to Sam, pausing to chat with a couple of guests along the way. When I got there, he looked up at me. "Ready to head out?" I asked.

"So soon?" He yawned then smiled. "Yeah, I'm ready."

"You don't want to overdo it," Becky said, getting to her feet. "You need to take it slow and easy for a while." She and Carlton walked with us to the door where several other people were waiting to see Sam off. It was almost twenty minutes before we shook loose from the well-wishers and went out the door that Livvie held for us.

I was at the car, Sam behind me, when I remembered. "Damn, I have to call Michelle." I pulled the paper out of my pocket and peered at it in the dim lighting as Sam edged around me. It was a packing list from a local produce company.

"Open up, okay?" Sam asked from his side.

I clicked Bilbo's control key and the car came to life. "Hey, Livvie!" I called out. "I forgot. I've got this receipt. I wrote something on it and stuck it in my pocket."

She stepped out onto the porch. "What is it?"

"It's an invoice for truffles and mushrooms. Do you need it?"

"Keep it," she called back. "I'll get it from you later. Get Sam home, he looks beat. Don't forget to call Michelle and tell her."

"I will." I thought about what I overheard while I lurked in the hall near the pantry. "I need to call the police about something she said, anyway." I got into the SUV as Sam carefully settled back on the seat and let his head drop back. I started Bilbo and plugged my phone into the Toothy adapter.

"What's that?" Sam asked.

"A Bluetooth Sync thingie." I spoke into the embedded receiver over my head. "Toothy on." I recited the phone number on the paper.

"Toothy?"

"I had to call it something." I carefully edged the SUV out of the parking space and headed for the road. As I did, Michelle answered through the speakers.

"Michelle, this is Cassie Whittington. Livvie told me they're at Methodist Hospital, on 169. She said something about surgery."

There was a brief pause, then Michelle said, "Thank you. I owe you one."

"No, you don't."

"I mean it. And I pay my debts. Take my advice. Have someone check the finances at the restaurant, especially the charges for imported items. You might find some discrepancies. Thanks again."

Before I could reply, the hum of static replaced her voice then the computer voice said, "Your party is disconnected."

"I wonder what that meant," Sam said around a yawn.

I drove onto the road and merged with the few cars there. "I have no idea, but I'll pass the tip along to the police, since I need to talk to them anyway." Headlights suddenly flashed in my rear view mirror and I shifted in the seat, unable to adjust the mirror because of my bound left arm. The lights were high, which meant it had to be an even bigger SUV or a pickup. The glare was so bright I bent over the steering wheel to see the road clearly.

"That car is close," Sam said, looking at his side mirror.

"Yeah, we've got a tailgater." I couldn't move over. We were on a two-lane road and it didn't widen for several more blocks. As we approached a T intersection I sped up slightly, hoping the guy behind me would make a turn.

No such luck. He stuck with me through the intersection, so close I swore I caught glimpses of his grill in my mirror. We drove that way for another block until I got to another intersection. I slowed this time as the road widened into four lanes, but the tailgater didn't budge from my bumper even when I moved to the right lane.

"Go left," Sam said suddenly.

"What?"

"Go left at the light. I want to stop by the store on the way home."

"How come?"

"Just go left. That road will bring us out behind the store."

I glanced in the outside mirror and saw a clear left lane. I couldn't signal easily because of my arm, so I took a leap of faith and swerved into the left lane then into the turn lane, barely squeaking through the yellow traffic light. Behind me I heard the screech of tires. I looked in my rear view mirror.

The tailgater was stopped at the intersection by a red light.

"Take that," I muttered smugly. We were now on a four lane divided road and I cautiously increased our speed. As I did, my phone chimed *The Boys of Summer*. "Hey, Charlie, what's up?" I called out.

"I meant to talk to you before you left. I need to drop by your house tonight."

I glanced at Sam. He looked peeved, his face set and hard. "We're pooped, Charlie."

"I just need a minute or two. We need to discuss something."

I knew what 'something' was. It probably had to do with Barlow's Nursery and C.R.'s decision to invest. "We're sort of tired, Charlie."

"It won't take long. We're driving by on our way to Janelle's house."

Sam and I exchanged a startled look. "Sure, why not?" he muttered.

"Great. Stop by when you're in the neighborhood. We'll be there. Sam wants to swing by the nursery on the way, but that won't take long."

"Okay, see you soon." His voice was replaced by static then the computer telling me he was disconnected.

"What's up?" Sam demanded.

"Hmm?"

"Why does Richie Rich have to stop by tonight?"

"I have no idea."

"You're not a good liar."

He was right. I was a terrible liar. I took a deep breath and decided it was time to tell him the truth, the whole truth, and nothing but the truth.

Chapter 17

"Is it about the loan?" Sam asked.

I glanced quickly at him. "What loan?" I turned my attention back to the road, thankful he couldn't see me clearly in the darkness surrounding us.

"Mary said the old man was going to make us a loan to tide us over."

"This is the first I've heard about that," I said, relieved to be able to tell the truth.

"She said he wanted to invest in the company. I figured that meant a loan."

"Oh. No. I think, um, I think he mentioned something to me about buying a share in the company." A car swung into place behind us, but it wasn't my tailgater. This one had regular headlights that didn't blind me. I bumped up the speed a tad and the car dropped back.

"He can't buy a share in the company unless Mary and I let him." Sam's voice wasn't sleepy any more. He sounded wide awake and pissed off. "Did you put him up to it?"

Once again I was relieved I could be honest. "No, I didn't. He mentioned it to me out of the blue when you were in the hospital."

"Why didn't you tell me about it?"

"We've been a bit busy, Sam." I let some of my own anger creep into my voice. "We had an accident and I've been going to physical therapy and you've been going to therapy and you moved in with me and I've had to adjust to having you in the house and…we've been busy."

"Okay, okay. Sorry. I thought you knew about it."

"I knew he wanted to invest in your company. I'm not sure how that happens."

"Why?"

"Why does he want to invest?" I glanced quickly at Sam.

"Yeah. C. R. Whittington the Second doesn't seem like a plants and trees sort of man. Why invest in an out-of-the-way landscape company?"

I thought furiously. I'm sure the Second didn't want me sharing his concern about doing the right thing as he faced the waning years of his life. "He wants to piss off Sheila," I said in a burst of inspiration.

"Sheila? What's she got to do with this?"

"She invested in one of his companies and told him," I paused, "or told somebody she'll have land soon in Pickaway that needs to be sold."

"What?"

"Yeah. Apparently she figures you guys can't stay in business too much longer." I let him digest that little nugget of information then I said, "If you would let me invest in the company, too, then you wouldn't need to worry—"

"No."

"That's what the Second said you would say."

Sam shifted in his seat to glare at me. "You guys just had a good old chat about me, didn't you? I suppose he wanted to know if my intentions were honorable."

I remembered the Second's comment about marrying and keeping the business in the family. "No, he didn't. I suppose this is just his way of helping me, that's all."

"No offense, but you have a weird relationship with that family."

I clenched and unclenched the steering wheel with my good hand. "You've said that before," I snapped. "It doesn't change the fact that I have a relationship with them." We were silent for several long minutes until I asked, "Where do I go from here? I don't recognize this highway."

"Take a right at the traffic light then a left at the next stop sign."

"How did you find this route?" I glanced in the rear view mirror again. The cars behind us were far back and when I looked down at my speedometer, I realized I was speeding. Anger had a way of doing that to me. I slowed down and glanced at Sam, happy he didn't notice or if he did notice, he didn't comment on my lead foot.

"A few years ago the road near the nursery was under construction and we had to find an alternate delivery route." Sam drummed his fingers on his armrest. "I don't know if I want business partners."

"You already have a business partner," I pointed out as I made the right turn. We were now on a four-lane boulevard leading through a residential neighborhood and I kept the speed within five miles of the posted limit. Cops were known to hang out on roads like this and I didn't want to add a speeding ticket to my evening. The cars behind me seemed to have the same idea because none of them sped up. "You have your sister. She's your partner."

"I meant strangers. I still don't know why a stranger would invest in my business. Doing it just to annoy Sheila doesn't make sense."

I stopped at the stop sign and made the left turn onto another four-lane boulevard, this one leading through a business district then on to more residential streets. "He's just trying to help me, I suppose. You know, help my guy, help me."

"That's a pretty big assumption on his part, isn't it?" Sam's voice was so low I barely heard him.

"What do you mean?"

"He's assuming we're serious. I mean, why else would he invest in a company if he thought you were going to dump me."

"Why would I dump you?" I stopped at the next stop sign. "Which way?"

"Straight then right at the next traffic light. You might want to dump me because I'm crippled, or because you don't care about me, or because you're getting bored."

"None of the above." I looked at the houses as we passed. This was an older suburb with low rectangular rambler-style homes, all tidy with attached one car garages and small fenced yards in the back. I had vague memories of such a home when I was a child, but my mother and I fled when I was only seven, so my recollections were hazy at best.

"So does that mean we're serious?"

Oh, man, I really don't want to get into this, I thought as I struggled to find a suitable answer. *I don't want to think about the future, or marriage or any of that.* "I don't think 'being serious' is like a mathematical formula," I said, keeping my voice level and reasonable. "It's not something like 'date two months plus don't see other people equals serious.' And it certainly has nothing to do with whether or not my ex-father-in-law invests in your company."

"What if I don't take his money?"

Don't look a gift horse in the mouth. Luckily I thought before I spoke. "Why wouldn't you? He's not going to interfere with daily operations. He doesn't know a pansy from a petunia." I frowned. "I don't think he does, at least. Face it—it's just money to him." We approached another traffic light. "Which

220

way?"

"Left then straight for about a half-mile. We'll come out on the frontage road behind the nursery, on the west."

I made the left on a green arrow as did two cars behind us. One other car slipped through on the yellow with a squeal of tires. I glanced at it in my mirror. Like my previous tailgater, it was higher than the other cars with bright headlights that momentarily bounced into my field of vision then vanished behind the intervening cars.

"I don't like being in debt to anyone."

"It's not being in debt," I explained patiently. "He's going to invest. In good years, you give him a dividend or something. In bad years, he writes off his investment on his taxes. Or something like that. If you want to know, ask Janelle. We'll see her in a few minutes. She and Charlie are coming to the house." I peered ahead through the darkness. This stretch of road wasn't well-lit and I slowed the car, not anxious to meet a deer face to face. "Where's the—oh, I see it." Ahead on the left I saw the white pole frame building of Barlow's Landscape Center. The retail building was dark, of course, because the place was closed but the exterior lights were on, highlighting the back of the building, the front parking lot and the side lot where pumpkins and other seasonal items were stored. Despite the yard lights, pockets of shadow made the place darkly mysterious. "Do you have a key? I don't have mine with me."

Sam pulled a key ring from his jeans pocket. "Got it. I just want to stop in for a minute. I haven't been here for so long."

"Just a week or so."

"It feels like a hell of a lot longer. If nothing else could do it, this accident proves to me I'm not cut out for a desk job," Sam grumbled.

I felt a momentary burst of concern. If my Big Plan worked, Sam would leave his main 'outdoor' duties in the nursery business and be focused in an office. How would he handle that? Was my Plan based on an incorrect assumption about him?

I decided not to worry about it until everything was in place. Who knew? Maybe Sam's preferences would change, maybe the deal wouldn't go through, maybe a million things would go wrong. *Focus on the now. Don't worry about the future.* The banal little aphorisms from Livvie's booklet popped into my head as I pulled up to the wrought iron gate separating the back driveway from the road.

Bilbo's headlights illuminated the scene perfectly. This was the truck entrance and because I didn't use it much I needed all the light I could get to show me the scene. I took the keys from him and prepared to step out.

"This is the longest I've been away from the place except for winter, when it's closed," he said. "I just want to touch base."

I leaned back in and smiled at him. "I know. Smell the plants. Touch some dirt. I feel the same way when I've been gone a while."

"I guess I'm just a guy who likes to play in the dirt."

"Hang in there. Soon we'll close up shop and you can head to Florida for some rehab. By the time you come back, you'll be put back to work." I didn't wait for his reply but went to the gate, managing to open it even with the awkwardness of being one-handed. My arm was healing and I could wiggle my fingers now without pain, but I wasn't taking any chances. I wanted that sucker healed, and healed fast.

I came back to Bilbo and drove through the gate, leaving it open behind us. Sam was so tired I knew we wouldn't be there long. "Do you want to go inside?" I asked as we drove slowly toward the retail building in the center of the big lot.

"No, I don't want to bother with the security alarm. Just go to the side lot where the pumpkins and straw bales are stored. The mums are still out, aren't they?"

"It's been a while since I've been here, but I think they are. We haven't had a frost yet." I drove past the big retail building and approached the outdoor lot, covered by a heavy canvas canopy. This was where we stored trees and shrubs in the summertime. Now it held corn stalks, scarecrows, pumpkins and yes, mums all in tidy rows waiting for purchase.

I parked Bilbo and got out. "Why don't you wait a minute? I want to make sure there isn't anything in the way. I don't want you falling down. If you do, I sure as hell can't help you up." I grinned at Sam. "You know—'I've fallen and I can't get up?' No kidding if you fall."

He paused, his hand on the door pull. "Okay. Just give me the signal."

I nodded as I closed the door behind me. The cold October air hit me as I stepped out, my breath making small puffs. I had to make this fast. Sam looked exhausted. With my luck, he would take one step on the uneven pavement and fall, hurting himself all over again. No way was I letting that happen.

I walked toward the hay bales separating the pumpkins from the parking lot, the pungent dry aroma filling my senses. To my right I saw the mums, nestled in their hay bale corral, which would keep them relatively warm in the chilly night. I paused to touch one plant, the blossom velvety but stiff to the touch. As I skirted the Great Pumpkin on display in front I saw the brief glare of headlights shine between the retail center and the small shed where we housed supplies and tarps used to cover the straw and the pumpkins in case of rain. I leaned to one side to see the source of the headlights, but either they moved or my position was wrong.

I moved into the pumpkin patch, walking carefully. Bilbo cast a good glow but only straight ahead. The ground under my feet was densely shadowed and more than once I paused to make sure of my footing. I started to turn back to Sam, to signal him to join me, when I heard the unmistakable sound of a car engine cutting off, not far away. I stopped and strained to listen. The nursery center was located on several acres of land, surrounded by fields on the south side and the county road on the north, at my back. The sound came from the southwest side—the open gate where Sam and I entered.

"Damn," I muttered. "Don't tell me somebody thinks the place is open?" As soon as I had the thought, I dismissed it. Nobody knew about that back gate except shippers and nursery personnel. It was hidden by the bulk of a storage shed from the general public. So how did someone find it?

Were we followed? That had to be it. But why? Was someone lost and thought we knew an alternate route? I thought about the traffic on the road behind us. When we left the residential area, most of the cars vanished. Only one remained, far in the distance.

One remained...one with bright headlights that sat high above the road.

I didn't give myself a chance to evaluate how intelligent my sudden fright might be. I reacted instinctively. I hurried back through the pumpkins, moving as fast I dared on the uneven surface of the paving stones set into the gravel lot. I was almost to Bilbo when I heard a car door open and close, the sound sharp on the cold night air. The almost-full moon cast disorienting shadows, turning night to pale day. I paused, peering through the dense darkness at the side of the retail center, back where the gate stood open.

Was another shadow moving there?

I slipped back into Bilbo. "Hey, what's the deal?" Sam demanded.

"I saw someone out there." I turned off the car but turned the key to 'accessory.' I flipped the headlights off and verified that my phone was still plugged in. "Get down."

"Why?"

"Because I think someone followed us. Get down. If they think we're gone, they might go into the store or the lot."

"But—"

"Damn it, Sam, get down!"

He shot me a disbelieving look but did as I asked, hunching over and leaning on the console as much as his busted leg would let him. I peeked out the passenger side window, over his shoulder.

Someone was moving toward us. "Damn. Somebody's there." I considered alternatives and decided I had none. Two wounded people were sitting in an empty parking lot and somebody was after them. "Toothy. Call police," I whispered.

"I'm sorry. I don't recognize police." The female computer voice was positively cheery as it relayed this devastating bit of information.

Sam glared at me. "It doesn't recognize police? What kind of thing is it?"

"It's a thing I trained and I didn't train it to know police." I thought furiously. "Call Charlie."

"Charlie? What's he—"

"Shut up, Sam. Normally I'd call you, but you're here and you can't do a lot to help." I peered up over the dash cautiously. The dark shape was moving closer.

"Cassie, what's—" Charlie's voice sounded

abnormally loud in the silence.

"Call the police, Charlie. We're at Barlow's and somebody is after us. Call the cops."

"What do you mean? How come—"

My door flew open and a hand reached in. The next thing I knew I was in agony. The man grabbed my broken left arm, jerking hard on it. I screamed and lights exploded in front of me. I heard Sam yelling but his voice was fading as I was dragged out of the car.

"Where is it?" someone shouted. "Give it to me. Where is it?"

My legs gave out on me and I landed on the pavement, hitting it with my knees and toppling over, thankfully onto my right side. Waves of pain washed through me—my arm, my head, my knees where I hit the ground. I tried to roll, tried to turn away but I was weak from agony and the nausea that rippled through me.

"You bitch! I heard you tell her you had it! Where is it? Give it to me!"

I managed a strangled yell. "What? What is it?"

"What did she tell you? Where is it?"

I tried to straighten, using Bilbo to give me support. As I did I heard the car door open and suddenly Sam was there, clinging to the side of the car and using one of his crutches like a weapon. He leaned against the front fender and swung it like a bat, but the man ducked, grabbing it out of his hands. Sam staggered and almost fell, his weight touching down on his injured leg. He yelled, his voice raw with pain but he stayed upright, clinging to the other crutch and Bilbo to keep his balance.

Headlights flashed across the scene and I peered around the bulky man groggily as a blue Jaguar screeched to a stop, almost running him over. The man whirled but Charlie was already out of the sedan. He tackled the man and they went down in a pile of flailing arms and legs.

Janelle sprang out of the passenger side of the car and came to us, pausing by Sam first. "Are you okay?" she asked urgently, her hand on his arm.

He nodded, his head bowed. "Help Cassie," he whispered. "I'm fine."

"Bullshit," I croaked. I tried to move but didn't dare. My sling was gone, my arm was pulled away from my side and any motion sent waves of agony pulsing along my left arm and shoulder. "I'm in bad shape, Janelle," I said softly. "I don't know what's wrong."

She knelt beside me and put an arm around my shoulders. As she did, sirens started to wail in the distance.

Chapter 18

"Why the hell was Mike Johnson after me?" I asked two nights later as Janelle and Charlie, Livvie and T.J., and Sam and I sat in my living room.

Sam and I had spent the intervening time since the attack at the hospital verifying no further injuries occurred except to set back our healing by several weeks. Then we spent most of Sunday talking to police over and over again.

"Talking to" was the operative expression. We didn't get a lot of answers in return. But Charlie and Billy Armstrong spent today, Monday, going over the facts and Charlie had promised us some answers tonight. I was keeping him to that promise.

"He heard you tell Michelle you had something incriminating about him." Charlie sipped his beer, looking smug with a black eye and swollen right hand.

"I never said anything like that," I denied, wincing with Charlie when the cold beer touched his cut lip. I had overheard the men talking in the kitchen about the fight at the nursery and I knew Charlie was suffering from injuries he wasn't discussing with us females, injuries involving assorted kicks and punches to his manly parts. From the way the men commiserated with him, it must have been pretty bad. I decided I didn't want to know the details. It was enough for me that Charlie jumped into the fray to help us. That really was going above and beyond the call of duty.

The doorbell rang and I got up to answer it, eyeing my bedroom door warily. Houdini and Truffles were stowed away but I wasn't sure how well that door closed. Truffles had apparently absorbed Houdini's fascination with the Great Outdoors and I had visions of two furry beasts making a beeline for the wide open spaces.

"Trick or treat!"

I evaluated the assorted gremlins on my stoop. I counted one Batman, one tiny Spider Man, a Wonder Woman, and a hobo. "Looks like the Justice League of America tonight," I commented as I held out my pumpkin bucket.

"Huh?" a chorus of shrill voices asked.

"Help yourselves." I rattled the bucket and hands dipped, then the small superheroes, hobo in tow, scampered away. I closed the door but didn't bother sitting down. My townhome development between six and seven on Halloween night was Candy Land.

"He heard you say you had an invoice. That would prove he was substituting American truffles for imported ones," Charlie said.

"So? Big deal." I sipped from the wine glass I kept conveniently on the table near the door and the kitchen chair where I perched in between requests for candy.

"He made almost three-hundred dollars a week on that scheme."

I choked on my wine. "What?" I gasped.

"He also was making money on other food switches. He substituted different kinds of salmon, spices, and other things. Mike Johnson was skimming a thousand or two thousand dollars a month, at least, every month." Charlie looked at T.J., who nodded confirmation. "The restaurant was also a good front for other activity. The police think he was involved in some drug trafficking as well."

"Holy crap," I muttered. "I suppose it is in a good location."

"It's a perfect location," T.J. said, his voice radiating anger. "Customers come and go on the lake side all the time and we even get some supplies via the lake. So no one would wonder if they saw activity there. And since it's a restaurant we always have trucks pulling in. All they had to do was slip in some drugs in a panel truck. Mike was in charge of the inventory and he kept the keys to the pantry cupboards." T.J.'s mouth thinned into a grim line. "And of course, I was an ex-drug addict. So if they were found…"

Livvie put a hand on his leg. "If they were found the police would blame T.J." Her eyes seemed to ice over. "It was a perfect setup for that bastard."

I heard the telltale patter of small feet and peeked out my spy hole. Yep, another pair was approaching. I waited for the knock then jerked the door open.

"Trick or treat, smell my feet, give me something good to eat!" a small dragon shouted. The knight with him/her laughed uproariously.

"Ah, an oldie but a goody," I said, holding out the bucket. "Help yourself."

The kids dipped, grabbed then dashed, the knight leading the way with raised cardboard sword as the puffy dragon followed clumsily after. I closed the door and turned back to the conversation. "So Mike heard me tell Livvie about the invoice."

"And you mentioned something Michelle told you about the police," Charlie added.

"No, I was just going to tell the police I overheard Michelle and Mike talking. It sounded like blackmail."

T.J. looked pained. "It was. Apparently Mike

found out about Michelle's past from Mickey, the dishwasher. They had become friends. And Michelle knew about Mike's substituting the local food for the imported food. So they were at a standoff. Robert wouldn't know a thing about it because Michelle handled the billing and accounts, and Mike handled food inventory and stocking the food as it arrived. It was just a fluke the invoice was still there and you could use it for scrap paper. Usually Mike grabbed them and created fakes, but he couldn't get in because the place was a crime scene and the police had it blocked off. Then I fired him and he had no reason to go in there."

"But—" The knock at the door prevented me from asking my question. I handled the tiny fairies, supervised by their bored older siblings, then turned back to the group in my living room. Whatever question I was going to ask vanished from my brain as I took another sip of wine. We were safe and that's what mattered. T.J. and Livvie were safe, Mickey Tolliver was recovering from his painful beating, and... "So Mike beat up Mickey? There're too many people with similar names at that restaurant."

"That's another coincidence," Charlie said. "Paul overheard Robert talking about 'Michel' but he thought it was 'Michelle.' It was really 'Michel.'" He looked expectantly at me as though his words made sense.

I stared at him blankly, as did Sam. "Say what?" I asked.

"Me-shell versus Ma-shell." Livvie said with exaggerated pronunciation. "Ma-shell is French for Michael. When Paul overheard Robert talking, he was talking about Michael and how he was worried about the profits because of Michael, not Michelle."

Sam looked from Livvie to Charlie. "So Paul thought Michelle was—"

I missed the rest of Sam's comment when I had to answer the door again. "Trick or treat!" four tiny goblins yelled.

I thrust my pumpkin bucket at them and small hands plunged in and grabbed. I smiled at the adults standing near the curb and closed the door.

T.J. smiled wryly. "I think Paul wanted to marry and start a family. If you find out that the woman you love has deserted a family that puts a damper on romance."

"Have you talked to Michelle lately?" Janelle asked.

"She called today and gave me an update. The police told her Mike went out of his way to be nice to the kid." I took another sip of wine.

"Now we know why he was so nice, of course," Janelle said. Her thin face stiffened with anger. "Mike put the pastry hook into the dishwasher and Mickey saw him do it. Later, when it came out how Robert was killed, Mickey put two and two together."

"Did Mike mean to kill Robert?" I asked.

Charlie shrugged then winced as sore muscles protested. "He's not talking. But the police think Robert looked at the accounts, he looked at the inventory, and he figured out what was happening. He made some phone calls then he confronted Mike."

"But to kill somebody over truffles—are you serious?" I know I sounded as incredulous as I felt.

"The police mentioned that a new shipment of drugs came into town the same night Robert died. His fingerprints were found in the pantry and the refrigerator."

"So? He's a cook."

"Head chef," T.J. corrected. "The under-chefs are responsible for gathering supplies. Robert did some cooking, but mainly he set the menu and worked with the sommelier—the wine steward," he explained when he saw Sam's suspicious look, "—

about purchases and pairings."

"Still, it seems thin. Why would Mike kill him?"

"The sentence for drug trafficking in this state is stiff," Janelle said. "Don't forget Mike had several other convictions. If he went to jail, he might not get out again. For some people, murder is a reasonable price to pay in order to prevent jail time."

The doorbell rang again. I took another sip of wine before pulling it open. I dealt with a Superman, Buzz Lightyear, and Princess Someone then turned back to the group. T.J. had resumed his narrative. "Michelle said she didn't even know Mickey was working there. She seldom went into the kitchen. She handled the books and the Feed Bag. The few times she was in the kitchen, Mickey probably wasn't on duty yet. He didn't come on until late in the evening. We had a different dishwasher for lunch."

"I wonder how he found Michelle." I sat down in the kitchen chair near the door to catch my breath. This Candy-Doling was tricky business with a broken arm.

"Michelle wrote to her mother occasionally. Mickey got the info out of the old woman." Charlie looked at T.J. "It sounds like Paul has been cured of his romance."

Janelle left Charlie on the couch and joined me. "Go sit down. I'll take over for a while."

"You're company," I protested half-heartedly.

"You're busted," she countered. "Go sit."

I compromised by dragging another kitchen chair out to sit near her. "So Michelle and Mike were in cahoots," I mused as I relaxed.

"Speaking of cahoots—that's why Charlie and I were stopping by to talk to you on Saturday. We found out Sheila Peavey and John are in cahoots."

I almost dropped my wine glass. "What?"

Janelle nodded. "John told Diane who told Becky

who told Carlton who told Charlie."

I didn't even blink at this convoluted family gossip chain. It was typical for the Whittingtons. "Who approached who?"

Janelle smiled. "You get right to the heart of the matter, don't you?" She was still in her lawyer uniform of navy blue jacket and skirt, white blouse with big bow, nylons, and pumps. As always, I felt like a pansy next to a rose in my *How do I set a laser printer to stun?* sweatshirt and my jeans. I glanced across the room at Charlie, who also was in lawyer gear, although he'd loosened his tie. Then I compared him to Sam in his flannel shirt, black T-shirt, and sweats. *Yep,* I thought. *Roses and pansies, that's us.*

"I believe Sheila approached John for funding. Diane is worried."

I sipped my wine. "She should be. The housing market is crap right now. I don't know how John can stay afloat with those pricy McMansions he builds."

Janelle got up to answer a knock at the door. "No kidding."

"Trick or treat!" a chorus of voices shouted. One added, "Wow, you're pretty."

Janelle handed over the pumpkin bucket full of treats. "Thank you. You're very pretty yourself."

I peered around the door at a Power Ranger, beauty queen, and small frog, complete with painted face. Janelle was talking to the frog, God love her. She closed the door and sat back down. "I wonder if there's a way to evaluate our society based on the popularity of Halloween costumes?" she mused. "It seems to me we have a lot of superheroes tonight."

"As long as there aren't any stockbrokers, we'll be okay," I grumbled. "So John is giving Sheila money? What's that about?"

"Charlie and I have a theory." Janelle looked at my ex-husband, who caught her glance and smiled.

His smile vanished when his split lip made him remember its presence. "He's so proud of the fact he was able to help on Saturday," she said in a low voice. "It's the first time he's been able to, well, compete with Sam."

I stared at her, my mouth ajar. "Say what?"

"I think he's been feeling a bit overshadowed by Sam. After all, Sam is so physical compared to Charlie." Janelle's cool, assessing gaze flickered over Sam, who sat in 'his' chair with his leg propped up on the hassock. "At least he used to be."

I felt a pang at that statement. She was right. Sam was losing muscle tone and weight, two things that bothered him and me. I had plans to turn my second bedroom into a weight room as soon as I could enlist the help of some Barlow's guys to buy the stuff and move the equipment in for me. "I talked to the physical therapist about that. She said he can start lifting weights for upper body strength soon." I finished my wine as another knock sounded on the door. "It will do Sam good to have something to occupy himself. So tell me your theory about Sheila and John."

Janelle doled out candy to a farm contingent—a scarecrow, a sheep, and a pig. It must have been a family group, maybe triplets. They all looked about the same size.

"It's simple, really. Sheila needs money to pay her legal fees." Janelle inspected the pumpkin bucket and refilled it from the bag of candy on my desk in the den. "John wants someone to distract you two while the probate is in progress. We figured it's a simple business deal." Janelle lowered her voice. "Charlie thinks Sheila hired someone to mess with Livvie's car and cause your accident."

"Did the police say anything about it?"

Janelle shook her head, her upswept black hair glinting in the light. "They still don't have any leads.

One of the investigators said he doubted they'd find any evidence to point to someone. They're hoping an informant or a suspect will drop a clue." She got to her feet when we heard footsteps on the porch.

"That's discouraging." I smiled at T.J. as he passed me on the way to the kitchen. "Can I get you anything?"

"Can you show me where the napkins are?" he asked.

I sprang to my feet and followed him into the kitchen as Janelle pulled open the door to the familiar shouts of 'trick or treat.'

"They're over here." I made a beeline for the drawers near the sink.

"Listen, I wanted to talk to you about Sam," he said in a low voice, glancing back toward the living room.

"Why? What's wrong?" I pulled the napkin package out of the drawer and moved closer to T.J., who obviously wanted a private conversation.

"He's pretty depressed about what happened."

I stared up at T.J., confused. "About what?"

"You know—there you both were, getting attacked, and he couldn't do anything to help you." T.J. glanced again at the living room. "It was Charlie to the rescue."

"Oh, for cryin'..." I slammed the napkins down on the kitchen counter. "Sam is hurt. He couldn't help me."

"You know that and I know that." T.J. put his good hand—his real hand—on my shoulder. "Look, I know what it's like. When a person is disabled, it affects everything. And for men, it can affect a lot of things." He looked away from me. "You know—a lot of things."

Oh, man. I remembered the previous spring when Sam and I laughed at the Viagra SPAM emails that plagued me. "I'll cross that bridge when I get to it," I said grimly. "So how do I deal with this? I take it logic won't work."

"I don't think you can deal with it. I just thought you should know. He's going to be feeling angry and upset until he gets mobile again. And depending on how his rehab goes, he may or may not be the same guy you knew." T.J.'s hook flexed and he smiled wryly. "If you know what I mean."

I nodded thoughtfully. "Thanks. The social worker mentioned stuff like that, but I figured it was something to worry about in the future. I can see I need to start thinking about it now."

T.J. took the napkins and gave me an awkward pat on the shoulder. "Don't worry about it. Just be aware of it. I'm sure you guys will work it out."

"Work what out?"

We both turned guiltily to see Sam leaning on his crutches in the door between the foyer and the kitchen. "Work out how to get dinner on the table," I said glibly.

T.J. walked back to the living room, napkins in hand. "I'll send Livvie in to help."

I started to follow him but Sam put a restraining hand on my arm. "Work what out?"

"Your physical therapy," I said. "It's going to be a long, hard journey to get you back to health." I started past him. "T.J. has been through something like it."

"And?" Sam demanded.

"And what?" I tried to avoid looking at him but he shifted position so I couldn't avoid his accusing gaze. "What?"

"I told you before, Cassie. You don't have to stick with me on this. I've talked to the doctor about what my outcome might be. I may not come back one-hundred percent. Are you sure you want to be with me?"

"Can we just face that question when we get to

it?" I asked.

The doorbell rang and Janelle got up to get it, glancing back at us apologetically. As she did a streak of yellow fur started racing across the living room.

"Sam! It's Houdini!" I yelled.

Sam turned as Janelle opened the front door. Three big kids stood in the shadows, out of the cone of light cast my overhead porch lantern. "Hey, lady, this is for you." One of the boys tossed something at Janelle.

Sam dropped his crutches, grabbed Janelle and spun, pivoting on his good leg and slamming into the wall of the foyer, his back to the door. Houdini skid to a stop at the doorway, yowling at the sight of a glowing, hissing cherry bomb on the front mat.

The resulting BOOM made me skid backward, the small rag rug near the doorway tangling with my feet. I went down into the kitchen chairs Janelle and I used, narrowly avoiding Sam and Janelle, who were still leaned against the wall, her face pressed hard against his chest and his arms protectively around her. My wine glass and Janelle's shot into the air and smashed back down on the wood floor in exploding shards of glass and wine. I landed hard on my butt and rolled to one side—thankfully to the side that was uninjured.

Houdini yowled once more, turned tail, and ran back the way he came from, followed by the black shadow of Truffles, his co-conspirator. The bedroom door slammed open as Houdini hit it with his shoulder and they both vanished inside.

Charlie, Livvie, and T.J. rushed to the front of the house. T.J. ran outside after the kids. Livvie was already on her cell phone, calling the police. "Are you okay?" Charlie demanded, peering down at Janelle.

I cursed softly as I unhooked my legs from the chairs. The kitchen doorway was nearby and I used it to straighten myself as Sam released Janelle. "Thanks, Sam," she said shakily. "That thing would have gone off right in my face."

Charlie put his arms around her and drew her to him. He looked at Sam over Janelle's head. *Thank you*, he mouthed silently.

"I'm fine," I said loudly. "Not to worry. I'm okay."

Sam grinned at me. He clung to the doorway, his crutches scattered near the front door. "Need any help?"

He held out his hand and I took it gratefully, getting to my feet with only minimal jostling of my wounded wing. I leaned against him. "My hero," I murmured. "Are you okay?" My heart was still hammering so hard I could barely talk. That explosive landed too damn close for comfort. If it was just six inches higher or a foot closer, Sam would have been...I peered up at him, a thousand conflicting emotions settling quickly into one: relief. I wasn't sure if I loved him forever but at that moment, I loved him so much I was weak with it. "You're okay?" I asked, needing the confirmation for what my eyes told me.

"I'm fine. How about you?"

"Bruised and not more broken, thank God. I'm already getting tired of this sling thing. I don't want to add more weeks to recovery." I smiled shakily at him. "I can't believe you did that."

He kissed my forehead. "Glad to help. Who do you think did it?"

That was so like him. *Yeah, I risked my life and don't worry about it.* Love, fear, panic, and relief made me dizzy. I released him as he bent over to gather his crutches. "One guess," I said in a shaky voice. "It must have been our nemesis."

"Sheila?" Sam looked thoughtfully out the door as T.J. came back into view, a squirming kid held tight by one arm.

239

"He says some woman paid him to do it," T.J. said, tossing the kid toward us.

Livvie glared at the boy, who glared back, his pug nose and greasy hair giving him the unfortunate appearance of a pig. "Asshole," she muttered.

"Hey, it's money." The kid jammed his hands in his jeans, which were already starting a precipitous slide down his scrawny butt.

"Use it for bail," Charlie said, his voice low and angry.

The kid backed away. "It's Halloween. This shit happens all the time."

We all heard sirens in the distance. "Think again. You tried to injure two lawyers. You're going to jail."

The kid's face got so white I was sure he'd pass out. "No harm done."

I tuned them out when Sam stumped over to stand next to me. "I'll bet Houdini doesn't make a break for it again," he said in a low voice.

I looked toward the bedroom where two kitty faces peered around the corner at us, frightened eyes wide in their faces. "I suspect he'll be sticking close to home." I put an arm around Sam's waist. "Our home."

He looked down at me, his eyes questioning. "Ours?"

"Yep." I squeezed his waist. "It's yours and mine, as long as you want to stay."

His dark eyes warmed then he brushed a kiss against my cheek. "That might be a long, long time."

That suited me just fine.

A word about the author...

J L Wilson is a Midwestern author who writes "mysteries with a touch of romance...and romance with a touch of gray."

She can be found on Twitter, Facebook, MySpace, and a few blogs here and there.

This link tells you where:
http://tinyurl.com/ak8hl8

www.ingramcontent.com/pod-product-compliance
Lightning Source LLC
Chambersburg PA
CBHW070916180626
46817CB00003B/1089